MW00489792

NOW THE NIGHT BEGINS

SEMIOTEXT(E) NATIVE AGENTS SERIES

Cet ouvrage, publié dans le cadre d'un programme d'aide à la publication, bénéficie du soutien financier du ministère des Affaires étrangères, du Service culturel de l'ambassade de France aux États-Unis, ainsi que de l'appui de FACE (French American Cultural Exchange).
This work, published as part of a program providing publication assistance, received financial support from the French Ministry of Foreign Affairs, the Cultural Services of the French Embassy in the United States and FACE (French American Cultural Exchange).

Published by Semiotext(e)
PO BOX 629, South Pasadena, CA 91031
www.semiotexte.com

Thanks to Noura Wedell and Frank Jaffe.

Cover Art: Klee, Paul, *Fire at Full Moon* (*Feuer bei Vollmond*). 1933.
50 x 60 cm, Mixed technique on canvas. Essen, Museum Folkwang
Photo: © Museum Folkwang Essen/ARTOTHEK

Author photograph: © H. Bamberger/P.O.L
Design: Hedi El Kholti
French Voices Logo designed by Serge Bloch
ISBN: 978-1-63590-005-7

Distributed by The MIT Press, Cambridge, Mass. and London, England
Printed in the United States of America

ALAIN GUIRAUDIE

NOW THE NIGHT BEGINS

TRANSLATED BY JEFFREY ZUCKERMAN

AFTERWORD BY BRUCE HAINLEY AND WAYNE KOESTENBAUM

<e>

This morning, I get up easily, it's beautiful outside, it's hot, even this early. I can't stop thinking about how it's almost the end of my first week of vacation, and I still haven't done much of anything, but then again that's normal, it's the first week, the point is not to do anything at all. I've got two more weeks, and this one isn't even over yet, maybe I'll get going on Monday. Actually, I don't know, I might just as easily not go anywhere for the whole break, even if I've got plenty of people I could visit by the ocean, the Mediterranean, I just know that after two days I'll be bored stiff and I'm perfectly happy here at home. And besides, I have to change the drive belt in my Safrane and I still haven't met the mechanic. I also told the banker that I'd have some time during break to come talk to him and renegotiate the loan for my apartment now that the interest rates have dropped. Also, I have to return some CDs to the library and write to the telecom company to get my cell phone insurance policy canceled, since it's been completely useless and I really shouldn't ever have gotten it anyway. On top of that, tomorrow is Daniel's birthday, he invited me to his party and I haven't found a present for him yet. And then I realize that it's Friday . . . Well, I might as well wander around the Trintaud market. After all, I'm on vacation, I'm not going to just sit here and torture myself. The problem with the

Trintaud market in July is that, unless I get there early in the morning, before ten at the very latest, there are just too many people. And it's a pain in the ass to squeeze past people, especially when I have nothing to buy, when I'm just here to walk around. So I go get coffee at Remparts . . . There are no ramparts in Trintaud anymore but there's still a Remparts café. Now that I'm here, I sit for a bit and watch the old men playing belote, just like that, from afar, but this morning it's not great, I get bored right away, so I go to Mariette's.

When I get there, the garage door is wide open. I wait a minute, look around, call out. Nobody. I go in the house. After all, we're close friends, if I tell her later that I hadn't dared, she'll say what she always does: "But you should have come in . . ." And besides, I'm intrigued. Inside, there's still nobody. I call out again. I walk through the house into the garden. Nothing there either. I'm starting to get worried, I wonder if they might both be dead, but I don't really think so, I keep my eyes on the clothesline. Mariette's done a lot of laundry and she's hung up tons of Grampa's underwear . . . Maurice is actually his name, but we've always known him as an old man, and even Mariette, his own daughter, calls him that, so we've always called him Grampa. I glance around, the windows on the second floor. Still not a soul in sight, I go up to the clothesline, I touch Grampa's underwear, briefs that are still a bit wet, hanging since the morning, I touch them one by one. Finally, one that's almost dry. Another careful look all around. Not a soul, not a single noise anywhere. I take the pair of underwear off the line, I'm really turned on with these in my hands, I'm nervous that I'll get caught, but this is stronger than me, and then I tell myself it's not a big deal, and, deep down, this little game makes me happy. I sneak in between two big sheets. A slight cough. From the end of the garden. Grampa comes out of his shed. He hasn't seen me. I have to hurry up, he's slow, he's turned his back to me, he's busy with a spade or something like that, maybe he's fixing the tool, I've got a moment to undress and slip on his underwear lickety-split. Let me give you a quick sketch of the situation, I'm in flip-flops, with shorts and a tee-shirt, but then I have no idea what to do with my own underwear, I shove it into the pocket of my shorts, and I go over calmly to say hi to Grampa. He's still fixing his spade as I walk right up to him, he doesn't hear me, he's a bit deaf, especially when he can't see someone's lips moving. So I get a bit closer, I don't dare say a word, I don't want to scare him, I walk in a big circle around him so he notices me casually. But when he sees me he's still startled anyway. Nothing dramatic, but he jumps a bit, as if he were about to be knocked over, I run over but he's okay, he stands up properly, straight as an arrow.

"How's it going?" I ask.

"Eh," he says. "Things are getting tricky."

"Okay, maybe you just have to take it easy."

"Nah," he says back. "Till last year things were going fine, but now, this year, I don't know what's happened, but now I can't manage anymore."

He's ninety-eight years old.

"Just look at your garden, you could have fooled us!" I tell him.

It's true that his garden is a very nice patch.

"Oh no," he says. "Don't you remember last year . . . All that was tomatoes, then over there were eggplants, and then that there was zucchini."

I look around, and there I can see tomatoes, there eggplants, there zucchini, I tell him I don't see any change.

"Right," he says, "but there were plenty more last year . . . Now, they've put flowers there, there and there, we've never had so many flowers!"

"Flowers are good, aren't they?"

"But we never need all those flowers."

And then he goes back to putting his spade together. And I've got my balls and my cock snug in his underwear, they have all the space they need and when I shift my weight from one leg to the other it rubs me just so, and I start getting hard ever so slightly. It's already starting to make a nice bulge in my shorts. And he's fixing his spade and in any case he's not talking to me anymore, I mean, he'd like to but mostly I feel like there's nothing else for us to say.

I ask him if I can help, I'm trying to figure out what he wants to do, he explains that the spade has gotten loose from the handle and now it's not getting weeds out right.

"But you can't fix it yourself," I say. "You've got to get a new one, at least a new handle, that's normal, it's worn down over time."

He's not convinced and he looks at me and then I hear, from the other end of the garden, by the house:

"Oh, it's Gilles!"

Mariette's alone, she said that more to let me know that she's there, she doesn't need to say she's there because I can see her perfectly well, but she says it anyway. She comes over to me. Then she stops, gets down to pick up something under the clothesline, and then she gets up, I see her looking over the clothesline. So I leave Grampa, I go up to her, I can tell something's not right.

And right when I get to her, she doesn't say hello, she says nothing, she shows me my underwear, yes, my red underwear, it fell out of my pocket, and she says:

"That can't be possible, it's the third time someone's stolen one of Grampa's pairs of underwear, right off the clothesline, in the garden."

I act shocked.

"Grampa's," she repeats. "Can you believe it?"

She must be counting the pairs of underwear when she hangs them up. And then I see her furious, and even, how do I put it?

Hurt deep down, as if someone had come and violated her privacy. And Grampa has no idea.

"But you must have counted wrong," he says.

"No, I counted, I counted twice, I hung up seven this morning, I even wrote it on this paper." She pulls a piece of paper out of her pocket, which she shows us, so we can see the number seven. "And there are only six."

Grampa doesn't believe her, he counts again.

"All right," he says. "This time you're right, but all those other times, how could you be sure? Surely you didn't count the other times."

"Of course I did, I counted."

"Even the first time?"

"The first time, I doubted myself, I couldn't be sure, and that's why the next time I started counting . . . and writing it down on paper."

Grampa has nothing else to add to that and finally, as if he knew, he says:

"But what would they do with it, anyway?"

In response, Mariette shrugs as if to say: My dear, if you're just going to be dense about all this, I'm not going to waste my breath.

And she goes into the house with my underwear in her hand.

Grampa looks at me and says:

"I mean, it's true? What would they do with it?"

On the doorstep, Cindy stretches her arms in her white Pink Panther tee-shirt. She yawns so wide she almost dislocates her jaw. Cindy is Mariette's granddaughter (and, thus, Grampa's great-granddaughter). She spends all her vacations here, I don't know her parents, but they must at least come to bring her here and then take her back. She's thirteen or fourteen, she's not beautiful, as she's grown up her face has sharpened terribly, every time I see her I'm surprised by that. It wasn't so long ago that I could still jerk off thinking about sucking at her tits, licking her pussy, or tickling her clit with the tip of my tongue . . . I also liked imagining her sucking me off at her grandmother's urging while rubbing my balls and finally, since cum would disgust Cindy and she was still a bit young for that, Mariette swallowing it all without losing a drop . . . but at the time, Cindy was still fresh and young, she had something cute and sweet about her, whereas now she sulks, she's even cruel, she spends her time yelling at her grandmother. Not so much at Grampa, but it should be said that Grampa acts like she doesn't exist. Anyway, it's not possible anymore to jerk off while thinking about her. It's pointless, it'll never be possible again. But I like jerking off in this house when Cindy's here. It adds to the sensation. I don't know why . . . besides, I don't even know why I like jerking myself off so much in this house . . . I don't have any desire for anyone here. It must be the house, plain and simple. Although I've tried to imagine what it would be like without anyone, and I know it wouldn't be the same. The house isn't all it takes. I need Grampa and Mariette, yes, at least Grampa and Mariette.

Now Cindy's coming to kiss me hello. How's it going, taking it easy? She yawns again and doesn't say anything, mumbles something I can't understand at all and then she goes back to her grandmother in the kitchen. Inside, they yell a bit, I look for a quiet spot to rub one out, I'm actually pretty turned on by this whole discussion about stolen underwear, deep down I'm not at all upset that Mariette noticed. And then the conversation between Mariette and Grampa and then my thoughts start wandering a bit and Mariette asks me to stay for dinner, she says "dinner" for the midday meal like all the other old people around here, it's a holdover from Occitan, and right then I don't have a chance to answer, for her it's a done deal, she absolutely loves when I eat with them, she offers me a drink. That's the way it is at their place, drinks at eleven thirty and at noon we eat. So I tell myself I'll jerk off during the siesta, it'll be so much better then. But dinner today is so boring. Grampa eating. Mariette passing around the dishes, still upset about this missing underwear . . . She doesn't talk about it, but I can tell it's bothering her. And finally Cindy, sulking and not eating a thing, it makes sense, she had breakfast not even an hour ago so she's not hungry. She doesn't stay put, she gets up, she walks around and then comes back, she slurps some Coke and leaves again, and then, in the hallway, we hear her saying:

"Grammy, what's this underwear doing next to the phone?"

And Mariette answers:

"Is that any of your business? What are you doing rummaging around everywhere?"

"I'm not rummaging, it's right here in plain sight . . . It's weird to see underwear here, that's why I'm asking you about it."

"Who knows, I found it in the garden!"

That's the only interesting part of the meal. Actually, I like to stay here for lunch because of the siesta. Yes, because after eating we all go into the living room for a digestive, some plum brandy, some Calvados . . . That stops us from doing much else and so we each doze off in our own armchairs. Even though he's ninety-eight, Grampa still has a bit of wine with every meal and some of the harder stuff after, especially when there's company. Well, just a little. It starts to get awfully hot, even inside, Mariette's with us, at the other end of the couch Grampa's sprawled across, he had his share of brandy and fell asleep. Mariette starts snoozing. We're quiet. Cindy's gone up to her room, at least I think so, even her grandmother is never sure where she actually is. And that's nice. It's calm here. The silence. Grampa's breath is loud. And I touch my dick in its underwear, I get myself hard and stroke gently, I almost bring myself off right there, while they're sleeping, I've never gotten quite so close and it's almost that now-or-never moment, I can tell they're all deep asleep and I'm rock-hard in

Grampa's underwear . . . That's it, I'm coming. I pull, I pull, I watch each of them in turn . . . It's so fucking good to jerk off in this underwear, I have all the space I need, the cotton glides over my balls every time I slide my hand over the head. I don't even have time to fantasize about anything, I'm so turned on that in no time at all I'm spurting in Grampa's underwear. And after that, I feel kind of like a fool, I tell myself I should have made myself last longer, I don't have anything to do all day, I could have waited . . . Even just to show Mariette my cock making a huge lump in my shorts . . . But now, great, what with everything that my balls have churned out, I'll have a nice map of France right in the middle of my shorts. They're still sleeping tight, but naps never last long, I get up and go to grab my red underwear off the telephone stand. I go out into the garden. The whole town's more or less numbed by the heat wave. Behind the clothesline, I take off Grampa's navy-blue underwear, I pull on my red underwear, I put on my shorts, and, without any witnesses, the deed's done. What am I going to do with Grampa's underwear? I could leave it on the ground, sure, but I'm sure I have better options. Sneakier ones. I have to think fast, they're not going to be asleep all afternoon. I look around, still nobody, the neighborhood's still fast asleep. Then a great idea hits me straightaway, I clip the underwear back on the clothesline, and, hanging there, it all adds up nicely . . . Mariette will have her seven pairs of underwear, she'll be happy . . . And she'll find the seventh one with dried cum or, better yet, if she's lucky, she'll find it still wet. Just thinking about it makes me smile. With that, I head back toward the house. They're still asleep, and there, now that I know nobody's seen or heard me at all, I just have to lie back down on the couch and shut my eyes.

We're all woken up by the doorbell. Mariette collects herself. Grampa opens one eye. It rings again. Mariette sits up properly on the couch, she says:

"That must be the police!"

And she goes to answer the door. Grampa opens both eyes. I wonder: "The police? Why the police?"

Then Grampa looks at me, still sluggish, and asks me:

"Is that the police?"

"I don't know," I say.

I hear Mariette talking with the men at her door but their voices are muffled, I can't make out what they're saying and then she lets them in and through the doorway I see two uniformed men go by. From where he's sitting, even though he's swaying from side to side, Grampa hasn't been able to see them. I tell him, nervously:

"Yes, it's the police!"

He seems satisfied. He slumps back into the couch. In the distance, Mariette calls Cindy . . . she calls once, twice, and then Cindy finally answers from upstairs, she says:

"What's wrong?"

"Did you take the red underwear from the phone stand?" Mariette bellows.

Grampa and I are looking at each other right then. He finally smiles at me, not really a smile, more of a face that means: "Mariette isn't happy, we're in for trouble." I'm half aware that Grampa doesn't really like Cindy. I keep listening.

"You're going to come down when I call you, not talk back from upstairs!" Mariette yells.

Cindy runs down the stairs. I keep on listening.

"You're positive it wasn't you?"

"Yes, I'm absolutely positive."

"Because this is serious, if I've made the police come for nothing, they'll be angry . . . And how do you think this makes me look?"

"It wasn't me!"

"If not you, who was it, then?"

No answer, and then some whispering, and then footsteps coming back down the hallway. And I see the police through the doorway, looking back at me.

"Could you come here, sir?"

Grampa makes another odd face, as if shit was really going to hit the fan. This whole thing seems to be funny for him. I'm in front of Cindy and Mariette again, with policemen on both sides watching me, Mariette and Cindy really bothered and also watching me but not for long, just a few furtive glances. And I notice right then that Cindy's breasts have grown a lot since last time, she's changed her tee-shirt, she's not wearing the Pink Panther one anymore, she's swapped that for another one that's gray and a bit tighter. She's got a nice set of tits, impressive ones. The policeman who seems to be in charge distracts me from Cindy's breasts, he asks me very solemnly:

"Did you take a pair of red underpants there, by the phone?"

I say no.

Everybody turns toward Cindy, especially Mariette, really, just how stupid are they, and, as if in reply to an accusation, she blurts out:

"But he did, I swear to you, I saw him."

"You saw him take them from that table there?" the chief asks.

"No, not there, but I was upstairs at the window, I saw him in the garden, by the clothes drying on the line, he took off a pair of Grampa's underwear, and then he put on the red one he was holding in his hand, and then he hung up Grampa's underwear on the line . . . And then he left."

I'm screwed now, but I tell myself that I have to do something, say something, I say:

"But Cindy, really, it wasn't me!"

"Yes, it was you!"

"But he was with us in the living room the whole time," her

grandmother says, and she turns toward the policemen and looks at them, shaking her head.

"Oh yeah?" Cindy says back. "After lunch, you slept so well that he could have done anything he wanted in the house and you wouldn't have heard a thing."

Mariette protests but the policeman cuts her off.

"Can you show us where he changed his underwear?"

"Definitely!"

And Cindy leads them into the garden. We all follow, even Grampa comes along, squinting at me, I don't know why he's looking at me that way, I feel like he's known everything from the start, but if so, I can't understand why he hasn't said anything . . . My heart is pounding like mad. And Cindy's tits in the meantime, she's running calmly toward the clothesline and then she stops, she shows the underwear in question to the policemen while Mariette counts Grampa's underwear again. It all adds up.

She takes the underwear in question off the clothesline, and then she sees something, she opens it, smells it, puzzled, she looks at me, but actually she doesn't dare to look at me, she immediately turns away and the chief walks over while pulling on gloves.

"We're going to need that for prints."

He says those words while carefully taking it out of her hands.

"Are we good now? Can I go?" Cindy asks.

"Don't go far," the chief says. He isn't looking at Cindy, his eyes are fixed on the underwear. But she's already run past me, barely glancing at me, without any cruelty or shame, only furtiveness.

"It looks like ejaculate," says the chief. "What do you think?"

And he holds Grampa's underwear under his partner's nose. The partner nods.

"This will be interesting to analyze."

I try not to lose it too much in front of everyone, I'm getting stares from all directions, and I hear the chief asking Mariette:

"So, you'll be pressing charges, I imagine?"

Mariette's really bothered, she doesn't dare to look at me. She's not sure, she wavers, she doesn't want to go quite that far, she looks over at Grampa, she'd like to hear his thoughts.

"Nah," says Grampa. "If it was just so he could jerk off in my underwear, it's nothing serious, we'll wash it."

I can't believe Grampa's answer. Mariette stays calm, doesn't show any feeling, but she's still thinking about it. The chief, however, is a bit pissed.

"Doesn't that upset you, that a stranger's masturbating in your underwear?"

"It's like someone's thinking about me!"

Mariette seems to think he's not taking it seriously. She looks up at the sky.

"Oh, that's a hell of a thing for you to say!"

And in any case, the policeman, who doesn't think any of this is funny, is infuriated.

"It might not bother you, but you've bothered us anyway . . . The next time, think first, we've got better things to deal with!"

"Don't get all riled up now, we didn't realize all this," says Mariette in the most soothing voice she could muster.

The chief cuts her off, he turns toward me.

"OK, could you show us the underwear you've got on?"

I'm flabbergasted and trying to buy some time. I glance at Grampa, then Mariette. She doesn't know what to do, she feels overwhelmed by what's happened. Grampa, though, still seems to think this whole thing isn't serious, that I just need to show him and that'll be all.

"Here, in front of everyone?"

"The neighbors might see us," Mariette adds.

The chief looks around. The neighborhood's waking up from its siesta, the neighbor to the right has poked his head out his window, when the policeman looks him right in the eye, he pulls his head back in. The chief brings me back inside the house and then he asks me to lower my shorts. Mariette and Grampa are waiting outside. I slowly pull down my shorts, I think that's enough, but no, he gestures for me to lower them all the way. And then he looks at his partner and says:

"Well, no question there, it's red!"

Then he says to Mariette: "Could you come here?"

Mariette walks over, she doesn't dare to look too carefully.

"Well?" the policeman asks her.

She doesn't know, and he starts to get infuriated by all these hesitations.

"Fine, take them off," he says, "so she can look at them more closely."

Grampa comes over, he looks at me sympathetically but also somewhat deviously, I'm thinking the whole time about what he told the policemen and then we hear Cindy's footsteps down the staircase.

"You can't do that here, I don't want Cindy seeing any of this!" says Mariette.

I pull my shorts back up. Cindy walks over, she's changed her tee-shirt, now she's wearing a tank top, I can already see her bra straps. I'm aware of the passage of time, like a mother seeing her children grow up.

The chief pulls me out of my thoughts about Cindy's breasts, at Mariette's urging he takes me into the bathroom, where there's also a toilet. And we're in this windowless room, not a small one but not terribly big either. We're facing each other, his hands are on his hips, the right one is just above his revolver, his gaze seems to say that he's not going to ask me twice and that his patience is almost completely gone.

I try to find something to say, I should revolt, but I'm in no position, or rather, I can't be bothered, I feel like it'll all be okay, Grampa and Mariette are on my side, she's even sorry she called the police . . . So I stay nonchalant, anyway, there's no getting around it, I take off my underwear. He takes it from my hands, leaves the bathroom, through the open door, I watch as he shows Mariette the underwear, she shakes her head no. Grampa mimics her. Then the chief is furious, he comes back to me.

"Give me your tee-shirt and your shorts."

I don't even have time to ask what for, he's raised his voice, gotten dangerously close to me, I tell myself that I have to push back . . . Yes, no matter what, I have to do something, he can't just take my clothes away, I get ready to scream my head off, but I don't see it coming, I'm hit hard on the head. It's too hard, I lose my balance, I fall, I'm hurt, my head explodes. I struggle to stay conscious. I can feel them pulling my clothes off, I want to fight back but I can't, behind the door, I vaguely hear Mariette saying:

"What did you do to him?"

And right after, the chief doesn't answer, he just says:

"We're taking it all for DNA analysis!"

I remember the DNA part very clearly and then my head really hurts, I can't take it anymore, I lose consciousness.

I wake up naked on the cold floor. I hear banging against the door, Mariette is calling, she's worried, she keeps knocking. Until I answer. But I answer softly, I mumble a "yes, what's wrong?" Mariette asks me if I'm okay. My head hurts, the light hurts my eyes, I remember that very clearly. Then I tell myself that's odd . . . Mariette knocking on the door when I'm locked out. I check, the key isn't on my side. I ask her to open.

"But they took the key," she replies. "They told us to wait until they came back."

"There has to be a crowbar somewhere!"

Mariette doesn't reply. I say it again.

"If we let you go, that'll make them furious!"

This story has upset her as much as me, she says that I just have to be patient, that they won't take long.

"Yes, but when they come back, do you really think they'll stop there?" I ask her. "You've seen the way they behave, it's going to be even worse."

She knows it, that there's something wrong with this whole situation, for that matter, she's called the police station to make sure those were real policemen since she was so shocked by their way of handling things, and they had confirmed it, the sergeant was actually irritated that she'd asked. In short, aside from the fact that we have to wait and that'll make them even more furious, she doesn't know what else to say. She's sorry for me but she can't do anything. I hear footsteps headed into the distance. Then I don't hear anything else. She doesn't answer. I tell myself that she'll come back and then no, she doesn't come back.

I sit in a corner. I decide to wait. I listen carefully. Nothing. I get worried. I watch the door. I look everywhere, I can't find a single thing that might help me, a screwdriver, a trowel, I don't know what but a thin, strong tool. There has to be *something* of that sort in a bathroom. And then I hear velvety footsteps, someone walking barefoot, and then a piece of paper slides under the door. I read it: "I'm sorry, I didn't want to do it but I had to, otherwise I'm always the one getting in trouble. Grampa will get you out of there. Cindy."

And immediately after, I hear iron striking against wood, and I'm positive that's Grampa attacking the door with a crowbar. He manages to break through, I can tell it's happening bit by bit, it skids once or twice, but he keeps at it, I'm hopeful again. No matter what, I'm happy that Grampa and Cindy are going to all this trouble for me. And suddenly, all at once, I hear the front door open amid the ruckus, footsteps in the hallway . . . The chief's voice asking: "What are you trying to do there?" The crowbar falls on the ground. Cindy yells: "Grammy!" Mariette runs in from the garden or someplace else, I'm guessing she wasn't in the house, and she says sharply:

"Can't you ring before entering someone's house?"

"Well, we have proof, it's him . . . That's it, have you decided?"

"To what?"

The chief doesn't answer. I can't see, but I can tell he's very upset. Mariette makes the mistake of repeating her question, and then it happens:

"All right, Grampa, time for the Tour de France, we're changing your diaper."

Everyone's arguing, Grampa's yelling. He's being dragged into the living room. In the hallway, Mariette digs her heels in:

"Just what are you trying to do here?"

And then her voice is more muffled but I can still understand her, so she must be in the living room:

"Just what are you doing to him?" she says, anxious.

"Since you want to leave it at that, we're giving him his underwear back."

"Hey, it's okay, you don't actually need to do that."

The crowbar starts its work on the door again, that has to be Cindy using the whole mess as cover to get the crowbar in deeper and deeper, I pull as hard as I can on the doorknob, I don't feel like I'm doing much, but if it helps at all . . . And Mariette says in the living room:

"At least let him keep his diaper on!"

"The underwear's already dirty anyway!"

Mariette shuts up.

In the living room, someone's turned on the TV, the ruckus of horns honking frantically and the muffled commentary all mean it's the Tour de France.

And then Mariette says at the end of the hallway:

"Oh Cindy, stop that right now!"

And the other cop, not the chief, the other guy, comes running and tells Cindy:

"Well, well, aren't you twisted . . . First you tattle on him, and then you try to let him out . . . Come here, you're going to help your grandpa watch the Tour de France."

And he pulls Cindy into the living room. Mariette follows, she's worried, all she wants is for everybody to calm down, and for the cops to free me and leave. She'd like that but that's not the way things are turning out, and her patience is endless. She's raised three kids, she's stuck with Cindy on every trip not to mention her other grandchildren, and her husband, if the rumors are true, wasn't much help at all . . . Always chasing after girls left and right and hitting on them or drinking at bars with friends until the wee hours.

She waits.

And then she says:

"What are you waiting for?"

Footsteps in the hallway, a key in the lock. I have no idea what to do at first, I'm looking for something to knock out the chief and then I stop, it's too late, the door is already open and, he's not dumb, he's sent Mariette in as a scout. Mariette stands in the doorway, then looks away. She doesn't want to see that. The policeman pushes her in:

"Go on in, he's not going to eat you!"

He follows her, shuts the door, I step back as far as I can, until I'm up against the toilet, I'm naked, but not trying to cover myself up, I'm not upset that Mariette can see my dick . . . It would have been nice if the circumstances had been otherwise, but even now, actually, I like it. And she still doesn't want to see.

"Do you recognize the facts?" the chief asks me.

I focus on him. I've been telling myself that the next time I lay eyes on him, I really should carve his face in my memory. Aside from his seriousness and severity, I hadn't remembered a thing. And, even if I concentrate on him thoroughly, all I know is that I don't like his face. His intense stare keeps me from seeing the color of his eyes, I actually think that, on another face, it would be a beautiful gaze. His long, broken nose convinces me he's not handsome. Tall and tough, he's a beauty of a beast. His height is impressive, his gaze is terrifying, but I steel myself and ask him:

"What facts?"

His eyes narrow and even though he wasn't easygoing before, now, I'm really in for trouble. He shoves Mariette even closer to me. In front of her, no question, I can't recognize anything at all. And I get the feeling that if I recognize the facts, it'll get worse. He doesn't seem like the kind of guy to wait for justice's wheels to turn. By not recognizing them, I tell myself that I'm not going to win much but at least I can sit tight in this bathroom. Mariette looks me in the eyes, oh she feels terrible for having called the police, she feels guilty and she wishes it would stop, she would like me to admit to it, it'd be so easy, and they'd leave again. Then she looks down.

"They've found your fingerprints . . ."

"And not just the prints, tell him the rest!"

Mariette pauses, she looks back up at me. He pushes her a bit again, not hard, she wavers.

"Go on, tell him!"

"And it's your semen in Grampa's underwear."

"And how do they know that it's his semen?"

"Because of the DNA!"

"You had no chance from the outset," the chief says. "So?"

I shake my head. I don't believe his story about DNA one bit. He looks at me as if to say, "Well, if that's how it is, we'll just have to see what happens." He drags Mariette and asks her, his hand on her back:

"Are you going to press charges?"

On the doorstep, she shakes her head no and immediately lowers her head, she can't look at him. He gets angry right away.

"Fuck, what's wrong with this place. I've had enough of this, all you wackos calling us when shit's gone wrong and after we work our asses off to fix the problem you give us the runaround."

"It's our choice whether or not to press charges."

"And when more of Grampa's underwear gets stolen, you'll just call us again!"

"But you can't just send him to prison for that!"

"That's not your decision to make!"

"Oh, but it is, at least a bit," Mariette says while looking at the chief's chest.

The other cop yells from the other end of the hallway:

"Grampa wants to go to the bathroom."

"All right, bring him in!"

And he pushes Mariette out of the bathroom, she keeps on protesting.

"But you're not going to let him . . ."

And she doesn't know how to finish her sentence but we all understand. The chief brings Grampa into the bathroom without listening to Mariette, he pulls the door shut in her face. Grampa is in a hurry. He's in his underwear and his undershirt, and runs over to the toilet, turns around, and just as he's about to pull down his underwear, the chief stops him, makes him sit down on the rim. Grampa refuses, he tries to get back up, the chief holds him down with one hand firmly on his shoulder, the other hand on his baton, I get close to the chief, I feel an urge to hit him but I don't do anything and, just as the thought crosses my mind, the baton strikes my forehead, I didn't even see him raise his arm, I stumble backward against the wall. The chief yells:

"Bring over the handcuffs!"

The other policeman comes in quickly, and the first one clicks the cuffs around my wrists. My head still hurts, I'm just a bit dazed, he has no trouble at all getting me face down against the ground. I can't struggle, and, worse, I don't even want to, I feel so weak, I feel like giving up, I'll never be able to. Be able to what? I don't know anymore.

I hear the chief telling his partner:

"Go get the chair!"

The chair? I don't understand. Something new's going to happen. This is far from being over . . . Then I think of Grampa . . . Yes, Grampa, I mustn't forget him, I turn over and push against the wall. I see his head slumped down and beaten. Humiliated, he's humiliated, he looks at me as if everything had gone to pieces, as if we wouldn't ever see each other again and as if we were stuck together forever. And he buries his face in his hands.

"Come on, Grampa, it's fine, we had to wash it anyway!" the policeman says.

He sets a hand on his shoulder and then he says:

"You can take it off now!"

Grampa doesn't react. He's listless.

"Let's go, you can't spend all day sitting in your own shit can you? Come on, let's go!"

Grampa's hardly lively, the chief helps him with a hand under the shoulder, he's encouraging. The partner brings the chair.

"Watch the lady and the little girl, don't let them lose their head!"

The partner goes off and then, above me, Grampa's standing, the chief's holding him up while he's laboriously pulling down his shit-filled underwear. I look away, I don't want to see Grampa naked in his shit. I don't want to humiliate him even more. If I see his penis, it's all over.

"Oh, good, I see that you've pissed yourself, too!" says the chief.

He doesn't seem especially satisfied, it's just an observation.

"Okay, good, now let's put this on your friend."

Grampa doesn't know what's happening, he looks at me, he looks at the chief, he looks at me again, I don't know why I'm still staying on the ground. I consider trying to do something but with the handcuffs I know it'll be tricky. I don't try anything. I know that I shouldn't look at Grampa's penis but my eyes move down. Then I see his balls dripping with shit. It doesn't even last a whole second. I straighten up immediately, I meet Grampa's eyes, I act like I didn't see, but he saw that I saw. The chief pulls him, Grampa looks away. I hear the chief saying:

"We're done with him, he can go wash himself now!"

Grampa leaves the bathroom, I recognize his padding footsteps.

"What if we press charges?" Mariette asks very quietly, her voice wavering.

She doesn't know what to do to make this stop. I'm still not looking.

"We'll see about that later!"

Then I see the chief coming toward me, pulling on his white gloves, he starts putting Grampa's underwear on me. I struggle, but the policeman is strong, he holds me down without any trouble and, in any case, I know that I'm not trying hard enough to really bother him. I feel Grampa's shit along my thighs. It reeks. I'm exhausted and scared. He pulls the underwear all the way up to my waistline. My balls and the bottom of my ass are swimming in Grampa's piss and shit.

He picks me up and sets me down on the chair, my handcuffed hands behind the back of the chair, and as I slump down, the base snaps under me, my ass gets stuck there. I can't move. My arms hurt as they're twisted behind the slats of the chair's back, but pain at least is something I can bear, I'll get through it . . . The gloves, the chair, just him and me . . . Fear rises up in me again, I know the next few minutes are going to be nasty.

He gets on his knees next to me, and with a gloved finger, he yanks Grampa's shit-filled underwear up my ass, I instinctively try to fight back, stupidly, but he holds me in place:

"Don't move," he says. "The more you move, the more it'll hurt! Relax, there, just like that, calm down!"

He's right, that's better, it hurts but not nearly as much, and the fact is, whether I move or not, this is going to happen, he's set on that idea, so much that I might as well let it happen without a struggle. And then he'll kill me but then it'll be over . . . Dying isn't something I really care about in the end, it's suffering that really scares me. So I grit my teeth, but when he pushes two fingers in, I can't help twitching.

"Quiet," he says. "Do you feel it, Grampa's shit sliding up your ass?"

I wasn't even thinking about that, I suddenly realize what he's thinking. I freak out. I twist around. It hurts. He tells me again not to move. I'm astonished by how calm he is, he's taking all the time in the world.

"I don't want to hurt you," he adds. He's not joking, he's very serious and his voice is still gentle and masculine.

I believe him. He just wants to push all of Grampa's shit into my ass, with as little pain as possible. And I tell myself there's that, at least, if he wants to hurt me, I'll let him, and just as I relax, he takes his two fingers out, that feels nice, but right after that, I feel a big thing, much bigger than his two fingers, harder too, and it's long, it goes in deep. It's the baton, I suddenly understand. It hurts, it really hurts. I thought I'd reached the peak of pain, I thought it couldn't possibly be worse, and now I realize that it'll never stop, that there'll always be something worse. I scold myself for being so stupid as to believe the chief, to believe that he didn't want to hurt me. So I start yelling, he shoves his hand over my mouth, not violently, and says:

"Don't scream, you'll just scare everyone in the next room, that's all screaming will do! Understand?"

I agree, I want to nod my head but I can't. My neck muscles don't work, I just drop my bruised head, I let my muscles relax, he pushes in deeper and deeper, the underwear's tight, he furrows inside me, the chief pulls the baton out a bit and then pushes it in deeper . . . And I drift off into a nightmare, I'm apart from all this. Like in an accident, I become a third man and watch myself facing the chief just accepting my fate, head down, in total submission, I contemplate the two of us facing each other, my ass stuck in the chair, and his knee on the ground as he pushes his baton all the way in. When he realizes he can't push any further, he steps back, but he still has me look at myself:

"I think that's good, you've got Grampa's shit all the way up your ass."

He still doesn't seem especially proud of himself. It's just an observation. As if he'd accomplished a disagreeable mission. I don't know what he's doing. I look up at him. He looks back at me. Even though I'm beaten up, at the end of my limits, I insist on seeing him one last time, I don't know why, it's not even to engrave his face in my memory anymore, I don't think that'll help me at all down the line, but it's more the way I'd look at someone I'd had an intense experience with. I can't say that he has a nasty face, he has the sort of frightening and mysterious face I've seen in dreams. I tell myself, that's a man. His forehead's covered in sweat, his lips are pressed thin. I don't want to meet his gaze, even though I won't see the color of his eyes. He sets a hand on my shoulder.

"All right, it's over," he says.

And I know that he's wrong. It can't end like that. He takes out the baton, I feel better but I can still feel Grampa's underwear all stretched out and twisted in my ass, I watch him washing his baton in the sink. Through the mirror, he throws me an empty, lost gaze. That, I tell myself, that means he doesn't want to kill me but he has to, and at that point I freak out . . . Deep within myself, I knew that moment was going to come one day. In my suffering, I hadn't really envisioned it, as if I'd decided deep within myself to take one anguish at a time. But now, there we go, it's happening. A panic, I don't want to die . . . Even if I have to, I don't want to, I'm going to sort this out, I want to keep going. I tell him everything, anything . . . That I won't say a word to anybody, that I won't try to get revenge . . . That I recognize the facts . . . And that I'll even get Mariette and Grampa to press charges . . .

He comes back, gets down on one knee, sets one hand on my shoulder.

"I know," he says.

And then, without any rush, as if he now only wanted to help me, he takes Grampa's navy-blue underwear out of my ass and all my own shit comes out with it.

"There's no use in pressing charges now."

He says that while unfolding Grampa's underwear. Suddenly it becomes absolutely clear that I'm going to die but I can't summon up all my strength again. I realize that I can't change the trajectory of things anymore. It's better to let this run its course. I watch him out of the corner of my eye, he's calm, I don't understand why he's just sitting there unfolding Grampa's underwear, and just as I think that, he wraps it around my head . . . I panic and start suffocating, it sticks to my lips, my nose, it fills my eyes, every time I try to take a breath, the shit gets a bit deeper into my mouth . . . Ugh, the smell, the disgust, the fear, I've held on for so long, my stomach begins to heave and I vomit everything that was in there. I shake my head to rid myself of this shit rag, I can't hear anything anymore, I struggle and wait until someone shoots me in the head. But I want to live. And I really don't want to die in Grampa's navy-blue underwear, suffocating under his shit and mine.

Evening. Night is falling gently. We're all together, Grampa, Mariette, Cindy, and me, in the living room. I'm afraid the policemen will come back but I'm even more afraid of leaving this house. I'm afraid that they're waiting for me outside or somewhere else, on the way home, I wonder if they know where I live. And besides, what else would I do? I don't have anyone to go see, even though I can always go see friends I don't have anyone I could tell this to. I don't feel like it. I don't want to take my car, I can't be bothered, I just want to get my strength back. Wait for this to blow over. Nobody's really suggested that I stay here for the night, but they haven't exactly said that I should go either. I stay put in this armchair. With Grampa, we're drinking plum brandy. Cindy is dipping sugar cubes in it. Not talking at all or very little. Mariette asks every so often if we want to eat something but no, nobody's hungry. For me, anyway, everything would taste like shit. Grampa, too, is lying prostrate on his end of the couch. Even Cindy isn't moving, she's right next to her grandmother. We haven't talked much about what we should do, but we're all more or less in agreement that this is like a secret that we mustn't ever let out of this house, it has to stay with us and we'll live with that. Even a doctor, we didn't really think that a doctor should come and examine me . . . And show him what, anyway? Yes, there was a little blood, but it stopped quickly, the chief had done it right, just a pair of underwear full of shit and a bump on my head from the baton blows. And the headache after . . . And, of course, my ass hurts, but what's to be done aside from some Tylenol and some patience? I know that Mariette doesn't want shame to fall on this house. And she knows I'd never do that to her. She told me that the police had been extremely menacing as they'd left the house . . . They'd promised her that they wouldn't hesitate to air the whole thing if ever . . . They hadn't said anything further, they just said "if ever" . . . Oh yes, they also added that they might as well express some gratitude for having solved the mystery of Grampa's stolen underwear so quickly. And Mariette thanked them. And that just set off Grampa. He's still pissed at her. He doesn't say a single word to her. However, he's talking to Cindy, he's being nice to her, the afternoon's events have brought them closer together.

As for me, I don't know where I stand, I don't know what to do. Mariette watches me for a while longer, I don't know what she wants, I can't figure out if she's angry at me . . . If she's angry at herself . . . I don't see much in her glare. After all, yes, I'm pretty sure this little bout of masturbating in her father's underwear hasn't made her happy. It's definitely broken something we had between us . . . Even as it's brought us closer together . . . I guess I don't know anymore. And since I really do feel happy in this house, since I feel close to them and know that tomorrow morning I'll have breakfast with them, I have to be sure, I ask her:

"Would it be all right if I stayed here to sleep?"

I look at all of them but it's really Mariette I'm asking.

"You can't leave now!" Grampa says.

Mariette doesn't think for very long, as if she were waiting for me to mention my plans, she gets up, she says:

"I'll make your bed!"

And she leaves the room. Grampa is happy for me to stay. Cindy, too. Grampa brings us out some liquor, we have to fortify ourselves, getting properly drunk will help us think about other things and it'll help get rid of the taste of shit that's still in my mouth and nostrils and won't go away. On top of that, a strong drink ought to help us get to sleep because there's no chance of that happening otherwise. And Grampa, who appreciates Cindy's company, asks her if she wants another sugar cube. Well, he doesn't have to ask twice . . . She dips it into Grampa's brandy, she soaks it completely, Grampa has to tell her that it's good now, it's been properly dipped, any longer and it'll dissolve in her fingers, she swallows it, and then she remembers that Mariette isn't there, she takes another cube, looks at Grampa with a mischievous smile, and she comes over to dip her cube in my own glass, I glance at Grampa, he waves that it's all right, no harm done, she raises her cube of sugar to us as if to say "cheers," Grampa and I follow suit, we raise our glasses, we drink, and she bites into the sugar with self-satisfaction. Then Grampa fills his cup up again. He's also taking advantage of Mariette's absence, and we clink glasses again and drink again. We forget, we're pretty close to being happy. I've always felt good in this house, this evening more than ever. And Mariette comes back down and she finds us there, she can tell there's some weird vibe between us, and in the end, I think she's happy that we're in good humor again, in any case she pours herself a glass and we toast . . . She even clinks her glass against mine, she looks me right in the eyes, smiles at me, and we drink. Outside, we hear a car going by with its radio blaring, its bass tones shaking the floor under us . . . It's Friday evening. I think about tomorrow, cool, after what's happened I don't need to go to Daniel's birthday party.

I feel all alone in my bed. Despite the booze, I'm not able to fall asleep. I'm used to sleeping by myself, but it's different here, I'd like to have someone near me, even someone who doesn't want me to cuddle with him. Just someone. Surely it wouldn't stop me from calling up these images again . . . I think back to Grampa on the toilet, I see my ass stuck in the chair, a baton stuck all the way up to my gut, I see the shit again, I even smell it, the odor hasn't gone away since this afternoon . . . When

Mariette took Grampa's underwear off my head, even with the handcuffs off, I couldn't get myself out of that chair, so when Mariette pulled me free, that was the first thing I had to do, wash my face, rinse my mouth, my nostrils, my eyes . . . And I didn't stop rinsing and scrubbing and rinsing again for hours . . . The smell was finally gone physically but the memory of that smell is still there. I try my best to push away that image of my face buried in Grampa's and my shit. But to push away an image, I have to put another one in its place, there's no way to live without images at that moment. . . And I don't have many options, either I go back to Grampa shitting on the toilet, or back to the chief, no matter what there has to be someone and someone associated with that moment. So I focus on the chief as much as I can. His face, his mustache, his gaze . . . These images seem gentle to me, I don't know if they are only in comparison to the others or if they actually are. And I don't like thinking these images are gentle, I consider Cindy's breasts, but that doesn't work, it's inappropriate, I don't want that, the chief killed anything I could have used for fantasy. I come back to the chief. His mouth, his nose, especially his mustache, his gaze. I recreate the chief's face bit by bit, it's still blurred, I try to detach myself, I reconstitute it, I add some feeling, his harshness, his seriousness when he asks me, "Do you smell it, Grampa's shit up your ass?" but also his gentleness when he sets his hand on my shoulder and tells me, "Okay, it's over!" And I add more, I add bits like that until it makes up a whole man.

I'm thinking about that when someone knocks on my door, softly, very softly. At first, I thought it was just a figment of my imagination, but then they knock again. I say yes very quietly, soft footsteps in the darkness.

"Can I get in with you?"

It's Cindy. I turn on the light. She hasn't even waited for an answer, she's already in my bed.

"Listen, Cindy," I whisper, "you can't stay there, go back to your bed, it's time to sleep now!"

"Were you sleeping?" she asks.

"I wasn't sleeping, but it's late for you, you have to go to sleep."

"I can't."

Typical. She's kneeling on the bed, she doesn't seem ready to leave, and I feel really bad about it. I do understand where she's coming from, though, and I'm not upset to have someone in my room, even if it's Cindy. But it's not possible, she can't stay here, I whisper:

"What if your grandmother finds you here?"

"It'll be fine, we're not doing anything wrong . . . And besides, I don't want to be all by myself!"

"Why don't you go sleep with her?"

"She'll yell at me."

"Of course not, she won't yell at you . . . Not tonight."

"You don't know much about her, do you?"

"All right now, go back to your room."

I must not have been persuasive enough. She insists.

"Go!"

She wants to get into bed, I stop her.

"No, Cindy, there's no way, if your grandmother finds you in my bed . . ."

"How would she find us, anyway? When she sleeps, she's deep asleep, she doesn't care, and anyway, nobody cares about me, my parents are off in Greece . . . While I'm stuck here with two old farts. They spend all their time sleeping and the less they see me, the happier they are."

"Don't say that, Cindy, it's not true, your parents care about you!"

"So why didn't they bring me along, then? Hmm?"

"They just need some time alone every so often . . ."

And even as I tell her that, I wonder what the fuck I'm doing. I'm not going to defend her parents' running off to Greece and sticking her with Mariette and Grampa. I stop. She retorts immediately:

"Well, they could have just not had me!"

"Okay fine, I get it for your parents," I say, "but, your grandmother, she really . . ."

But I stop there, I've heard a door opening, we both listen carefully. Footsteps on the wooden floor, we're quiet, then Mariette calls out: "Cindy." Cindy answers: "I'm here." And when Mariette opens my door, Cindy's still sitting at the end of my bed, I'm still under the sheets.

"What are you doing there?"

"I didn't want to be all by myself."

"Why didn't you come to see me instead of bothering Gilles?"

"Because you were asleep!"

"Actually, no, I wasn't sleeping."

"You were! Maybe you didn't realize it, but you were asleep."

Mariette looks at me with profound exhaustion, she's sick of this, she's worn out, having to deal with a teenager for all of vacation, she's too old for this, she can't wait until her parents come back and everybody's life goes back to normal. I understand. I wave at Cindy to get off my bed, calmly at first and then forcefully. Cindy doesn't move, or only a little, as if to acknowledge us. Mariette goes to pull her out.

"Come on!" she says. "Enough of keeping him awake."

"But he wasn't asleep," Cindy says. "Right? I wasn't keeping you awake."

"She's right, I wasn't asleep, but I'm tired anyway."

Mariette's patience is infinite, she goes up to Cindy, takes her hand.

"Come on, Cindy, let's go to your room, I'll stay and sleep next to you, okay?"

And Cindy knows that she can't win and just has to go along with her grandmother's proposition, she gets off my bed quietly, lets out a huge sigh, and Mariette leads her out, slowly. Before leaving my room, Cindy wants to act nice one last time, she turns around with a smile that sticks in her throat, she says "good night," and her grandmother pulls her away.

And I'm alone again. Even Cindy staying would have been better than nobody. That's funny, I think, she's a pain in the ass, she's a moron, not all that cute, she doesn't have a lot going for her, but I think I do like her, deep down . . . Likewise for Mariette, there's not much for us to talk about, we don't worry about the same things in life, we'd both end up bored together in the long run, but still . . . And ditto for Grampa, too, we have even less to talk about, with two back-and-forths we've exhausted all topics of conversation, but still . . . Still, I feel happy when I'm with them. Always have, actually. We met one morning when I was with one of their neighbors to make an estimate for building a veranda, and Mariette was sweeping the sidewalk in front of her door. Her neighbor wasn't answering the doorbell, so Mariette tried to help by yelling his name, because she was sure he had to be out back in his garden and so he wouldn't be able to hear the doorbell. But when he still didn't answer, we got to talking about the weather (it was still cold, and for May, that wasn't great, we were actually a bit sick of winter), the construction at the Trintaud entrance which was making a huge mess in the town. And every so often I rang the doorbell again, in case the neighbor had come back in from gardening. And then Mariette said that since we were talking, we might as well have a conversation where it was warm, and she invited me over for some coffee . . . Inside, Grampa was reading *La Dépêche* at the kitchen table. We settled in, had our coffee. We didn't have much to talk about and fortunately her neighbor finally turned up not too long after . . . But I did feel at home there, so I came back to see them two or three weeks later, just like that, to say hi, and I could tell right away that they were delighted I'd come back to see them. They were already both on their own, him a widower, her long since divorced, she had come back here to take care of her father. My visits broke up their tête-à-têtes. . . A father and his daughter at that age, that can't be fun every single day. They did like talking, they were both inquisitive in the best sense of the word, they took interest in what I did . . . I told them about my life, but not too much, and they listened happily without asking further. Then Mariette invited me to come eat, once, twice . . . And every time I'd bring a bottle of wine or some flowers. And after dinner we'd kill some time drinking plum brandy or watching TV or both. And I really did like being bored with them. It was always nice. I just felt better every time I was at that house . . . Enough that, little by little, I began jerking off at their place . . . Not out of any desire for Grampa or Mariette . . . Just for the warmth of their welcome, I'd found my peaceful haven . . . And I cast my mind back to those days of happiness and boredom . . . But I'm an idiot, I shouldn't think about that . . . Again, I see Grampa on the toilet, holding his head in his hands because he'd just shit in his underwear . . . Because maybe deep down he knew what his underwear full of shit would be used for. I don't want to think about that. The memory of that smell comes back. I think of the chief. His mustache, his calm gaze as he pushes the baton and Grampa's underwear up my ass, the vague feeling coming over me at that moment, the fear, the pain, the fear of pain, the anguish of not knowing when it would all end and that of knowing that even when it really hurt, it could hurt even more . . . And in the middle of all that, a sort of trust that I had in the chief, he's not far from being my friend, I have to be careful, it's fragile . . . The image is fragile, I have to hold it all the way through . . . And poof, it falls apart, the shit-filled underwear surges back into my mouth. I turn in bed, and then again. I turn on the light. I can't stay in the darkness anymore. I can't be by myself anymore.

Sitting on my bed, eyes wide open, I see Grampa in the garden again, telling the policeman, "Nah, if it was just so he could jerk off in my underwear, it's nothing serious . . . He's just thinking about me!" I think about that again and keep coming back to that image of a tranquil Grampa, devilish and happy-go-lucky, without a single worry, always seeing the good side of things, and beneath that comes the image of a more anguished Grampa, alone in his bed, unable to sleep, knowing that he's not long for this world, hoping that someone's thinking of him. So then I no longer feel alone. I tell myself that I have to go down and join Grampa, that great stranger . . . The man living in this house a bit like a ghost, living his little life, who's called Grampa these days just as he once was called Baby . . . We're amused or amazed by his age, we forgive him everything because at heart it's not serious, he's alive, there, in his corner he's made his own little world. When we talk and he's nearby, we act as if he's not there, the modern world's more or less passed him by, he's already twenty years out of touch . . . And he's grown accustomed to living that way, after all, nobody's unkind to him, he's a bit deaf and it's better that way, he falls asleep in front of the TV, he waits for life to go by, he could live for eons that way, just watching everyone else move . . . So long as there's someone next to him, he can bear it all . . . But at night, all alone in his bed, is he all right? Tonight, that great stranger is doubtless my best friend. I'm off.

By the time I'm in front of his bedroom door, I'm already less sure of myself. I knock twice, not very hard. And immediately after I hear Grampa asking: "Who is it?" I open the door.

"It's me, Gilles," I say. "Can I come in?"

"Come on in!"

He turns on the light. He's lying on his back with his head propped up on his pillow, he wasn't sleeping and he wasn't close to sleeping. In his pajamas and beneath the covers pulled up to his neck, despite the heat, he seems to be cold. At first I think I should ask if it would be okay for me to come sleep next to him but I'm nervous that the suggestion might be too abrupt, I reconsider, I just say:

"You're not sleeping?"

He pats the bed as if to say that I should come sit next to him, and I do. We're finally looking at each other, but it's more me looking at him. This is the first time I've seen Grampa without his hat, his hair is uncovered and I feel a bit embarrassed looking, as if this was an intimate part of him. He doesn't have much anymore, most of it is white, and it makes his head look completely different, actually I realize that I've never really taken the time to look at him properly. I suspect I've had a mental image of Grampa that bore no relation to reality and now, tonight, I'm discovering him as he really is. I examine him, I want to unravel the mystery of Grampa, I notice his eyes turning away, they're wet and reddening, as if he'd just been crying, he tilts his head up to the ceiling, he still hasn't answered my question, he wipes a long finger across his eyes, then I understand that he's still crying. He doesn't want me to see him like this, and I lean my head against the wall, now he just sees my profile, I'm not looking at him anymore. It's the first time I've ever seen an old man crying. It's like a revelation. I've always thought that crying was something only kids did, and that the older people got, the less they cried, until they didn't cry at all anymore. I let him cry in his corner, he's being very discreet, crying somewhat inwardly, without sobbing, without sighing . . . But even though I want to respect his privacy, after all I'm here, he invited me in, I can't help looking at him, not for long, just long enough to see his own profile, his head on a pillow, his eyes lost in the ceiling, and a tear making its way past his crows' feet. I'd like to talk but I don't know what to say. I don't know what to do. I can't leave, either, how would that look to have come here only to leave right away? And, deep down, I know he wants me to stay. I wait. Little by little, I get onto the bed, I pull up one leg, then the other, I slide down, I stretch out. I feel comfortable here. I'm happy that Grampa's crying next to me, every so often I try looking over again but it's always a delicate, fragile moment that could blow apart if I did a single thing wrong, I'm afraid of meeting his gaze. All I can do is wait for him to do something. I have time, though. Finally, I sense that he's looking over and I can feel him staring at me, I slowly turn toward him, very slowly. Maybe he's also thinking this is a fragile moment. I wouldn't want him to look away at the last minute. We find each other in our locked gazes, he smiles at me . . . He's smiling the way I do when I've just been crying, and he says:

"It doesn't affect me, you know."

I have no idea what he's talking about, I wait for him to say a bit more.

"It's the same every night . . . Until last year, everything was fine . . . from eleven at night, eleven thirty, until five in the morning, I always slept like a baby and at five o'clock I was up and ready to go, I went into the garden and had a nice nap in the afternoons and that was all well and good . . . But now, nope, I never make it all the way through, I'm suscing[1] all night, I wait for day to break, and when it does, at five or six in the morning, I fall asleep . . . I used to be such a morning person, and now I never get up before nine or ten . . . And after that, the whole day, I'm just dragging myself around, I'm . . ."

He stops talking, he's listening, he says, "Yes . . ." He says that loudly as if he was talking to someone else. The door opens. It's Mariette. She sees me lying on Grampa's bed, bare-chested but

---

1. From the Occitan verb soscar, which means to be lost in thought, to meditate, to hesitate, or to reflect.

with shorts on. She's a bit taken aback and then as if it didn't matter, she says to Grampa:

"I was wondering who you were talking to."

And then she looks at me again, then at Grampa. She stands there, in the doorway, her hand resting on the doorknob.

"Well, you've got to get to sleep now, Grampa!"

She looks at me again. She said that so I would leave. And then I wonder why she always calls him "Grampa." Why not "Papa"? It's her father, after all, she's annoying like that. And Grampa replies:

"You can tell me I should sleep as much as you want. As long as I'm not sleepy, I'm not falling asleep."

But she's not paying attention to his words at all, she says to me:

"Are you going to let him get some sleep?"

She says that very quietly, without any ill will, almost affectionately. Of course, she's a bit tired of our idiocy, she wouldn't like to spend her entire night making sure everyone was properly asleep in their own beds . . . And here I am, trying to show her that I'm not there to stir up trouble, I'm just there to be with Grampa. I'm just about to relent, so there'll be some peace in this house, just for one minute, I think about leaving Grampa's bed . . . Even if I have to come back later. And Mariette's still waiting in the doorframe and we're all still in the same place when Grampa says:

"What are you waiting for, Mariette?" He's abrupt, biting, so much so that we're all caught off-guard . . . "Are you waiting for him to leave so I can spend two more hours suscing all alone like a nimwit? We're talking. We're not doing anything wrong. What are you afraid of?"

"But you're not gonna to sleep together, are you?"

"We're not sleeping!" Grampa says sharply, as if for him that put an end to the conversation, but in fact, it doesn't, so he adds:

"And really, what does it matter if we sleep together? Well?"

And with that Grampa's glues us to the spot. Even Mariette doesn't have anything she can say back to that. She looks at me, she looks at Grampa. She still hasn't let go of the doorknob, she tries to think of an answer, and then she walks over to me, very bothered, she gives in, she says:

"All right, fine! But you can't stay like that!"

And Grampa, looking up, exclaims:

"What exactly are you implying here?"

Mariette's very bothered that the thought's crossed her mind, but she's firm.

"Alright, fine," Grampa says. "Just give him my yellow pajamas if you care so much!"

"Your yellow pajamas?" Mariette asks.

"He's not going to sleep in overalls, is he?"

I can tell Mariette is at her wits' end, she gives up, she just wants to get some sleep and we can do whatever we like but, since her patience is infinite, she rummages in the big oak armoire where all Grampa's clothes are, she pulls out a pair of yellow pajamas, she gives them to me, she says "Good night" to us, and she goes through the door. I stay there with the pajamas in my hands, I look at Grampa, I'm overcome with admiration for him, for this great unknown friend I'm just now discovering. This is a new Grampa who's been revealed to me. And if he doesn't reach a hundred years old, despite the sleepless nights and his long years of masonry (he began when he was thirteen) . . . He's still very serious when he says:

"Put those on, she's going to come back to make sure!"

I'm delighted and pull on Grampa's pajamas. They're a faded, pastel yellow, they still smell like the closet they came from, they smell Grampa's room, they smell like Grampa, smell comes back to me, nothing smells of shit anymore, Grampa clearly had a good idea. I don't know if I should get under the covers now. It's still hot, and it doesn't feel like a moment when I can get away with something. If I'm getting under the covers, it's not going to be until he's asked me to. So I lie on the comforter. I can feel Grampa's eyes on me.

"You happy in my pajamas?" he asks.

I say yes, and then keep looking at him, his head's turned toward me. Tonight, I have to see this new Grampa . . . See him properly, I mean, I want to examine his face, but it's hard because his gaze is locked on mine, so all I can do is meet his eyes. These little brown eyes buried under his wrinkles and his weary, worn-out eyelids half-covering them, and then I don't understand, I don't know whether he's embarrassed or just exhausted. Grampa looks away, he shifts his head on the pillow. I keep my eyes focused on him. His cheek, he has cheeks darkened and etched by time, here and there are little burst vessels that darken his skin even more with bits of blue, and his skin has cracked . . .

"You know," he suddenly says, "I've known for a while."

He doesn't add anything further, as if that were enough, I keep on looking at him, I don't say anything, I assume he'll keep going. And he does.

"Actually, I wasn't sure of anything, but I had my suspicions . . . Well, this morning, I had a feeling you were the one who had taken my underwear, I didn't know what you were up to there, by the clothesline, but I could see you. And this afternoon, in the living room, during the siesta, I heard you, I heard you rubbing, even with my eyes shut . . . I didn't open them at all . . . I knew it was you. Everybody always thinks I'm asleep, but I keep one eye open . . . When I take a nap, it's never good to fall deep asleep. But today, I wasn't sure that it was my underwear you were masturbating in . . . It was when you went into the garden, I heard you and you took so long that I knew you were in the garden . . . And after that I was sure."

And he stops there, he turns his head toward me, he looks at me, I lower my eyes but I end up raising them again and I'm about to tell him something but I don't know what, something so I don't leave it at that, but he's faster than I am.

"I'm telling you this so that you don't think I don't pay attention to anything . . . I'm not telling you this because it's embarrassed me, if it had actually embarrassed me, all I'd have had to do was open my eyes and you'd have stopped."

And then, once again, he doesn't say anything else. His head tilted toward me again, he probably wants to see what I'm thinking. And of course I do feel like an idiot for having thought they were both deep asleep, as I go through my memory of that moment, I realize they didn't seem fully asleep, their breathing wasn't heavy or slow, he's right that they were dozing more than anything else, it was a siesta, nothing more . . . And then I stop feeling ashamed. After all, I kind of like that Grampa knew I was jerking off in his underwear, and even Mariette. I smile at Grampa. More to let him know that I'm sympathetic than to clear away any embarrassment between us . . . No, there's no embarrassment here, it feels good to be together. Grampa smiles in turn.

"I want to ask you a nosy question."

He says it as if he's asking my permission, and I gesture that we're past that point now, he can go ahead, so then he says:

"Were you thinking about me?"

And with that, a hundred thoughts come into my head, I have no idea what Grampa is getting at . . . Of course I had to be thinking about him, and Mariette too, they were right in front of me and I was terrified that they might suddenly open their eyes. But I don't want him getting any ideas. I shake my head no. I get the feeling he's a bit disappointed, or maybe I'm just imagining it, I don't know. He thinks for a couple of seconds, and then he asks again:

"You were masturbating in my underwear, right in front of me, but you weren't thinking about me?"

"No!"

"You're a funny one."

"Okay, I must have been thinking a bit about you, I was looking at you, but not the way you're thinking."

"And what do you think I'm thinking?"

"Or what you might be thinking . . ."

He opens his eyes wide. I clarify:

"I wasn't thinking about making love to you."

He looks at me, I feel like has even more questions now. I have to keep talking.

"I really liked jerking off in your underwear. I like being with you this evening in your bed . . . I like talking . . . But I don't actually want you!"

I stop there, that seems clear enough to me. But he's still looking at me, I don't know what he's thinking about all this. His head falls back on the pillow, his eyes aimed at the ceiling.

"Well, I guess that's best," he finally says, without looking at me.

And suddenly I can't decide whether I'm relieved or disappointed to hear that. On the one hand, relieved because, after his argument with Mariette, the yellow pajamas, and our conversation, I was starting to flip out about Grampa liking me. But also disappointed . . . Certainly I'd have liked for him to have feelings for me. And the way he says that, gently but insistently, makes me afraid that our budding friendship has just been nipped. I'm afraid that Grampa might not want us to stay together. To be honest, I'm afraid that he'll send me off to sleep elsewhere. But then he says:

"Come on, get under the covers, day's about to break, we can fall asleep at last."

And I do it straightaway. I slide into bed, Grampa turns off the light, then he turns over and once he's found a position, he immediately starts breathing deeply, he's sleeping like a log.

Through the window, I can see the sky brightening, I think: "Well, Mariette hasn't come to make sure I've put on Grampa's yellow pajamas." My head still hurts but I'm so happy to have finally met Grampa, I feel like my whole life's been a path toward this single moment that I fall asleep without even knowing it.

I wake up with a tightness in my stomach. A dry mouth, my head foggy like I've got a hangover. I'm hot. Between the sheets and the pajamas, I'm actually too hot, I get out from under the covers. The tightness in my stomach increases when I see Grampa isn't in bed anymore. It doesn't even make me happy that I didn't fall back into nightmare during the night. I don't even remember my dream anymore, I don't like that, I don't like dreamless sleep when I feel like I haven't existed at all . . . So I try to make the night last a little longer. I try to bring back the dream . . . If only even a small, distant image I can grab hold of. But all I could remember was the chief's face, still vague and imprecise and unreal. I'm surprised it hasn't been firmly fixed in my mind, as if his face had escaped me and I still can't understand why he let me stay alive. And how he was able to be so sure that we'd ever tell anyone. I mull over all that in my head, and since I'm getting nowhere, I ask myself why I was so stupid as to grab one of Grampa's pairs of underwear and then jerk off in front of the two of them in the living room. I can't stop thinking about how much of an idiot I am. I turn over onto my stomach. I try not to think about anything but I realize there's no getting past it, I'll eventually see Mariette again this morning. So I get up properly, I sit on the bed. I look at the walls of the room, the ceiling, the alarm clock, eleven o'clock, and then, little by little, I start to feel just plain happy that I'm in Grampa's personal space. Real happiness. The shame fades away, and I'm very pleased that my balls are warm in his pajamas after all these ordeals . . . I even think to myself that somehow this was worth all the trouble. But immediately after, I say, okay, I slept next to Grampa . . . In his pajamas . . . So what? What are we going to do now? See where this has got me . . . I'm not going to spend the day with him . . . And this tightness in my stomach just grows bigger. So I look out the window. The blue sky. Grampa's busy by the shed at the far end of the garden. Even though I can't imagine what else he'd have been doing, it bothers me that he's gone back to his normal routine and I realize that life's going to go back to the way it always was . . . And that's a real bummer. So I summon up my courage, I walk out of the room. I go into the kitchen . . .

"Well, you slept a really long time!" Mariette says.

She says that so simply . . . As if nothing had happened the night before. But I see Cindy drinking hot chocolate and with the smell of milk, the smell of chocolate, it all comes back, everything from the day before in a huge rush, the underwear full of shit, the shit on my lips, in my nostrils, there's nothing for me to vomit up, thankfully, I retch but nothing comes. It hurts terribly. I hold my hand to my chest.

"What's wrong?"

Cindy's staring at me.

"Are you wearing Grampa's pajamas?" she asks.

"What of it?" Mariette says. "Yes, he put on some of Grampa's pajamas. Are you being nosy?"

"I'm not sticking my nose in anything . . . I'm just asking, that's all!"

Cindy scowls into her mug of chocolate. Mariette asks me if I want some lunch. I don't know. I feel like it would be better if I waited for Cindy to finish, especially when she's just dipped her toast into the hot chocolate and I can tell nothing good is going to come of that. I'd rather not look. I'm going to take a shower, that'll make me feel better . . . Actually, no, I'm not going to take a shower, there's no way I can go back to that bathroom . . . Considering what happened there yesterday but also considering

Mariette and Grampa, that would be breaking some sort of taboo, even read as a provocation . . . My thoughts are muddled but I know there's nothing for me to do in that bathroom. And really, what am I doing, going into the kitchen in Grampa's pajamas, like I'm at my own place? I go take it off, I put on my shorts and my tank top since the chief kept my red underwear. Mariette's busy preparing the meal, I'd like to see Grampa, I take a step to see the garden, I see him at work by the shack at the far end. And then Mariette, still stirring the mixture in her saucepan, says:

"It's best if the policemen don't find you here if they come back."

She says that nonchalantly, she doesn't want to be disagreeable, she doesn't want to push me out either . . . That's what bothers her the most, she'd have me stay to eat and she's sincere, I know . . . It wouldn't be wise for me to stay in this house, the police would get annoyed if they found me here. And, no matter how much I'd like to stay here, I know she's absolutely right, and I really don't know if I want to stay that much. No, I can't stay.

"I'm going to head out," I say.

"But you'll come see us again," she says. "You just have to wait until this is all sorted out."

And, again, her words are sincere, that's Mariette for you. As if it was just a matter of waiting a few days until this was all sorted out . . . Now I'm not so sure what she means by "sorted out" nor what exactly "this" is, because many things happened . . . And I'm not sure that she wants me to come sleep with her father again. I say:

"Of course I'll come see you again."

And I go to see Grampa in the garden.

"All right, I'm headed out."

"You're not staying to eat?"

I shake my head. I say no. We look at each other. He's put his hat back on, his overalls, it's no longer the same Grampa as before, nor is it really the Grampa from last night either, but the night's long gone, it's somewhere else. We look at each other again. We know that this can't last the rest of our lives. And even if I stayed, what would I do? For now, we know we're friends for good, and that'll be the case, no matter what happens. We can imagine what our reunion will be like. I'm sad to leave Grampa all alone in his garden but I tell myself that before last night, he had been far more alone.

"Will you come back to sleep with me?"

"I hope so!"

"Don't wait too long," he says as he shakes my hand. I feel a strange surge of feeling for Grampa, I want to kiss his cheeks, but I hold back, I tell myself that it's much too soon, and I'm also sure that Mariette is watching us from the kitchen window over there.

I don't do much over the next few days. Actually I don't do anything. I lie around. For starters, I don't even want to stay at home, I don't want to see anyone or maybe just some strangers, I like to go have a drink at a café, doesn't matter which one, I don't care . . . And even if it's empty apart from an owner scowling behind the counter, it doesn't matter. I read the paper, I look at the bottles, I listen to the radio, and the less chatter there is, the better I feel . . . Or maybe I only like that chatter when the words disappear into the hubbub of the room and I can't understand anything they're saying. It's still very hot, around here I think it's hitting a hundred degrees. I go shopping, I buy a tee-shirt, a pair of flip-flops, some shorts, *Asterix and the Soothsayer,* it's my favorite volume in the Asterix series and I don't have it at home anymore, someone must have borrowed it and never given it back, I also buy the DVD box set of *Star Wars* episodes IV, V, and

VI, and some books, but I don't look at them or read them. All this has me running around town. I keep my cell phone with me, when it rings I answer. But I answer irritably, I say "yeah?" and then I cut the conversation short or I say that I don't have time, that I'll call back, but I never call back. François calls me, too. He wants to meet up. He wants to hook up. I don't. Actually, I don't know, I do like François. Maybe I'll want to in a couple of days, I tell him that right now I can't, I have way too many things to do, we'll just have to see if I can make it happen, but I can't promise, I'll call him soon . . . But he shouldn't be surprised if it takes me a few days to get back to him.

Daniel left me a few messages. First, he was disappointed that I hadn't been there for his birthday, especially when I could have let him know . . . Then he was worried that I hadn't checked in with him . . . Then with the third message, he was clearly upset . . . Practically ready to call the police. I don't call him back right away, first I have to think about what to tell him and then I realize that the longer I wait the harder it'll be. I call him. He's happy to finally hear me. When I hear his voice, though, I realize that I don't really want to see him anymore, but maybe that will change in a couple of weeks, I'll feel the urge again, I'm evasive, I make up a pathetic excuse, I hadn't been in the mood to go out, hadn't felt like seeing anybody, hadn't been feeling well . . . All right, yes, I could have called but I really wasn't feeling it, I just wanted to be by myself and I dig myself into a hole, deeper and deeper, and Daniel's on the other end of the line saying nothing, and then I don't say anything either and to break the silence I tell him that I'll call him later and I say good-bye and I hang up.

And then, having called Daniel, I decide I should call Paul . . . Because it'll do me good to talk to him, and also because I feel like we haven't seen each other in ages. He's really happy to hear me, he thought I'd been sulking, he'd tried to call me several times but never left any messages, since he figured he'd try again later. He'd like to meet up . . . Spend an evening, a night, two days, the week together . . . He misses me . . . His wife is away at a training somewhere . . . It's the same spiel every single time, every time his wife isn't around, he wants us to live together. Now I sort of wish I hadn't called him, even though I do want to see him, I tell him that I can't do tonight, that I already have plans, but tomorrow's different, we can have dinner and then spend the night together and maybe the next night, but I'm not sure. And when I hang up, I feel like I'm an idiot, I should have told him to come the day after tomorrow instead . . . I'm not so sure that tomorrow I'll want to make love with him. But I know Paul well enough to know that if we don't have sex, he won't be upset, so in the end it's a good thing that he's coming tomorrow. Then I spend the whole afternoon walking along the Alzou, that's the stream that runs through Roquerolle, and Roquerolle is the town where I live, I think about Grampa . . . Actually, I've been thinking about Grampa since this morning, I guess he's been hovering over all my thoughts, maybe I'll go see him again one of these days, stay for dinner, and then we'll get in bed together and sleep together for the whole night. I remind myself that it'll be a bitter pill for Mariette to swallow, that yesterday it wasn't so hard for her to accept after the ruckus with the policemen but now that that's over, it's a different story . . . And then I decide that it'll be okay in the end, we're all grown-ups here, I'm in my forties, he's about to hit a hundred, we're safe, consenting adults, we can get in bed with whoever we like . . . And I can trust Grampa on this, he's not easily taken in. That's what I've been thinking all morning, but now, with my eyes wandering aimlessly over the Alzou's waters, I suddenly realize how impossible it is to do anything with Grampa . . . Sleeping with him one night, two nights, three, four, five, six, and more . . . Sleeping with Grampa to do what? The first night was the one that mattered, and it'll never come back again. So it's clear that there's no use in going to Grampa's tonight, it would be too soon. I'm scared. I'm scared it'll all fall apart. I'm scared Grampa won't want to sleep with me again. And I'm scared that it's not going to go anywhere. But mostly I realize that tonight, I'll be unhappy if I'm all by myself in my bed.

So I call Paul to let him know that I'm actually free tonight, and I'd like to see him. And when he says all right, he'll come over, I'm so happy that I tell him if he wants to come now, he can. But he can't right now. So I go to the butcher's and then the bakery and then the grocery store, I come back home and I wait for him.

As soon as he gets here, Paul immediately knows that something's off. He's known since I called, actually . . . All that time I took to call him back. But he's calm as always, he's not pushy about it, he lets me take the lead, if I want to talk, he's there, if I don't want to, that's fine, I don't have to, no problem. But I don't say anything. Sometimes I really get the urge to tell him, I don't know why I haven't told him but then I think that just the story about jerking off in Grampa's underwear, since I have to start at the beginning . . . So, even then, and maybe not even the part about jerking off, even just the part about putting on Grampa's underwear, I can't tell him that. I'm almost sure that Paul, who really cares about me, who's known me for ten years already, my oldest partner in crime, I'm sure that even he won't understand what the fuck I'm doing. So there we are, not talking about anything in particular, sipping our drinks, pastis for him, whiskey for me because I'm getting sick of pastis. Paul asks some questions. But they're pointless questions, completely stupid. Whether my parents are doing well. What does he care about them, he's never met them. And he asks me again if work's going well, it's fine, and I've already told him over and over that it's fine, especially since I'm on vacation now. And Paul's annoying me more and more, since he just wants to talk for the sake of talking . . . We could just stay there, just drinking and not saying anything and that'd make me perfectly happy, but not him . . . He always has to be having sex or eating or talking. And since I don't feel like having sex . . . Of course, he asks me if I've met another guy. That's already more interesting. I'm this close to saying yes . . . Partly because that would solve our problem, that'd save me from having to explain so much, Paul's already seen me in love with someone else and he knows what that's like . . . Pretty close to the way I'm feeling today. And partly because he's right, sort of . . . I met another man. But I shake my head, I say no. Maybe I'll want him later, after eating, when we're curled up in bed . . . That's how it often happens with Paul, I don't want him while we're having drinks, or while we're eating, I even wonder how I'm going to deal with spending the night with him, and it's only when I feel his warm body against mine in bed that I finally get hard and I stay hard until the morning. Paul's used to it, he goes with the flow. So we sit down for dinner, we have some wine, I feel like talking, we gossip about this and that, it takes my mind off things, but after we're done, once we're both in bed and Paul's snuggled up to me, stroking my dick, I really do have trouble getting hard. He licks it and manages to get me hard but it's almost mechanical, and I end up getting soft right away. He doesn't understand, but he acts like nothing's wrong, like we've got all the time in the world, he stretches out next to me, I can feel his worry, he caresses me, he doesn't ask questions. He knows something's not right and it's worse than he'd thought. I'm sure he's thinking I really have met another guy. He thinks I lied to him. And then I think about Grampa and I start sobbing, at long last, I've been holding it in for so long. Paul has no idea what's going on. He wants to know what's happened. I tell him things aren't good, I'm unhappy, but I don't explain any further. But that doesn't help, so he won't let things be, he keeps asking for more details. I'm so close to telling him the whole story about Grampa's underwear, I feel ready, I open my mouth, I take a breath . . . I really do think it'll make me feel better to let it all out . . . And then, at the last minute, I change my mind, I hold back . . . I'm ashamed that I jerked off in Grampa's underwear and especially right in the living room, in front of them all . . . And really, even if I got to the end of the story, I know what he's going to say, he's going to urge me to press charges, that I can't just let it go, I can't just let the bastard who did that to me stay in the police force. And I don't want that. Even if it's just out of respect for Mariette and Grampa . . . It's clear that they don't want this whole thing to leave our little circle, and I can understand that, in a small town like Trintaud, even if it didn't have anything to do with them, it would just stir up trouble . . . As for me, I could never even think of going back there. But that's not all it is, it's not just about gossip . . . It's mostly that the chief gives me the shivers, I was already wondering about it while I was stuck on that chair after he cleared off with his partner, while Mariette was pulling the underwear full of shit off my head . . . I was just starting to catch my breath but I was still wondering why he'd let me live. And the question's still bouncing around in my head. Sure, he wanted to teach us all a lesson, make us mind our manners, but how could he have been so sure of himself . . . So sure, I mean, that we wouldn't press charges, that we wouldn't go talk to other policemen or the commissioner to tell them what happened. I see him again, near me, his hand on my shoulder, as I swear up and down that I won't press charges, that I won't tell anyone, I see him again just saying: "I know." At that moment, I thought to myself: "There, there, you poor thing, it's over, he's saying that because he's going to kill you in two seconds," as if he was actually saying: "I know . . . But I'm not taking any risks." Until Mariette had taken off my handcuffs and until I was sure that they were really gone, I thought my time had come. When I was in front of that perfectly normal policeman, I couldn't make sense of what was actually happening. At that moment, I was out of my depth, I was just taking each thing as it came. It's only afterwards that the real terror appeared . . . With that memory, the fresh memory of what happened. As I played the film in my head again the chief came back like a sort of psychopath with good-old Gallic features . . . But I have no idea what a psychopath would look like, much less a pure Frenchman. I can't stop thinking about this "I know" . . . it makes me feel like a pathetic thing, a poor guy who's lost his mind . . . A poor guy you might calmly tell: "You have no more secrets from me, I don't have to worry about you." All right, he understood or thought he understood what was happening between Grampa and me, especially with Grampa's attitude, that must have been part of what was annoying him. But that's not enough . . . His "I know" was so calm, so sincere, so confident . . . And not one bit of irony. There was no ambiguity at all about that. As if he had total power over me and as if he was so sure of having it that it was no longer playing out as violence at all . . . As if now we were bound together by full complicity . . . And maybe it was more than mere complicity. How did he know? What did he know? And that weighs down, that weighs down on me like a word on the tip of my tongue, I have a distant feeling, a vague knowledge of a strange moment, and I dig, I dig, I try to catch the thread just like when I try to summon up a forgotten dream, to recover various memories in order to grasp its essence even though it all fades away and is gone for good. The mystery of the chief is still slipping through my fingers. I don't want to talk about it but I don't want to forget it, either. And it's very simple: when I think of Grampa, I think of the chief.

Thankfully, Paul is here with me. He's the person I like sleeping next to the most. And I know he feels the same way, he really likes sleeping against me. And even tonight without having sex, although that hasn't happened often . . . Then I realize that I've never even spent a night with Paul without having sex. He's still so patient, he lets me bury my face in his shoulder. Ten thousand questions go through my head, I can tell from his breathing that he's also having trouble sleeping and he's got just as many questions as I do. We stay that way for several hours. Little by little, I hear Paul's breaths slow down, he breathes with his mouth open, and then I know he's asleep. I huddle against him. I think of everybody, it's a mess in my mind, I mix up everyone, Paul, Grampa, the chief, Mariette, Cindy, and a lot of other people with no connection. And then, by disappearing into this crowd of people, I fall into a half-sleep in which fantasy and reality are commingled. I know that I have Paul's penis in my hand but little by little, I realize it's the chief's, but that doesn't terrify me, on the contrary, it feels very agreeable, full of love and then immediately after I caress the chief's body only to find when I'm done that it's Grampa. And I fall asleep that way, without really knowing where I live, I think that when I fall asleep I wonder how I managed to do so in the middle of all this mess. Paul and I stay together like that for the whole night, we stroke each other, we love each other without having sex, but when I wake up, I'm not very happy that he's there, my first thought is that I hope he won't stay long. And I'm afraid that because his wife's in training and he's alone for the whole week, I won't be able to get rid of him. But it's over quickly, Paul's tired of seeing me scowling, and given I'm not much of a morning person already, this is even worse, he really doesn't know what to say to me. He doesn't dare to ask any more questions, he doesn't even dare to say anything at all. I tell him to piss off every time. He walks around my apartment, he's bored, he takes his shower, and once he's done that, he's even more bored.

"All right, I'm going to go!" he says at last.

And I say back:

"Well done, off you go!"

I'm not sad that he's leaving. We kiss, he wants to kiss for a while longer but I cut it short . . . I don't walk him out, he knows the way. And then he comes back to the door, he tries not to look sad, as if none of this mattered, as if things would be just fine.

"If you want to meet up again, just call me."

"Sure, I'll call you."

And he leaves. I'm not happy, I'm pretty upset at myself, I wasn't satisfied with him but I wouldn't have been any better without him. I sit on the couch and think. I'm not actually thinking, it's already self-evident, I have to call Grampa . . . I need to hear his voice. I miss him. It's ten in the morning, he ought to be in the garden. I look through the window and see the men walking down the street, the cars going by. I linger. It's already very hot and I know I'm still afraid. I'm afraid that this won't go well, that Mariette will tell me to piss off, that Grampa's enthusiasm will have abated and he won't want to see me at all. And I don't really know why but I'm afraid. Come on, I tell myself, and I call them. Mariette answers. She's happy to hear my voice on the phone, that I'm thinking about them, that I haven't forgotten them . . . That's just like Mariette . . . She was worrying, she had my phone number, but it never occurred to her to call me. We make small talk, she's doing fine as far as I can tell, almost as if nothing had happened . . . She seems to be in good shape. And she's not asking me too many questions . . . Yes, she was worried, but now that she's hearing my voice, it's enough for her . . . Then I ask her for news about Grampa. He's not doing well, he's had trouble recovering, he goes from the bed to the couch, sometimes he walks around the garden for a short bit, like a lost soul.

"Could you put him on the phone?"

"Of course, he'd be happy to talk to you."

She hands the phone to Grampa, and right before doing so, I say in a rush:

"I'll come see you before long!"

"Well," she says immediately, "be careful, the police come by every so often. They're not doing anything bad, they stop by to say hello and look around. I don't think they'd be happy to see you here. Hang on, Grampa, it's for you, it's Gilles."

And she gives him the phone. I ask him how he's doing, right away he answers:

"I'm bored."

"Me too, I'm bored . . ."

And we don't say anything. Then he asks:

"When are you going to come see me again?"

"I'd be right over, but with the policemen . . ."

"Come at night . . . They don't check at night . . . And you can come sleep here."

When I hear that, a huge weight inside my chest vanishes. It's all the anguish of those last hours without Grampa going away. I float off toward unhoped-for tomorrows. I savor the moment. I hear Grampa's breath on the other end of the line. We don't say anything. I have to speak up, so I say:

"All right yes, I'll come see you soon."

"Tonight?"

"Maybe, yes . . ."

And then there's nothing else to say, we both feel really stupid with the phone in our hand. We say good-bye and hang up. And then I realize why I was afraid to call Grampa. I knew this was how it would turn out, that we would only be sad not to be together. Worse yet, that it would make us doubt each other's feelings. Because we didn't tell each other everything. I ought to have told him that I missed him. I know that perfectly well: on the phone, we have to say everything out loud, lest the most important thing go unsaid, we can't see each other's faces or gestures, only hear our voices and it's not enough. Phones are fine for business or technical discussions, but here, between Grampa and me, it's useless. All I have is confirmation that it's not over, this whole situation, what good does that do? This is stupid. This phone call was a joke, I have to go see him for real. But I didn't even figure that one out, if it was so simple, I would have already done it. There's still the problem with the police, Regardless of what Grampa said, there's no guarantee they won't show up after dark or early in the morning. And there's also the problem with Mariette, which goes hand-in-hand with the police problem. If she didn't say to come see them, it's because she knows exactly how that's going to end, and she doesn't want to see me sleep with her father for another night, the police seem more like an excuse than anything. Which leaves the problem that I don't know how things stand with Grampa, I don't know what to do with him, and even if I came and slept with him tonight, tomorrow I'd be no better off than I am now, we'd still both be clueless, and that bothers me more than anything else . . . Everything else, after all, I can handle somehow.

But even so, the phone call with Grampa has perked me up, so I go swim in the lake in the afternoon. On my towel, among families, I look at the people, children crying, bawling, a little girl with a diving mask over her face going head-first under the water and then coming back up with a pebble in her hand that she proudly shows to her mother, saying: "Look, Mommy, look!" And her mother answers: "Oh, what is this pebble?" "I found it at the bottom of the lake." "You have to find nicer pebbles, this one is normal." And the little girl goes back in. Further off, teenagers are mucking around on a paddleboat, I can't tell how many of them are on it and then one of them falls into the water and then another goes after while they're all shouting. It gets annoying very fast, it's hot out. I head into the water. I swim and, as usual, I discover all over again just how nice it is to swim and I go a long way, when I start to tire since I don't have the lungs I did when I was twenty, I turn over on my back, and I look at the shore gently moving away and the water slipping across my body. Once I'm in the middle of the lake, I think of the catfish . . .

Apparently a sixteen-foot-long catfish has been sighted in this lake . . . Some people say it isn't possible, others say it is . . . Some say that they've never seen a catfish attack a man, others say that just because they haven't seen it that doesn't mean it can't happen. As for me, I always end up thinking about it at one moment or another, especially when I'm all alone in the middle of the lake. My first instinct is to be very afraid, but, the more I think about it, the more I realize that I'm afraid mainly of being afraid. And, it's odd, I'm no more afraid of the catfish today than usual. And it's so nice to swim, I'm in the middle of the lake, which must be more than half a mile wide, I know that if I go back now, after this, I'll be bored out of my mind on the shore and where will that leave me? I decide to go all the way and, eventually, I'll reach the other side, where everybody sunbathes in the nude. Before I get out of the water, I look around the beach . . . If this can really be called a beach, since nudism isn't allowed, we're on the rockiest part of the shore . . . The least welcoming part, then. My eyes sweep the shore. The men are all sprawled out on their towels, tanning like crazy. I only recognize one guy whose name I've forgotten (if I ever knew it) who I had a great fuck with, right here in fact, one afternoon last summer or the one before. But I don't feel like making a move, so I just wave hello. He doesn't recognize me, he turns over to see who I'm waving to. I don't bother, I look away. A bit higher up, on the path just above the bank, I can make out men moving in the woods and among the ferns I see the face of a man I've come across several times here, a man I don't like at all. He looks at me insistently, as if he'd never seen me before, and I don't understand why he's staring at me. I get out of the water. I want to be relaxed, I stand off to the side, by the hedges, but I still take off my swimsuit, because it's nice to dry off in the nude by the lake shore. But once I've taken a good look at the lake, at the hill on the opposite side, about ten or fifteen minutes for me to see my fill, I'm over it, I pull my

Speedos back on, I head toward the woods to pee. I find a nice spot, away from the cruising area, I try to pee but nothing comes, I push because I know that if I don't pee now, I'll want to in five minutes, and right then I see four naked strangers coming out of the ferns, I don't even know where they came from, and they rub their balls and get themselves hard looking at me and I start to freak out . . . I tuck my dick back in immediately. I turn away and go straight back to the lake, I don't even look back. Once I'm in the water, I feel completely stupid. They're not zombies, after all. I don't know what came over me, four guys jerking off in front of me and just because of that I freak out like a teen, as I think about it I realize that they weren't all playing with themselves and I'm not even sure they were jerking off to begin with. Well, I stayed dignified, I didn't yell out, I didn't run, I simply left without peeing but I'm still ashamed anyway. Honestly, if I'm upset it's in regards to them . . . What did it matter if they had been jerking off, anyway? It's not my role to treat men fondling themselves in the woods like the plague. Okay, sure, they didn't have to come crawling out of the ferns like that, without any warning, but even so, maybe they were already clearly in sight when I came, and I was the one too busy with my nonexistent need to pee to see them. I feel like I'm the worst traitor of all. As if I'd been running away from unknown comrades. And really, what am I thinking swimming so quickly? I'll never keep going at this rate. I slow down, I float on my back, my arms outstretched, kick my feet every so often, I look at the shore I came from, its monotonous stillness, the men still sunbathing nude. Near the path there's still a bit of movement, men must be pairing up and fucking each other a bit higher up in the woods. I regret leaving this place. I linger, telling myself that I'll come back soon, maybe tomorrow. And then I think about the catfish again, I switch to a front crawl. But I quickly forget about the catfish, because even while I'm doing a front crawl, I'm thinking about

Grampa again. I'm too happy that he exists. I know that I'll see him again and we'll sleep together and this thought alone carries me the rest of the way back.

On the road, driving my Safrane, I head straight west toward Trintaud. It's around eight thirty, a quarter to nine, I've put this off as long as I can, I don't want to arrive while they're still eating and I know that sometimes, during the summer, they end up eating late, perhaps eight o'clock but never later than that, given that they had lunch early, they won't wait too long to eat . . . And I definitely don't want to come just when they're headed to sleep, I've keep thinking about these questions of timing over and over in my head before hitting the road and I'm still undecided. I know that for Mariette, I absolutely can't look like I've come just to spend the night, or just to grab a free meal if I end up coming while they're at the table, I have to make it look like a normal visit. I have to show up at the right time and I've come to the decision that between a quarter to nine and nine o'clock should be just right. In the meantime, I'm nervous about everything. Mariette might use that excuse about the policemen to tell me I shouldn't stay, that it's too risky, and if Grampa's not at the door with her to make sure I come in, then I might end up leaving without seeing him. But I don't think Mariette would actually do any such thing . . . Although, if Grampa's gone to bed, which he might since he's so bored right now, yes, if the urge's overcome him to head to bed early, then there's no question that I'll go right back home. I'm anxious at the prospect of going all that way for nothing, not seeing Grampa for even five minutes, and then his spending the night wondering what I'm doing, thinking that I've forgotten him, that I don't care about him . . . And I'm also anxious about possibly running into the policemen, I'll be safe once I'm at Grampa and Mariette's, I'd be amazed if the police came to bother them after nine o'clock, although with them you never know . . . In any case, while I'm on the road, anything could happen, at first it was fine, I took a detour, if they'd stopped me then, I could have said I was headed somewhere else, like Brignac or even Bosc, but now that I'm almost there, less than a mile away and entering Trintaud . . . And just as I come around a bend, what do I see a hundred yards away, at the Courrèges intersection? A blue van. Two policemen on the side of the road. It's too late to turn around. After the initial shock, I'm calm again. It's fine, my heart's pounding but not as much as I'd expected. In the distance, I can see the two men, no familiar faces, phew, I haven't had anything to drink, I have my papers, I'm not driving too fast, it's all fine. I think about everything, turn on the blinkers, come to a stop by them. Hand brake. I turn off the engine before they ask me to. My papers, a breathanalyzer test. Start the car again, check the headlights and taillights. And then:

"So where are you headed?"

"Going home to Roquerolle."

"And you're driving through Trintaud?"

"Yep!"

I say that straightforwardly, but I'm already starting to feel nervous . . . What are the police doing asking me where I'm going and acting surprised by where I'm driving through? And he looks at me, he nods, and goes to meet his colleague. Then he gets into the van, I can see him through the windshield making a call on the radio, and it lasts and lasts, and then he comes back and he just says:

"All right, the boss wants to see you, follow us."

"What did I do?"

"He wants to see you."

And of course I start to panic, I don't want to see the chief, I say no, I want to know why. He doesn't answer, he just says that the chief will tell me himself, that the police station is a stone's throw away and it'll just take five minutes. I stay in my seat, determined not to go anywhere. There's no way the chief could have perverted his whole team, surely not every single policeman in Trintaud has to be at his beck and call without asking any questions. But he's very patient, he walks around my car, he looks at every single thing. The more I think about it, the more freaked out I get, nine o'clock at night at the Trintaud police station, that's not going to be nice. I see a car in my rearview mirror, I get scared, I start imagining scenes of torture, so I get out of my car and I try to get the driver's attention, I wave my arms, I yell: "Help me, come help me!" But the policeman comes over to me, the car slows down, the lady driving the car (it's a woman behind the wheel) looks at me, she asks me what's going on. I can feel the policeman's hand on my forearm as his partner waves for the lady to keep moving. He tells her it'll be fine, there's nothing to worry about. I start to realize just how ridiculous I'm looking. I take a deep breath.

"Listen," says the policeman who had been talking to me earlier. "We have your papers, we know where you live, so where are you going? It's no big deal to see the chief, right?"

And then I realize there's nothing else I can do, I'm on my own against the national police force, I won't get out of this, I surrender, they put me in their van.

When I go into the chief's office, I'm very quiet, he's sitting behind his desk, he's wearing a sky-blue polo shirt, it's still very hot, the window is wide open, it shows a square with people going past, children playing a bit further off, and as long as the sun doesn't set, they won't go home to sleep. That makes me feel a bit better. The chief doesn't look the same as the one I met the other day. He's the same one and yet I'm surprised to see him looking so different . . . I can't really pinpoint how, it's not in his gaze, not in the particulars, it's more in the sum total of his face. I wonder if it might be the light and then I realize that this is actually not uncommon, we think we've examined someone carefully and then, the next time, when we see them again, they're not the same as what we thought they were. Especially people we've thought about often, we've probably turned them into myths or created a personal image of them so much we've wanted to keep it in memory. The chief welcomes me from behind his desk. Yes, he welcomes me in as if we were old acquaintances, not like a friend, more as if I were a regular at the police station, but the good kind, a troublemaker he's happy to see every so often. He waves for me to sit in the chair across from him. I tell him:

"Okay, I'll have a seat, but I want your colleagues to stay in the room with us."

And as I say that, I see the two policemen behind me looking at each other and at the chief. I'm very proud that I had this idea, even if the window is wide open and people are walking past in the square (it's never just the policemen and their gang), but one can never be too careful. The sun sets, the lights go on. The chief says:

"If that makes you happy!"

He gestures to the two policemen, who each take a chair. In fact, that doesn't reassure me at all. Once I'm sitting as well, the chief looks at me.

"What are you coming to Trintaud to do?"

"I'm not coming to Trintaud, I'm going to my place."

"So you weren't planning to stop here? To visit anybody?"

I act surprised, I shake my head no. He asks again:

"You weren't planning to spend the night at anyone's house?"

"No!"

I'm firm, that's all I have to say. But he keeps asking, he doesn't believe me.

"You weren't planning to sleep with someone?"

I hold on, I think of the underwear filled with shit, and I think of the baton up my ass but I hold on . . . In any case, if I admit it, shit will hit the fan, I know it. I glance at the two policemen sitting behind me, they're not moving, they're not showing any surprise, they're listening. I tell myself that I can hang on as long as the window's open, and the children are playing outside. But the sun is setting, and I might not have so much time left. And just as I think that to myself, he says:

"I know you slept with Grampa last week. I thought that was clear."

"What was clear?"

What the hell, I might as well try to learn something, turn the interrogation around, that could piss him off, but I can't think of anything better to do. And it doesn't piss him off so much, he gets up, comes to sit on his desk, and says to my face:

"You have to forget about Grampa."

I want to match the chief's stare, show him that he's not scaring me, but I can't, it's not really because of fear, I actually find myself really bold, but because his stare is so intense . . . Intense enough that I feel like he's going through my thoughts with his eyes and I can't bear that . . . I look down, my eyes land on his gaping fly, I'm fascinated by his fly, it's not wide open but it's open all the same, and I tell myself that he's going to see where I'm looking and I don't want him to notice that, I look back up and I say:

"I'll sleep with whoever I like!"

I hear the two policemen burst out in laughter behind me. The chief smiles at them. I think to myself: "That's it for me, they're all in cahoots." And to top it off the chief gets up and looks out the window, as if to make sure nobody's listening. I realize that it's happening, night's falling. It feels like it was still daylight at ten o'clock in the evening not so long ago. The chief comes back to sit on the desk. His fly's open a little more, I can make out the color of his underwear, a little more, I'm not entirely sure because of the light but it seems to be red. I feel panicky. I start to get this strange intuition. Quick, look up before he notices.

"But we didn't do anything we shouldn't!"

That's dumb, but I had to spit out something, that was a close call, he was looking at me, he was just about to figure out what I was looking at. The two policemen behind me burst out again. And I start feeling like their bursts of laughter had been planned in advance, as if the chief had told them to do that when I said something stupid.

"Listen, when you sleep with someone, you can do whatever you want, we're not following you."

As he says that, he leans toward me, his fly opens a little more, and it's definitely red . . . I'm actually sure that it's my red underwear, maybe I'm just getting ideas but that wouldn't shock me, coming from him. I look away quickly, I drown in his gaze again. But he's staring above my head, one of his men is calling him, the chief seems not to understand, the policeman whispers something to him, I don't understand what he's saying either, the chief goes back to his men, I watch out of the corner of my eye but I don't see everything, I don't dare to turn around completely. I just feel the chief walk around me and, when he sits down on his desk again, I glance and see that his fly is zipped.

"A good-looking man like you," he says, "athletic, in the prime of life, what are you doing with Grampa?"

I want to tell him he can't treat people like this, especially when he's a policeman, and for that matter I'm free to do whatever I like with my nights, my days, my life, that I'll sleep with whoever I like and even that I'll hook up with whoever I like, but like an idiot I don't say anything back, nothing comes out.

"Are there so few handsome men for you out there that you have to go slum it with this old geezer?"

And, just as before, I want to tell him that he's not an old geezer, and so on and so forth, but like an idiot I just say:

"There's nothing sexual going on between us!"

And they all snicker but not for long, the chief gets up, he goes around his desk, and he starts giving me hell. He's really yelling now, he's harsh, inflexible:

"Who the fuck do you think you're fooling? You were masturbating in his underwear and when we asked him if that upset him, he said, 'No, that means he's thinking about me' and you dare to suggest that there's nothing sexual between the two of you! I must be dreaming . . . Why were you masturbating in Grampa's underwear?"

I don't answer. I'm really surprised that he's yelling like that, when everybody outside can hear him, even people in the apartments nearby. I look at him, his thin gray mustache, his piercing stare, I shake my head, I have nothing to say back, he knows it.

"You don't know?"

I look down, I'll never get out of this by shaking my head or telling him that I don't know. I have to tell him something, anything, some stupid thing, otherwise I'm fucked . . . No, being stupid won't get me anywhere, he'll never believe me and that'll just make everything worse, he doesn't like being made to look foolish, and from behind me I hear:

"Sir, I think we might head out, it's getting late."

The chief checks his watch and waves his hand to let them leave. I don't think about this for long, I don't care that much whether they leave or not, as long as I can see outside, as long as he doesn't close the shutters, I'm not too worried. Knowing that both of them are sitting behind me hasn't really helped me to focus on my answers. I hear the door shut. The chief and I are alone. Yes, in the end, I think I like this better. I have an idea, I look back up.

"Why are you doing this?" I ask him.

He does not reply, he keeps staring at me and then he gets up from his desk, turns around as if he were deep in thought but he still doesn't answer, instead he goes on the offensive.

"Explain to me, very clearly, and maybe I'll believe that you haven't slept together!"

"Because I like it!" I answer.

"Why do you like it?"

"Because it gets me hard."

"So Grampa gets you hard?"

"Grampa's underwear."

"Why his underwear and not Grampa himself?"

"Because Grampa is too old, he's wrinkled, and he doesn't appeal to me, is that so hard to understand?"

"And his underwear?"

"What about his underwear?"

The chief's impatience is clear, he presses his lips together, drops his head, his hands stop short, as if he were going to slap me if I kept acting like this. I answer.

"His underwear? It's for the fabric, they're huge, I'm comfy in them . . ."

I'd stop there, but that's not enough for the chief, and I keep going:

"And they remind me of someone!"

"Someone?"

"A man I liked when I was young . . . A teenager."

"Who?"

"You wouldn't know him."

He keeps on staring at me, he asks again, he wants to know.

"Monsieur Escandolières!"

And now I've really got his attention. He wasn't expecting me to give him a name like that, straight out, a name that couldn't be made up, it came right back to me, because it's the truth . . . And the chief knows I'm not bullshitting, now he has to come up with something else. But he does.

"Well, you could have gone to the store, found a few pairs just like that one, you didn't have to go steal Grampa's."

I don't know what to say back, he goes on.

"Why did you go put them back on the clothesline?"

I don't answer that, I'm tired of this interrogation, I had been hoping that by playing the game, we'd be done more quickly, but that hasn't done me any good, the more answers I give the more questions he asks.

"You wanted them to see, didn't you?"

I still don't say anything.

"You wanted one of them, Mariette or Grampa, to see, didn't you?"

He doesn't give me a chance to answer, he keeps going.

"Was that fun for you, messing with those two old folks?"

I shake my head, I can't see where he's going with this. He says nothing. He gets off the desk, walks around my chair, as he does his hip rubs against my shoulder, very lightly, I don't know what this touch means, did he misjudge the distance? Did he want to make an impression on me? And then he takes a few steps behind my back, I watch out of the corner of my eye and he comes back around the other side of my chair, then he goes to sit in his armchair, as before.

"Gilles," he says. "If somebody was masturbating in one of your underwear, would you think it was because of the size or its material or because it reminded him of someone? Would you ever think about that?"

Now that he's on the other side of the desk, it's easier for me to look at him, but I don't take advantage of this to act a fool. I shrug a bit, I don't know what I'd think, I wait for him to tell me.

"No, you'd never think about any of that!"

His voice has softened, as has his face.

"You'd tell yourself that someone, somewhere, not too far, wanted you!"

Yes, I would have thought that. He's convinced me. I nod my head.

"That someone loved you!"

And his stare bores into my own. And I hang on. He said that as calmly as he said "I know" in the bathroom at Grampa and Mariette's, right after pulling the baton and Grampa's underwear out of my ass, but also right before shoving Grampa's shit-filled underwear over my mouth. I know this is the end of the interrogation, but I also know that now is when I have to expect the worst. So I have to hang on, as long as I keep my gaze fixed on his, nothing can happen to me, I feel strong, I've summoned up all my courage in order not to shirk away, if I give up now, I'll give up all the time. I'm going to try to figure out the color of his eyes. He's too far away, I can't, but at least I'm not in his gaze anymore, I'm only in his eyes, and he takes that moment to get up, he comes back to lean against his desk, and he says:

"We're going to stop there for tonight. You can go."

When I hesitate, he looks down and then, with a wave of his hand, motions for me to get up, and when I don't get up quickly enough, he says: "Go." So I get up. I don't dare to go to the door, I keep my eyes fixed on his, and as I try to see the color of his eyes, I wonder what else is going to happen to me. Blue. They're blue, normally I'd notice that, blue eyes, but no, up until this moment I've never noticed and I still don't know if the chief is a handsome man (or what I, at least, would call a handsome man) or not, but I can see in my mind the red of my underwear through his open fly . . . And then I turn around and go to the door. Before I open it, he says:

"And forget about Grampa . . . An old man who lost his wife thirty years ago, don't you think that's a bit too easy?"

I mumble an answer, I don't say either yes or no, but yes a bit . . . I look at him properly one more time before going through the door. In the hallway, the policeman who inspected my papers is typing at a computer, I walk right in front of him, we look at each other, I don't dare to ask him to go back to my car with me, since it has to be a good mile and a half away, and he doesn't offer . . . I start walking, I don't really understand what the point of this interrogation was, I go through it in my head, but it's too fresh, there's no point. I walk in the night and every time I hear a car coming, I take cover in the ditch. That means it takes me a long time to get back to my car.

Afterwards, I'm not sure what to do . . . Or rather, I know. I still want to go see Grampa, but now I'm not sure how to do so. It's past midnight, I can't just stop by and ring the doorbell. Grampa won't be sleeping, that's for sure, he's thinking of me, that's also for sure. I have a feeling that the chief and his men are watching the house, maybe not up close but probably they drive past it every so often, just like that, on their rounds. And as if that weren't enough, I'm fixated on that image of the chief's fly revealing just a sliver of my red underwear. I'm sure he was wearing my red underwear. I'm also sure that he specifically kept it open to show me that he was wearing it . . . But in front of his men, come on . . . That brigade at Trintaud is an odd one, for sure. And sometimes I see the chief's stare in my mind again, not his face, or his mustache, only his gaze . . . That I won't forget easily . . . And that fly keeps coming back to mind. But oddly, this evening, in the night, I'm not afraid . . . I even feel very brave, I park my car in a lot full of other cars, that way, there's less of a risk it'll be noticed, and I walk down the streets of Trintaud. I can see how I might get to Grampa and Mariette's house by going down this side street, I walk without making a noise, just when I get to the entrance of the square where the market is, a police van pulls up across the street, and I think to myself that this is crazy, they're already looking for me. I'm shocked for a full second but then I catch myself. I hide behind a pickup truck, I want to see them leave, but I don't dare to poke my head too far out in case they see me, which is why I won't actually see them heading away, it's okay, I focus on the sounds, I hear the engine fading away, I make my way around the place by sneaking down the arcades, in the shadows cast by the street-lights, and I cross Trintaud that way, from back street to back street, and then I see a very small side street, actually an alley that isn't even paved, and I have a hunch it goes past Grampa's garden, I'm pretty sure that's right, but then I have to find the right garden, at night, and that's tricky, plus with the hedges so tall, I won't be able to see the houses . . . But then I realize that's not really a problem, I just have to get into one garden and if I remember right I'll be able to go from one garden to the next . . . Except . . . Right, except all the gardens have a prickly hedge between them and the side street, and where it's not prickly it's too dense for even my arms to get through. But I'm here, I can't just give up when I'm so close, if I go back without seeing Grampa I'll have to do this all over again tomorrow. There has to be an entrance somewhere. So I keep looking. And I'm right, a minute later I see a small opening, grass, shrubbery. Under the shrubs there's some space, I get down onto my belly and I'm just able to crawl beneath the low branches, I sneak through, but I should have figured, it was too easy, I hit a fence. And just when I touch it to see if there's a hole in the fence, I hear light footsteps . . . The sound of footsteps in the alley . . . And just as I curl up to be even more discreet, a foot trips over my calf, someone falls, I pull out right there and then, and I'm face-to-face with someone I can't see in the darkness . . . Especially because there's a flashlight shining right in my face.

"Gilles? What are you doing here?"

I know that voice. It's Cindy.

"What are *you* doing here?" I ask.

"I'm going back to Grammy's," she says, and then she waits for my answer. But I don't say anything. I'm trying to figure out what I could tell her and there's nothing.

"You want to see Grampa?"

She says that half as a question and half as an affirmation. And when I still don't answer, she gets insistent.

"Well? You're coming to get in bed with him, aren't you?"

"To sleep," I clarify, "I'm coming to sleep with him."

"If you do that, Grammy's going to tell the police!"

"Right, so I don't want her to know."

I feel like Cindy and I understand each other well, and in order for us to understand each other ever better, I ask:

"Does she know you're spending the night out?"

"Don't you tell her that!" she shoots back.

"Will you show me the way in?"

"Yeah, we can't stay here."

She turns off her flashlight, gets up, holds out her hand, and I follow her. Further off, she's made a small entrance through the hedge, she just has to go through a hole in the wall by pushing a large bit of wood to the side, and then she pushes it back and that's it. It's not quite that inconspicuous, but when her grandmother hardly suspects that Cindy's up to these sorts of things, there's not much chance that she'll get caught anytime soon. It feels safe in the garden. We stay there. Cindy doesn't seem to feel any urge to go back to her room. It's nice outside, after all, it's vacation, she isn't sleepy at all. And she has plenty of time.

"What are you doing out at one in the morning?" I ask.

"Look," she says quietly, "don't tell anyone you saw me, and I won't tell anyone that I saw you, and you come sleep in my bed."

I try to look at Cindy properly, I can't see her face clearly, but even in the darkness I can tell she's looking back at me, her eyes are fixed on mine, I say:

"Are you crazy, can you imagine if your grandmother finds us together in your bed?"

"What if she finds you in Grampa's bed?"

"That's not the same at all!"

She thinks for a bit, she agrees, it's not the same, but she doesn't let up.

"But when she's asleep, she's deep asleep, all you have to do is leave early and she won't notice a thing."

It's clear she's determined. And I start thinking that Cindy wants me, and that thought doesn't reassure me, I wonder how I'm going to get out of this mess, she adds:

"I really want to sleep with you!"

"Just sleep?" I ask.

"Yes, just sleep . . . What else would you want to do?" Her answer is immediate. And then she says:

"Well?"

"All right," I say.

"All right, what?"

"I'll come sleep with you."

"Really?" She acts like I have a choice, as if I was giving her a huge gift of my own volition. I nod my head once more, as if I had lost. She gets up immediately, takes my hand, and pulls me into the house. When we walk past Grampa's doorway, Cindy, very authoritarian, pulls me hard, she doesn't want me to stop. I don't argue. We go up the steps barefoot and stealthily. She's very excited, but like a big girl, she's not in a rush, when there's a slight creak she turns toward me, and she holds her finger up to her lips to shush me, as if it were my fault. I step lightly and follow her. She holds my hand the whole way, she only lets go of it once we're in her room. She doesn't even turn on the light, she whispers that it's cool, now there's nothing to be afraid of anymore but it's still better not to talk, and then she goes to her closet and she brings me some pajamas, once they're in my hands I can tell they're one of Grampa's pajamas, their fabric, their scent of the old days.

"Where did you get this?" I whisper.

"I took it for when you come again."

"Because you knew I would come again?"

"I had a sneaking feeling . . . Go on, put it on!"

"But I'm not going to put it on . . ."

"Just in case Grammy comes."

"You said she wouldn't come."

"You never know."

"But what would happen? If your grandmother found me here and in one of Grampa's pairs of pajamas, on top of that?"

"Better that she find you in those pajamas than naked."

And as she says that, she puts on a long tee-shirt, the Pink Panther one, I think. And then she twists around, under the tee-shirt, she pulls off her shorts, her bra, and her panties, and she gets under the sheets. So I put on Grampa's pajamas, at least I'll feel a bit like I'm with him. I'm happy to be in the house. Cindy won't take long to fall asleep and then I can go wherever I like.

"Good night!" I say as I get under the sheets.

"Are you tired?" she asks.

"Yes!"

"I'm not," she says.

I don't answer, and I wait. In her bed, which is smaller than queen-size but bigger than twin, it must be a full, we're right next to each other. As I'm lying on my stomach, I shut my eyes and listen to Cindy's breathing, then I start to slow mine, as if I were falling asleep, and I wait for her to do so as well. But she really isn't sleepy, after five minutes she asks:

"Are you sleeping?"

I don't answer. I think that if I say anything, she'll start talking. I just have to be patient, I slow down my breathing even more, then, eureka, I shift onto my side, turning my back to her, I'm sure that'll force her to go to sleep. I'm having trouble thinking about anything other than Cindy, what she actually wanted by dragging me to sleep in her bed, with her Pink Panther tee-shirt and nothing under it. What I do know is that Cindy wants something that she doesn't dare to ask for and it's just my luck that she wants me, disconcerted, I think about that for a while, and after a while, I decide that I don't want her. Then I think about Grampa, alone in his bed, not sleeping and just suscing and waiting for daybreak, when he'll finally be able to sleep. I feel bad about being stuck here. I just want to see him again, it's frustrating that I have to waste my time this way. I wonder again about my desire for Grampa, I churn him around over and over in my head, with or without his hat, in overalls, in his pajamas . . . The chief's interrogation flustered me, his questions come to my mind again . . . I try to imagine what might happen if I wrapped my arms around him, if I stroked his skin through his pajamas and then slid my hand through his fly . . . But no, it doesn't work . . . It isn't appealing, it doesn't get me hard, it's so far from what I really want with Grampa . . . I just want to sleep beside him. Why do I want to sleep in the same bed as him? And why does Cindy want to sleep with me? It can't just be so that she's not alone, it has to be more than that . . . If it's more than that, she'd come over to my side, she must think I'm asleep, I'm breathing loudly and slowly, I'm doing a perfect imitation of someone asleep. She still isn't sleeping at all, I can tell from her breathing. We hear a car, a van to be specific, going down the street. Cindy sits up in bed, she gets up and goes to look behind the curtains, then she turns around and shakes me, she tells me to come see, but she stops me before I get to the window, tells me to be careful. I fear the worst, in fact, I know what's going on, we're in darkness, behind the curtains, but with the streetlights, people can see us. I poke my head out slowly. There's no point in having been careful, I'm caught. The chief and his partner, the one who was with him the day of the shit-filled underwear, are walking up to the house. We hold our breath, we step back behind the wall next to the window. To my dismay, in the night's silence, I hear a bolt, then a second one, and the front door opens . . . As if they had keys to the house. Their footsteps go down the long hallway, then another door opens, it has to be the one to Grampa's room, we hear a short, muffled conversation, as if they were simply getting some news from Grampa. I imagine him petrified in his bed, frightened that the chief could come into his house like that, at any hour of the day or the night. I don't dare to move. I don't know what they're doing but I'm stuck there, Cindy holds her breath next to me, she looks at me with terror. Then footsteps go down the long hallway again but in the other direction and the door opens and closes, the keys click, the bolts lock again. We don't move, with a quick glance I make sure that the policemen are actually going back to their car, but I don't really check, I'm too afraid of poking my head out the window. We still don't move. Thirty seconds later, we hear the engine start. They leave. My first thought is to go see Grampa but I stay where I am, I have to think carefully about all this, I wait a few more minutes to listen for Mariette's door, I feel like even when we're deep asleep we always seem to know when someone's broken into our house. So I don't dare to leave Cindy's room. Mariette still hasn't left her room. Then I think she must have woken up, but stayed in bed, she can't have been sure that she heard something, she's waiting for confirmation, she doesn't want to get up for no reason. She's waiting for some noise, any noise. And then I start worrying that the policemen only pretended to leave simply to come back and catch me. I'd rather wait a bit, I stay in Cindy's room, we get back in bed. I'm listening carefully, suddenly it makes sense why the chief let me leave the police station with so little trouble . . . he wants to catch me in flagrante delicto. And other things start making sense, as well, he could only have gotten into the house this quickly by already having the keys, and I'm sure Mariette must have given them to him, that's why she didn't get up, maybe she didn't even wake up . . . Yes, Mariette has to be on the chief's side, against Grampa and me . . . But then right away I think I'm going too far. I tell myself that Mariette doesn't deserve that, that I'm unfair to her and even stupid. And in that way, little by little, I start to relax, it's so odd, I tell myself that I'll go to see Grampa later, I have plenty of time for that, since day hasn't broken yet, now I'm thinking that Cindy's actually saved me tonight and maybe it's not so bad to be in her bed.

In the living room, Mariette is sitting on the couch next to me, she tells me that she'd like to school Cindy in the ways of the world because she can't bear her anymore, she's always running off . . . She wants to have sex, she wants it so much, but if that's going to happen, Mariette thinks it might as well be with a man she knows. On her knees in front of me, Cindy's wringing her hands, she's looking at me like a downbeat dog, I realize that I'm naked on the couch, and at that moment I know this is a dream. I look at Cindy, I look at Mariette, the living room, it all seems so real. This situation is so strange but it's all set in reality. I fixate on the details, the TV, the green plants, I touch the couch, it's definitely the couch I'm used to seeing here. And then I tell myself that if I touch Cindy's breasts, I'll know for sure. I touch Cindy's breasts.

"Go on, Cindy," Mariette says. "You have to do something, take him into your mouth!"

But Cindy shakes her head, she doesn't want to, she says:

"I want to make love!"

"But this is part of love," Mariette says, "and if you want a man to make love to you, being that you're already not all that pretty, you have to make him want to."

I look at Mariette, astonished by the way things are happening and distressed by this authoritarian grandmother, she takes my hand and holds it tight, she holds it really tight to make it clear she's with me. Then she looks sharply at Cindy, and

Cindy does it, but I don't get hard, I can feel her drool and her teeth, as if my cock was in a bowl of water with a fish biting me, it's a very unpleasant feeling, I expect she'll be gnawing on my head any minute now.

"Apply yourself," Mariette says. "If you can't get him hard, how will he be able to make love to you?"

Cindy's crying. I want to stop this torture, I look at Mariette and tell her:

"It's okay . . . It's not Cindy's fault, it's my fault, I can't do it, I don't want to."

"What does that mean, you don't want to?"

"It happens, sometimes, I just don't want to."

I'm lying. I really don't want Mariette to think that I don't like women. To keep them from getting upset I act like it's nothing, as if some other time I'd be able to get hard in Cindy's mouth. Mariette understands, she tells me that her husband was like me, that sometimes he had trouble getting hard and she did this for him . . . She takes my cock and rolls it between her fingers. And just like that, she gets me hard. Really hard, even. I'm so hard that it hurts. Really hurts. I wake up.

At first, I'm not sure if I'm really awake. The first thing I see is Cindy's head, her hair close to my chest. I'm as hard as I was in the dream, it still really hurts. A hand is sliding up and down my dick, I look down, my cock is sticking out of the pajamas and Cindy's stroking it very gently with her two fingers up and down, and when she slides over my frenum and then the head with her dry fingers, I can't take it. I grab her hand to stop it.

"You're so hard!" she says in astonishment.

"It hurts," I tell her.

I keep my grip on her hand. We look at each other, she's sorry, she didn't want to hurt me. I put her hand on the bed and I tuck my dick into the pajamas. Suddenly, I panic, I realize where I am, what I'm doing here, there's no way I can stay here, the sky's brightening behind the windows, and then I realize that it's not the night getting brighter, it's the day about to break. In five minutes, it'll be too late. I get up, I grab my shorts, my shoes, and my tee-shirt.

"What did I do wrong?" Cindy asks sheepishly.

"Be quiet," I say. "I'll come back!"

And I tiptoe out of her room. And she, clearly because she thinks she did something wrong, lets me leave. I can't believe it. On the steps, I only have one thought: I have to keep my erection until I get to Grampa's room. In my half-sleep, that's all I think about, showing my hard dick to Grampa. I don't even think about the chief, much less Mariette, I go into Grampa's room, he's lying on his side. He's sleeping, I think to myself. My erection's still firm, my cock stretches the pajamas, I'm proud of it, and I'm sure it'll make Grampa happy. The day's about to break. Grampa isn't really sleeping, he turns over.

"Somi?"[2] he asks.

"No, no, I'm really here!"

"Qué fas aquí?"[3] He's shocked.

I'm happy. My erection is still solid. My cock actually sticks out of the pajama's fly. But I'm nervous, Grampa's never talked in Occitan to me before, it's as if he were unconscious. But his eyes are wide open, he looks me over from head to toe.

"Soi ieu que te fau quilhar coma aquò?"[4]

"Benlèu!"[5] I answer in Occitan, I figure that'll reassure him, but instead he gets up from his bed, he's frightened.

"Te cal pas demorar aquí, los gendarmas son venguts . . . Te cercan."[6]

---

2. Am I dreaming?
3. What are you doing here?
4. Am I the one making you hard like that?
5. Maybe!
6. You shouldn't be here, the police came . . . They're looking for you.

"Mas son partits, ara,"[7] I reply.

I have trouble remembering my Occitan. I'm a bit ashamed, I'm so touched that Grampa's talking to me like this in his mother tongue, because this really is his own mother tongue . . . I don't want to force him to talk in French again.

"Los as vist?"[8] he asks.

I tell him, half in French, half in Occitan, that I've been in front of their place for a while, I'm lying, I say that I had to wait for them to leave and then to be sure that they wouldn't come back and then to make my way through the garden, and finally I ask:

"Cossí son dintrats?"[9]

"Lo sabi pas,"[10] he says irritatedly.

"Marietà lor balhèt la clau?"[11]

"Benlèu,"[12] he says, and then he realizes, and asks me:

"Mas cossí siás dintrat, tu?"[13]

"Per la pòrta de l'òrt . . . èra dobèrta."[14]

"Ah!" he says in astonishment. I think he's wondering why the garden door was open, and little by little a smile grows across his face, he looks very happy to see me. He gets a grip on himself. He pats the bed with his right hand.

"Ven aquí . . . Ven dins lo lièch amb ieu!"[15]

I don't hesitate, I get under the covers but I tell him right away that I can't stay, that I have to leave before Mariette gets up. He knows. I turn toward him, I look at him, first his eyes are

7. But they're gone now.
8. Did you see them?
9. How did they come in?
10. I don't know.
11. Did Mariette give them the key?
12. Maybe.
13. But how did you get in?
14. Through the garden door . . . It was open.
15. Come here . . . Get in bed with me!

focused on the ceiling, and then he turns his head toward me, and then he turns his whole body and we're looking at each other. I notice the color of his eyes, hazel, small eyes amid wrinkles in every direction, his face covered in tiny bruises and dark stains and his skin cracking here and there, the skin of his neck dangling, this Grampa is definitely not the same one I'd kept in my memory, there's some love here, I idealize him, and now, seeing him again, there's still affection, of course, but as for the rest, desire, need, all that vanishes at once, I even feel guilt at telling him that maybe he was the one to make me so hard. In fact, I'm not hard anymore. And in fact, he's lying on his back again, his head on the pillow, his eyes on the ceiling. I have to talk, I have to get the latest news.

"Cossí vas?"[16] I ask.

"Oh, not great," he says in French.

And it stings that he's not talking in Occitan anymore.

"Contunha en occitan!"[17]

He looks at me. His mouth trembles, as does his nose, his face, all the way down to his shoulders. As if to say "What's the use?" He's from that time when saying a word in Occitan at school got you a painful slap on the wrist . . . Now it comes back when he forgets himself like this, caught off-guard so early in the morning, but once he knows what's going on, he goes back to French. He's still pensive, his eyes are lost somewhere in the ceiling.

"Was it me that got you hard or wasn't it?"

I had said "maybe" in Occitan. And now I answer, in French: "No."

He nods gently a few times, as if that was what he preferred, but I can't be totally sure. I take a deep breath.

"Would you have liked that?"

---

16. How are you feeling?

17. Keep talking in Occitan!

He doesn't answer, he shifts onto his side, facing me. He isn't really looking at me, his eyes are unfocused, I don't know if he's sad, he tries to smile at me, a melancholic smile.

"I've been pining for you," he says.

"I have, too."

"What are we going to do?"

That's the right question, except that I really don't know what we're going to do. I don't even know what I want to do with Grampa, and I don't think he's thought this out any further than I have . . . We just know that we want to be together, to sleep together, oh yes, sleep together, that's important. But if I'm just going to say "I don't know," I'd rather hold my tongue.

"What do you want us to do?" I ask him.

"You know, at my age . . ."

But the door opens, he stops. It's Cindy, she runs over to me.

"Grammy's just gotten up, you have to leave!" she whispers.

I stay in the bed.

"Quick, if you ever want to come back, she can't find you here!"

At first, I wonder if she's exaggerating a bit like all the other girls her age, and then I look at Grampa. He's nodding. He agrees with Cindy.

"Come back soon," he says as he takes my hand. I'm amazed he'd say that in front of Cindy and we hold hands for a minute more.

"Quickly!" Cindy says.

Then we hear Mariette calling from upstairs:

"Cindy! Cindy?" Grampa doesn't let go of my hand, he holds it tight. Cindy goes through the door, she says "Yes!" We can hear Mariette's steps on the stairs already. I pull away from Grampa and as I take off his pajamas to put on my shorts and shoes, I hear Mariette saying:

"What are you doing?"

"I came down for some water."

"How much time do you need to drink water?"

"I'm just having a glass!"

I smile at Grampa one last time, I say "see you soon," I climb through the window, and I escape into the garden. And as I run, I have a strange feeling, I'm terrified, I'm actually panicking a bit, but at the same time I don't care at all. I have faith in the future, I feel like a free man. I can't be far from what they call happiness.

Once I'm back home, I'm wiped out, but I can't get to sleep. I toss and turn in my bed. As soon as I shut my eyes, my mind goes through everything that happened. The chief staring at me. Grampa's shit-filled underwear over my mouth, the baton up my ass. I try to think of Grampa in his bed, in his pajamas, without his hat, I try to focus on his face again, or rather, on the image I've created of his face, his eyes, his neck . . . but it doesn't make a difference, I keep seeing him in his underwear and wifebeater, coming into the bathroom as fast as he can and then, immediately after, the underwear full of shit, the baton up my ass, the chief saying "I know." I'm too nauseous, there's no point trying anymore, I get up. My stomach growls but I'm not hungry at all, I yawn so wide my jaw clicks but I'm not tired anymore. On my balcony, I watch cars going down the road but that bores me quickly, there's nothing exciting to see, I go out to buy the paper. I see a shortish article on the second page, I read it, and once I've gotten to the last paragraph I don't even remember what it was talking about, I read it again because I'm interested, it's about pension reform, I try to focus, it's a bit technical but nothing too tricky, it has to do with both technology and politics, that's what I need, but just like the first time, when I get to the end, I'm not able to explain what's written there, not even in a general way. I yawn again. It's not worth it to lie down again, I know I won't fall asleep, it's all too shaky, even as I skim the headlines all I can see is Grampa, the chief with his gloved hand, Grampa's underwear coming out of my ass, I stop there, quick, another image . . . The chief in his office, that's better already, the open fly, the red underwear . . . My red underwear in Mariette's hands in the garden, the navy-blue underwear on the clothesline, Grampa in his underwear on the toilet, the shit coming out, the underwear over my mouth, the shit in my mouth. I get up immediately, four quick steps down the hallway. No use. I'm upset, and the more upset I get the more my mind plays these images, I have to get out, yes, getting some fresh air will do me good. I walk in the streets. It's noon. It's hot. It feels good in the shadows on the side streets, my mind is blank, I look at the stores and feel no urge to buy anything, I look at the buildings off in the distance, I haven't lived in Roquerolle for very long, although it's actually been six years. . . I feel like I know all that by heart, I do like this little town but I wonder how long that'll last . . . How long will I like Roquerolle. Then I push the idea away, I decide that, for now, I'm happy here. I walk past people, I meet their gazes, quickly, they look away, and when they don't look away I'm the one who averts my gaze. I keep going in a circle, but at least that circle is a bit bigger. I have a strong feeling that I shouldn't disconnect myself from all this, the town, the people here, everybody, although I am a real individualist, I know that, essentially, it's through them that I live . . . Without them, there'd be no more point to my being here, and in the end, it's only when I'm here that I feel well, amid all these faces at once unknown and familiar. I'm on my third lap around the town when I start thinking about Grampa again, calmly this time, without any image in mind, just the idea of him, he's there, in my heart, I miss him, we'll see each other again soon. It'll be complicated. My heart wrenches. We'll sleep together. Soon. We won't do anything more than that, we'll just sleep in the same bed together. I like that. For scarcely a second, I'm able to be happy. And then I tell myself that I have to go to the police station, to press charges against the chief. The idea scares the shit out of me, but I slowly convince myself that I have to . . . That it'll help with everything else . . . To forget, first of all, although no, I don't think I'll forget this so easily, but mainly it'll help my relationship with Grampa . . . At least if the police chief isn't there anymore, that'll make things easier. But when I come to the police station, I change my mind. It suddenly seems too complicated, I'm not sure I've properly thought about all the ins and outs of this case and how it will turn out. I'd rather wait a bit. And I'm hungry, I go have a rib steak at Jean-Pierre's restaurant. He's very busy in the kitchen, we only exchange a few words before I go sit down, and so I talk to his wife, Danielle, we never catch up all that much, she asks me how I'm doing, I say I'm doing fine, and it's going to be hot this afternoon. I eat on the terrace, I watch the cars and passersby, and when I'm done, I stay at the table for a bit longer. And then Éric comes by with his friends from work. He asks me if I'm all by myself, he's dismayed, he would stay with me but he feels obligated to eat with his colleagues. It's no problem, I've already eaten. He sits down anyway for a couple of minutes so we can catch up. I tell him that things aren't going all that well, but when he asks what's happened, I don't really know what to answer so I talk about the general mood, the crisis, all those arrogant rich people, they want to do away with us all, we'll never get out alive . . . The lower classes are going to take a beating. He tells me we're all already taking a beating. And he's right. I flip out. He flips out, too. We're all flipping out. So Éric checks on his colleagues, he orders something and he comes to sit with me. I'm grateful. I really like Éric. It's too bad, after his youngest child was born, they all went to live in the countryside, with his girlfriend, and we don't see much of each other anymore. But, as he reminds me, it's really nothing more complicated than just picking up the phone, calling, and then getting in the car, he's only a few miles away. I know, but I don't call . . . All right, yes, I do call, but I never come over . . . Or rather, yes, I come over but without checking in first and that never works out well, either they're not there, or they're busy with something else . . . Maybe I'm not all that interested in seeing them. To be honest, I don't really know why I'm gradually withdrawing from my friends. It's the same thing with everyone else, I like running into them here and there, by chance on the street, I also like when they invite me over to eat, to parties, birthdays, housewarmings. I like being invited, but once I'm there, I usually don't stay long. It's not that my friends bore me, but for some time now I've preferred to celebrate with strangers . . . Or at least with friends amid strangers. I can't figure out why and I don't think I'm really set on finding out why either. That's just how it is. I'm not trying to change my feelings, either.

Seeing Éric eating across from me makes me feel hungry again, and it'd be good to keep him company properly. I order some dessert. He says that everybody is just fed up . . . When people go back to work in the fall shit's going to hit the fan . . . We're headed toward some huge social movement, it'll be even worse than 1995. I'm actually scared of war, I feel like we're not all that far away from savagery. I don't really understand how civility and respect for others and negotiations when there are conflicts . . . I don't really understand how all of that still works. And then I feel like one day or another we'll have to defend ourselves from all these super rich people profiting off of the deserts and deaths and starvation they create around themselves . . . Otherwise they'll kill every last one of us. So the war's coming soon. Éric's pensive, he nods, he's thinking, he hadn't been thinking about war, he thinks that, in any case, the war's already here . . . But in economic terms. And democracy just serves to maintain an artificial status quo that does us no favors . . . It might stay that way for a long time, he concludes. But I'm still wondering if we really give a fuck whether the human race keeps on existing. Starting with me. Éric looks at me oddly, he doesn't know what to say, then he goes:

"Well, yeah, I give a fuck!"

"If we really did give a fuck, then we'd get off our asses, wouldn't we?"

"But we are doing what we can, what do you think we're doing?"

"But what can we do?"

"You tell me . . . What do you want to do?"

I look at him, I can't decide if I know what he's talking about.

"Do you want to live or do you want to die?" he says at last.

"I want to live."

"See!"

And that's how he ends the conversation . . . As if the answer was obvious, and as if I had the solution right there in my hands. And I tell myself that he's got a point. I'm actually feeling better about myself after that moment spent with Éric. I promise him I'll come up to visit his family one of these days. I promise him this with a genuine desire to see him again and to have more time to talk about this . . . We should spend a whole evening together! Once he's gone, I finish off the pitcher of wine and decide to go back to the police station to tell them everything that happened. And then halfway there, I'm scared of the shame again, I'm scared of the chief, I don't trust the police. It's really hot now. It has to be more than a hundred degrees outside. There's nobody in town, I don't want to sit around at home, I grab my towel and my swimsuit and go to the lake. I park my car by the spot where everybody sunbathes nude, I don't really want to get hit on, but I don't really want to swim either, I just want to take an afternoon nap in the sun with everybody around me, but not too close or too far away . . . After all, it wouldn't upset me to see someone I know. I stretch out on my towel, the sun beating down, the children making noise over there, far off, on the other shore, the muffled sound of the water, everything that I like, I shut my eyes. I don't even have time to think about which thoughts I might focus on, I hear footsteps a few feet away. I open my eyes, a fifty-something man in shorts and an unbuttoned shirt revealing his hairy chest looks at me as he walks by. I look back at him. He stops, says hi to me. I say hi back, he gets closer. He asks me if he can sit down. I don't like him, that much I know, I'd never want to do anything with him. Whenever that happens I never know what to do, I never know if it'd be better to tell him that right now so he doesn't waste his time, but on the other hand, we're not dogs, there's a time and a place for seduction, you never know, and in the end it's not nice to push away people like that, right off the bat. So I tell him to go ahead and sit down. I stay outstretched, my cock in the breeze, I'm tanning my whole body, my hands are behind my head . . . I think that's been my favorite position all my life. He just takes off his shirt, and keeps on his shorts and we don't have anything else to say to each other. Finally, he decides to say something.

"The water's surprisingly low this year!"

Always the same tune. The lake is a reservoir that's used to irrigate fields. So the water level goes down over the course of the summer. But I never pay attention to that, I never have any idea whether the water level's higher or lower than last summer. So I say:

"Yeah?"

"Last year, at this time, it was six or seven feet higher."

"But it rained so much this spring."

"Not that much," he says.

"It didn't stop raining until the middle of June,"

"Yes, but the summer's been really dry," he explains.

And after that neither of us has anything to say. I look at him. I try to see if there's couldn't be some little thing I like about him.

But no, there's nothing. He has an odd-shaped head with a pointy nose, big brown eyes and thick lips, he does have a nice body, but that's not enough. I'm not into him, I don't want to get laid this afternoon, I just want to do nothing. Well, no, I do want to talk. I ask where he's from.

"Corignac," he says. "You?"

"Roquerolle."

And then there's silence again. He looks over my body, my cock, my face. From the way he's looking at me, I can tell he's horny, he's not here to chitchat. I'm reluctant to say anything right away, I don't know how to tell him, so I decide to let him make the first move. And I don't have to wait long.

"Want to walk around the woods?" he asks.

"Nah, I'm not in the mood," I say.

It always happens the same way, even though I say it amiably, it feels weird, even to me, I feel like I just blew him off. But he's cool, he doesn't take it personally, doesn't try to make me explain, he's not interested in chitchatting, he's only here to fuck, no time to waste, he gets up and he goes cruising further off. He says good-bye. I don't want to be cold, it's better to end on a friendly note, so I get up on my elbows. I tell him good luck, but I regret it immediately afterwards. The way I'd said it, I feel like I'd said "With your face, you haven't got a chance." He doesn't pick up on it, that makes me feel better, he says goodbye with a nod. I watch him walking off, I hope he'll turn around one last time, but no, I don't really hope that, I tell myself that's what should happen. He doesn't turn around. Farther off, two guys are standing and talking right by the water. Muscular, buzz cuts, completely hairless, they're in really good shape, well tanned, they must spend every day on the beach. They must even be good swimmers, I'd like to see them get in the water but they're just talking. And then they see that I'm checking them out. I look away. I lie down on my towel again. The sun on my skin, on my dick, I'm sweaty from not doing a thing. I tell myself I should have brought some water and a hat, and then, even though I'd like to be thinking about Grampa, I start thinking about Cindy. Yes, Cindy, at first I think that I haven't thought about her since I left her during the night, and that wasn't nothing. As I shut my eyes, I see her again stroking my cock, I see her talking to me again, self-satisfied: "You're so hard!" I ran off like a thief, I left her without any explanation, she must have ten thousand questions, poor thing, I have to go back and see her . . . We have to talk, I have to explain. I realize that I do like Cindy. It makes me smile that she's sneaking out at night, that makes her more sexy, she's alone, she's bored, and even so I'm sure she's watching over Grampa, in fact, she's watching over everybody. I still don't think she's very attractive, in my head I fix her face just a bit, let's say I make her a few years younger. And then I imagine her going into raptures over my cock, stroking it, gently rubbing it. She takes it into her mouth, she pays attention to it and sucks it slowly. And then I imagine Grampa with us, next to me on the couch, he holds my hand, he squeezes it, he's with me. I'm hard in the sunlight. Where do all these passionate feelings we have with Grampa come from? I didn't expect it at all. I go through my memories for moments that might have given me reason to believe that Grampa might want to sleep with me one day. I consider the numerous times when we shook hands, to say hello or good-bye . . . But there's no point, it was never tender or affectionate. His handshake was still frank and manly. Sometimes, when we sat in the living room, after dinner, he'd tell me to sit next to him on the couch. I'd do it, but it was never very practical, since Mariette was in the armchair on my left, and so when I turned toward her, I would basically have to turn my back to Grampa. Yes, I turned my back to him, since I was always talking to her. He was interested, he tried to join in the conversation, every so often I'd look back at him but we never paid

Grampa much attention, as if we thought he didn't have anything interesting to share. We wrote him off. He was too old. And so after a while he'd give up, he watched TV instead, read the paper, or dozed off. And those few times that I was sitting next to him, I don't remember him trying to touch me, to hold my hand, even though that's what old people tend to do. They like to touch whoever they're talking to. And then I think back to that winter night. I was coming back from a thing in Cahors, it was snowing but not hard, a few small flakes that melted as soon as they touched the ground, I stayed to eat with them, then we had a few glasses of digestives after the meal and when I walked out, I saw that the ground was completely white. Immediately, Grampa said:

"You're not going back to Roquerolle!"

"It's just ten miles, I'll be fine!" I'd replied.

"But that's not safe!" Mariette had said.

"We've got space," Grampa said. "By tomorrow, they'll have cleared the roads."

And I was feeling so comfortable in the house, this cozy spot one snowing evening but it was barely nine o'clock and I was scared of getting bored in the few hours before going to bed, I wanted to be back home and I insisted. They kept begging, both of them, I can still see Grampa's disappointed face. More than anything, it reminded me of the faces I made as a child when I wanted our guests to stay overnight at our house . . . It would make my family bigger for a night, and I liked the idea that my family could incorporate others. But I hadn't taken that as any indication of affection. I was touched that Mariette wanted me to stay the night, as if I had found a safe haven in case things took a turn for the worst . . . Or just for a night when I felt especially alone. But that one time, I left.

I keep looking for signs. A smile, a tap on my shoulder, a hand on my thigh I hadn't noticed at the time. Nothing. And then I think back to the first time I jerked off in one of Grampa's pairs of underwear. I had been telling the policemen the truth, it wasn't out of any desire for Grampa, or because I felt like fucking around . . . It's true that Grampa's underwear remind me of those M. Escandolières used to wear. He was the father of my old friend Patrice, and I often had slept over at the Escandolières' on weekends or vacations. M. Escandolières was a sturdy farmer, he must have been around forty back then. He was tall, intelligent, with blue eyes, and I secretly liked him . . . One day, I found one of his pairs of underwear in the bathroom. I jerked off in them, then I put it back with my hot semen in it, like a signal I wanted to send. But it didn't work at all. I did it one more time. And then he stopped leaving his underwear in the bathroom, and since I stayed friends with Patrice because I had a crush on his father, knowing that this love was impossible, I slowly pulled away from Patrice. However, I'd never forgotten M. Escandolières. But as the chief had said, for navy-blue underwear, all I had to do was go to the Trintaud market or any market at all, they were sold everywhere, no need to take Grampa's. M. Escandolières was a man I definitely wanted to have sex with. On the whole, I like older men, Paul's fifteen years older than me. And I've slept with men older than him. But not Grampa . . . Not at all . . . It's not possible. I try once again to imagine making love with Grampa. Just trying to imagine him naked doesn't work, it feels wrong, I can't do it, I just see him coming into the bathroom in his underwear and wifebeater, then on the toilet shitting into his underwear. I stop. I open my eyes. The sun is still high in the sky, I keep my eyes open as I try to follow a train of thought, not Grampa naked, I focus on the feeling and the actual act. I see him asking me last night if he's the one making me so hard, I see him on the first night asking me if I think about him when I masturbate in his underwear. Those aren't just empty questions, asked for the sake of asking. And those questions are also what link me to him. What could I possibly do with Grampa?

Kissing him is impossible. Taking him into my arms, yes, but that's the extent of it, and even then I'm not sure. Caressing him through his pajamas, too, I can see myself doing that, although . . . Putting my hand on his chest, on his stomach still covered by his pajamas. Holding his hand. Talking in Occitan. Assuming I could spend all my nights with Grampa, I wonder what else we'd do together. And yet I miss him. He's always in my thoughts, in my heart. As much as a man I'd like to have sex with.

It's already six thirty, it's still very hot, when a paunchy, hairy, self-assured man comes to say hi to me. He pulls me out of my haze, I haven't even replied and he's already taking off his shorts and lying down on his towel next to me. I remember we hooked up this spring, well, hooked up is a bit much . . . I've been with more generous guys. He gets people to suck him off, the most he does is pull on their cock, and once he comes, he pulls his shorts back up and leaves after a handshake. I'd talked about him with other men, and they all agreed that was how he did things. He doesn't recognize me. He asks me directly if I'll go into the woods with him. I say no. And then I give him the rundown. It wasn't even that long ago, just two months. He tries to remember, no, it doesn't ring a bell, but it bothers him. He tries to put a finger on what we did, as if he usually did all sorts of things. I tell him. And then he shakes his head, no, he definitely doesn't remember me. He's really completely clueless, he asks me what went wrong. Apparently I have to tell him every single thing. So I break it down for him. I'm not sure if he understands, but clearly it's not all that important to him, he puts his shorts back on and he leaves. The sun's harsh, I'm sweating, I realize that I still haven't gotten in the water, come on, it'll clear my thoughts. As I go down toward the lake, I take a minute to look around, I notice a pair of men I hadn't seen before, they're in the shade, close to the hedges. I know them, they're very nice, they live together in

Roquerolle, I had sex with the younger one, fifty years old but he looks older, and it was really nice, I'd also really like to have sex with the older one, who's fifty-five years old and looks much younger, but he doesn't want to and I think he'll never want to. Really, I'd like to have sex with both of them at the same time. They wave hi to me. I go back up to say hi to them. The one I've already hooked up with, the younger one, flirts with me a bit, he'd like to go walk around the woods. He does this discreetly, behind his man's back, but I don't flirt back, I'm only interested in the other man's dick, which is half hard between his legs. But he's the same as ever, he doesn't want to keep the conversation going, he must have only come to sit by the lake and be with his man, maybe to keep an eye on him. I don't know why I'm thinking about this so carefully, I don't even want to have sex this afternoon, I just want to swim, now. I go to the water. I start with a front crawl toward the middle of the lake. I swim lazily, using only my arms, just kicking my legs every so often, enough to keep me horizontal. I'm not exerting myself, I'm gliding, I'm thinking about nothing at all, just the water on my body, and when I turn my head to breathe, I feel the water flowing over my face. Once again, I wonder why I dawdle when it comes to getting in the water since I enjoy it so much. Why am I always so lazy and slow to do what I have to do? Once I'm in the water, I'm happy, not on the banks. I know that. What was I thinking tanning until this late? I turn onto my back, I look at the naked men on the beach. They're far away now. I recognize a few shapes. I watch them come and go between the beach and the woods . . . then I realize it's not really coming and going, the shadows of the trees stretch along the lake, the afternoon is stretching toward its end, the men are gradually leaving. I glance at the other shore, there are no more children yelling, the families are leaving the beach. It's still a long while until nighttime, it's still very hot, as if at the stroke of seven, everything was supposed to stop, it makes me sad, we could all enjoy this for as long as possible. It's my fault, I should have come earlier. Nobody else in the water, I don't want to be all by myself in this lake . . . I'm not afraid of the catfish, or some kind of heart attack, or any sort of accident . . . No, I'm afraid of the unknown. Alone in the middle of the lake with nobody around, I don't even dare to imagine it. I think this would be too much solitude for me. I make my way back to the banks. I take my time, and in any case, even if I didn't take my time, it would have taken me a while since I'm so far. By the time I touch the shore, all the men have left, the couple I really like included. And I don't see any movement around the trees. As for the opposite shore, the families have deserted it, I just hear one last car engine starting in the distance. I go to my towel, and there, as I want to stay naked to dry off and as I'm possibly the only one there, I bring it all the way over to the hedges. That way, I'm less visible. It's always like that, when you're alone, you don't want to take too many risks. I stretch out, I shut my eyes, and I think about Cindy stroking my cock, next to me, on the couch, Grampa holding my hand. Noises off in the distance, feet slashing water. I get up on my elbows. Two men down there are walking naked in the lake water. I see their backs, they're far away. A very young body, thin and olive-skinned. The other one seems older, strong, tanned. The latter one catches my fancy and I'm really fascinated when I see just how easily he's swimming. A perfect front crawl, high above the water, he glides effortlessly, in just a few movements he's several lengths ahead of his friend, he waits for him to catch up and then he's off again. I love watching good swimmers maneuver through the water, I could sit there for hours. The two of them head toward the open water, they both seem ready for a long swim. Further off, the stronger waits for the younger one, they are close, they kiss and caress each other. But it doesn't last long, the stronger one goes off even faster, never getting tired, his strokes are steady for a hundred yards, while the other one works to keep up. But he's not a bad swimmer either, and since the bigger one waits, the other's quick to catch up. In the middle of the lake, the hug each other again and then begin playing around. They try to push each other underwater and this game is where the stronger and better swimmer is clearly winning, but the other one pops up to the surface every time, he takes a deep breath, and then they're at it again, the two bodies intertwined disappear under the water, while I wait for them to come back up, it's getting a bit long now, maybe they'll reappear farther off, then I start worrying and they come back up to the surface at the same spot, they've overestimated their strength a bit. The tougher one is out of breath, he pushes himself abovewater to catch his breath, the other one stays in place while beating his arms, he seems to be panicking. And that seems a bit scary, even with my best friend I wouldn't want to play around like that in the middle of the lake. And actually he sees his friend coming over to him, he holds up his hands to tell him to stop but the other man doesn't stop, he grabs him in his arms and pulls him underwater with him. Once again it lasts long. My heart's pounding, I'm worried, and still waiting for them to come back up. More time goes by, just when I think there's no way they can stay underwater any longer, I see them break the surface again. I look more carefully, no, it's not the two of them. The stronger one is the one who came back up. He stays where he is for a minute, he dives down again, and then he comes to the surface again, he looks all around, I curl up by the hedges but keep watching. The other man still hasn't come back up. The stronger man comes back to the beach using a backstroke. And even on his back he's a fast swimmer. I check my surroundings. I'm alone, completely alone. And if the man let himself do that, right in the middle of the lake, he'd have checked to make sure there was nobody. I'm afraid of being seen. I'm even more afraid of leaving. If he sees me running off and he comes after me, he's good enough of a swimmer that he'll definitely be fast on the ground too, I wouldn't be a problem for him. And I want to see his face. I hide in the hedges, they're prickly but it doesn't matter. I have to be brave. And I am, I stay in the hedges without moving, safe behind a tree. For half a second I think about the drowned man, the body falling to the bottom of the lake, I wonder if he'll stay there. I've forgotten whether a drowned body rises to the surface . . . I'm not sure if I ever knew. The man switches to a front crawl, he's still gliding easily over the water, not the least bit worn out from the effort. In no time at all, he reaches the shore, gets to his feet, stumbles a bit because of the rocks on the ground. Water is dripping off his body, the front of his body is even more beautiful than the back, his pecs are hairless, his groin is shaved smooth, I have a foreboding feeling and two seconds later, when he raises his head to look all around him, the feeling turns out to be right . . . It's him, it's definitely the chief. Hidden in the hedges, I can't turn my gaze away, but I'm worried that he's going to sense my eyes fixed on him, he has to feel it. But I also tell myself this isn't the moment to waver, I have to pay attention till the end . . . If he sees me, I need to know that he did. I'd never thought the chief could be so handsome. I wait, at once fascinated and terrified. This was well worth my staying here, but I feel pathetic in my hedge, I should have been farther away, I'm sure that if he puts any effort into it, if he just takes a few more steps in my direction, if he looks at the hedges carefully, he'll see a bit of my body behind the tree, a bit of my red towel by my ass. But he doesn't make the effort, he goes the other way and rubs his body dry with his hands. He turns around one last time. I still haven't moved. Where he's standing, he can't possibly see me anymore. I keep on waiting, I wait for the engine to start, for the car to leave. And then I suddenly remember my own car, the only one in the parking lot, there's no way he didn't see it. I'm not sure that the chief knows my car, but Safranes aren't all that common, he wouldn't have any trouble recognizing it. And a single car in the parking lot, that'll catch his attention, he'll wait for the driver, and if he doesn't see the driver, he'll come back to look around the lake for him. And even if I walk back home, this car that nobody's driven off is going to seem even fishier. The only solution is for me to get to the parking lot before he does. I have to beat him. But, just looking past the tree, I know there's no way to do it. Even if it were possible, I'm too scared to move. I forget the idea.

Around me, everything is quiet. Night is falling gently.

Normally, the chief would need a good fifteen minutes to get to the parking lot by foot. I count the minutes in my head, alert to any noise at all, every second I expect to hear footsteps on the path behind me . . . It's possible he parked his car in the other lot on this side of the lake, at the other end . . . It's father off but more secluded. And that would be better for me tonight. But no, it's already been five minutes since he left and still not a single noise behind me on the path.

The crickets start chirping. The lake is a huge, dark, solid mass. I still don't dare to move in the hedges. I haven't ruled out the possibility that the chief is still there, on the shore, waiting . . . I don't know why . . . That's what we often see in the movies, in books, killers staying at the crime site, lost in their thoughts. And maybe to make sure there really were no witnesses. I'm stuck on that thought when I finally hear a car starting. The noise is coming from the parking lot, I'm sure of it. The car runs slowly for a while, it backs out, and then it leaves, it's headed up the hill. It stops at the stop sign. For a long time. Finally, it turns onto the road toward Corignac, I think. I'm relieved and, immediately after that, disillusioned, I feel like it's all happening too fast, the chief must have seen my car, it's odd that he didn't come back to check the lake shore. I stay and don't move. I take a moment to think. I spent the afternoon lying in the grass, my eyes shut, maybe the chief saw me. Why wouldn't he have noticed me? He wouldn't have had to be very close to recognize me. Maybe he drowned this poor guy just to send me a signal, just to tell me: "Be careful, this is the kind of thing I can do!" And that slow gaze when he came out of the water, there's no way he didn't see me . . . I was hidden in the ferns and bushes, but even when I was behind the tree I could see him, so why wouldn't he have seen me? And my car sitting in the parking lot would have been a paltry detail for him . . . Just the confirmation that I definitely saw everything. It's nighttime, I finally step out of my hiding spot, I go back to the parking lot by going along the shore, here, I don't know why, I feel safer going this way rather than up the path where I have a feeling that the chief might catch me at any moment. But whenever I hear a fish splashing, a frog diving in, a bird flapping in the air . . . It freaks me out. What if it was the chief's accomplice who'd left in the car a little while ago? What if the chief was hidden in the parking lot? I stop. I listen. I think about everything and wonder if I'm ready to die. At first, I don't think so. And then I think again, I start walking again, I tell myself that it would be a difficult moment to go through, but then it would be over, I wouldn't be around to be upset about anything. I don't think I have much left to expect from myself or from this world . . . When I take the time to think about it, it all seems futile, increasingly futile . . . Working so that the humanity of the future might be better than the present one, I don't know if I'm all that interested anymore . . . I feel I myself have such a long way to go, I haven't figured everything out, I'm running on empty . . . At forty, the best of my life is behind me, and to think that I'll have to live that many years again, with soccer games on TV, lunches with friends, movies, concerts, hookups by the lake or online or wherever. And that's where I am in my thoughts when I get to my car, all by itself, under the trees in a dark corner of the parking lot. I'm not afraid of anything in the night now, I walk intently. I think that only Grampa's love could make me upset about dying tonight, but, in any case, even with Grampa, life doesn't seem to be really leading me anywhere. So it wouldn't be a big deal. I get into my Safrane, it starts right away . . . For a second, I'd thought that it might not start. Then when I turn my head to back out, I expect to see a shadow rush toward the door, but nobody rushes forward. As I drive off, I stop worrying. I'm really not afraid of anything anymore. But when I get home, as I park my car on the other side of the road, I see something odd on my building door. A bit of red cloth on the doorknob. Deep down, I know what it is, but I walk over anyway, I look around, check to see if anybody's watching me, I pick it up, it's my red underwear, it's moist, I unfold it, in it there's still-wet semen.

I had to move several times over the last few years, I'd already had this horrible recurring dream where I became poor again, where I have to live in a hovel . . . No more work, no more money, humiliation, I knew it was just waiting to happen, as with everybody else. So now I live in a little attic apartment, a dilapidated building with damp, stained carpets, daylight barely comes through the little window overlooking a narrow street. Across the street is the old town hall, tall and massive, it blocks all the sunlight, I have to lean out the window to see what the weather's like. But the worst part is that I don't really have the right to be there, I didn't really inquire before and now that I'm in the apartment, I don't dare to ask to make sure. First, I don't really know who I should ask, and second, I tell myself people will be suspicious, I don't want any problems. So I just let things be. To get to my attic apartment, I go up winding stairs that end so steeply they're practically a ladder and then a little door that I have to bend down to go through. Really, even though it's the twenty-first century in Roquerolle . . . It feels more like being in a Zola novel. Once I'm inside, it's miserable, I'm bored, and with the stench, a moldy smell that lingers and which I haven't ever been able to get rid of, I always want to leave immediately. I don't sleep well. I'm still half-asleep when I freak out, I feel an overwhelming need to get out of this place immediately, in case there's a fire or some kind of war, I'm increasingly scared of war, I have a feeling this is going to be horribly complicated. I'm afraid of staying stuck in here. So I'm alert, ready to run out. I'm scared that it's going to be like this all the way to the end, until my life's finally over . . . And it might get worse . . . Maybe this crappy apartment is my last stop before homelessness. The chief comes to see me regularly. Sometimes he stays and sleeps with me, he helps me as much as he can, but it's not easy for us to love each other. I like running my hands over his body, he got a good tan over the summer, every so often, we kiss, we tongue kiss endlessly, he's an amazing kisser but I know I should be on my best behavior. If I ever mess up, that'll be it, he'll be pissed. So I stop getting hard as often. He gets upset, he thinks it's because I don't want him anymore, I assuage his fears right away by taking his dick in my hand, he has a beautiful dick, not too big or too long, it's exactly right. It feels nice in my hand, nice in my mouth, nice up my ass . . . The perfect dick, indeed. By that point I've learned that he's not married, and that he never has been, and when I learn that I'm amazed that he's been able to work his way up the hierarchy without a wife or kid. He says that in the police force everybody knows that he's gay and it hasn't been a problem. He's lying, I'm sure of it. Why wouldn't he bring me back to his place, then? He says it's too early, that we don't know each other well enough. I don't believe a word of that. He keeps a company apartment so that he can fuck all of his colleagues. And he keeps me here, like a prisoner, I had to sell my car, I don't even have any money to buy a cup of coffee, I have to hope he'll feel like giving me ten euros to buy some pizza. And tonight, he comes over without a care, he says:

"That's one less thing to deal with. Grampa's dead!"

At first I don't believe him, I'm sure he's just saying that to make me upset, but then I look at him properly, he's not joking, he doesn't actually look sad but he's shaking his head very gently, he's silently confirming what he said, he does it for so long that I start to believe him finally. And then everything falls apart. Even though I hadn't seen Grampa for a long time, he was still a reason for me to go on living, a light at the end of this dark tunnel.

"He was ninety-eight," he says. "It was to be expected."

"But he was planning to live to a hundred!"

The chief looks right at me with fury.

"You didn't forget him!"

I shake my head . . . No, I didn't forget him.

"You promised!"

And he grabs my neck and starts to kiss me. And that's when I realize that he's the one who killed Grampa, he knows that I've realized it. He keeps his hand on my neck.

"Show me that you love me!" he says sharply but lovingly.

And as he says that, he pulls out his dick, it's stiff, he always gets really hard when I'm with him. There's no way out, I have to wait a few more minutes, I'll run away when he's at work. I suck his cock, but it's not like usual, he's being forceful, pulling in and out of my mouth and shoving it deeper down my throat. And he comes quickly, a huge torrent spurting into my mouth, it's endless, quarts and quarts of it, he doesn't pull out, I can't breathe anymore, I'm suffocating. I wake up.

Alone in my bed, in a cold sweat, drool on my lips, I stay there, paralyzed. It's night outside. I slowly stretch out my arms to turn on the lamp but I hesitate, I'm afraid of what I'll see. In the light, I'm happy at first to see my room and my apartment, but I'm not relieved for all that. In fact, I tell myself, it's only starting. I'm worried about Grampa. But I can't call him now, it's four in the morning, I walk around my apartment, out onto the balcony, I look at the sleeping town through the window, I get a feeling the chief's going to come see me . . . Normally, with the building entrance downstairs and the intercom, I'd be safe here, but all he has to do is ask one of my neighbors to buzz him in, they'd never say no to him, and he won't have any trouble making his way up to my apartment door. I freak out, I go back in to turn off the light. You never know. In the darkness, it's worse. I go back out onto the balcony. I slowly look from one end of the street to the other. Nothing's moving at all. I take a risk. The chief has to sleep at times. I sneak down to my car. On the road, I check my rearview mirror. I took the side road along the Alzou, it's safer, nobody ever goes this way. I can't stop thinking that the chief might actually suspect that just because nobody ever goes that way, that'd be exactly the route I took. I get to Trintaud without seeing any cars, but when I get to the back door of the house, on the garden side, it's locked. I'm surprised. I have to wonder why Mariette decided to lock that door. Did she know about my intrusion the previous night? But I tell myself that maybe she locks this door every single night, and it was only unlocked last night because Cindy hadn't locked it behind her. So, I need to knock on Grampa's window. No answer. Day's about to break, so maybe he's fallen asleep. I knock again, a bit harder, but not too hard. And Grampa comes to open the window at last, hushing me with a finger to his lips. And I'm so happy to see him alive and safe.

"Espèra!"[18] he whispers.

He disappears into the darkness of his room again. A few seconds later, he opens the big door and comes out into the garden, wearing his pajamas and slippers.

"Ven amb ieu,"[19] he says as he takes my hand and takes me to the far end of the garden. We huddle between the hedges and the apple tree.

---

18. Wait!
19. Come with me.

"Te cal pas demorar aquí!"[20] he whispers again.

"Ai somiat de tu,"[21] I tell him, because I have to.

"Ieu tanben," he replies. "Èras mòrt! Sabi pas cossí, lo legissiái dins lo jornal, èri malurós coma las pèiras, podiái pas m'empachar de plorar . . . E ploras que ploraràs . . . Lo chef es pas encara passat mas va passar, lo me prometèt ièr de ser . . . Nos cal pas veire d'un brieu . . . Tot lo mond deu créser que nos vesèm pas mai."[22]

"Quant de temps?"[23]

"Ne sabi pas res . . . Doas setmanas . . . Benlèu un mes."[24]

It's the only solution, he's really sorry, he just wants to live without being bothered. It feels like I'm being stabbed in the heart, I want to insist, tell him that he can't give up, but I really don't know if it's worth it, I look at his face to see what he really wants . . . But when I meet his gaze, when he looks back at me, it's no help, there's a glint of either determination or resignation . . . A glint I can't interpret . . . And I don't have any more time to think about what it might be. The light in Grampa's room turns on. I jump, I can see the chief's silhouette fill the window. Mariette's up, she's calling Grampa in the whole house. She stands in the doorway, she's calling his name in the garden. Grampa goes.

"Good-bye!" he says as he touches my arm. He's speaking French now, that's even harder to bear. And he walks over to Mariette. I fall to the ground, in the shadows of the hedge.

---

20. You can't stay here!

21. I was dreaming about you.

22. I did, too . . . You were dead! I don't know how, I read it in the paper, I was unbearably sad, I couldn't stop crying and crying . . . The chief hasn't come by again but he will, he promised me last night . . . We can't see each other for a while . . . Everybody needs to think we're not seeing each other anymore.

23. How long?

24. I don't know . . . Two weeks . . . Maybe a month.

"What are you doing out in the garden in your pajamas?"

"Pòdi pas dormir!"[25]

Grampa goes back inside, the chief's silhouette disappears from the window, once he's gone I feel ashamed and escape into the Trintaud streets to find my car, but I was too fast . . . Or not fast enough . . . Just when I turn the key in the ignition, I see the chief looking at me through my windshield. He's all alone, in his police uniform, I don't know where everyone else went. And I have even less of an idea how he got here before I did. He goes around the car, he opens the side door, gets in, sits down.

"Drive!" he orders.

So I start the engine, then I take a moment to think. I turn off the engine.

"No, I'm not driving," I say.

I'm tired of this chief, he can't treat me like this forever, I feel sure of myself now, I'm trembling but if I have to die, it's not going to be in a thicket all by myself early in the morning.

"As you wish," he says. "I take it you got my message?"

I'm astonished by how calm he is, as if he wanted to move on to something else. The tone of his voice is almost reassuring. I nod.

"Well?" he says.

"What?"

"So what did you think of it?"

"That you're going to kill me!"

I keep looking straight ahead, through the windshield, there's nobody in the area, just a car driving by at the end of a street, it has to be six in the morning, something like that. I can feel the chief's gaze on me.

"Look at me!" he says.

I don't look at him, he leans over.

"I said, look at me!"

---

25. I couldn't sleep!

I look at him.

"Don't you think that if I wanted to kill you, I'd have done it a while ago?"

I have to say something back, but instead I'm riveted by his round face, his gray mustache, his blue eyes. I catch myself, I look away and out the windshield, and I say:

"Maybe you like playing with your victims."

"I'd say I've already played with you enough."

"Maybe not enough!"

"Well, I'm not playing."

And I can't help looking at him. He shrugs and presses his lips together. I don't know what that means.

"All right, I went too far . . . The cudgel up your ass then the pair of underpants full of shit, that was too violent . . . I was upset . . . I'm sick of people doing whatever they like, I wanted to teach you a lesson . . . Both you and them. I went too far, okay!"

I can't believe what I'm hearing. Not only is he making proper amends, but he really does seems sincere . . . Not seem, he actually is . . . He's sincere. I can't let myself be won over, I can't turn my head toward him, I'll just end up mesmerized by his handsomeness. I keep my eyes fixed on the windshield wipers, a man is crossing the square in the distance.

"Grampa, though," he says. "That's serious, you need to understand that Mariette's worried about him, she doesn't want her father to get fucked up the ass . . . Not even by a good-looking man like you . . . At his age, can you imagine? She's keeping an eye on him, isn't that normal?"

I don't reply.

"Hmm? Don't you think so?"

Yes, he's right, I nod. And anyway we've already had this conversation, we're wasting our time.

"And Grampa has no idea how this whole thing is going to turn out!"

"What do you know about that?"

"He's losing his marbles!"

"What the fuck makes you say that?"

"He's speaking patois again!"

"First, that's not patois, it's Occitan . . . Just because he's talking in Occitan doesn't mean that he's losing his wits!"

"It's proof that he's senile."

I shrug, I look at the chief in dismay. Then he adds:

"He's going back to his childhood language."

I don't want to reply to that. What I really think is that Grampa's switching back to Occitan because it's a more tender language for him than French, it used to be the language of troubadours and it's still the language of love. But I'd rather not say that to the chief, that would take us too far.

"But he really doesn't want to turn into a fag when he's about to hit a hundred . . . You need to realize that!"

"I haven't asked that much of him."

"Do you think we're all idiots? Sleeping together . . . Nobody ever sleeps with someone else just to sleep."

I have to say something back, I have to show him that I don't agree, but I'm still confused, I think for a while about this last statement, in a way I don't think he's wrong, I finally just blurt out a ridiculous "Oh really?" The chief looks at me, he nods, I'm sick of this conversation, I feel like I'm losing, I'm angry at myself for not being more combative, I know that I really don't agree with him, somewhere in my mind I decide I'm done, I don't have any more energy to deal with this. I don't want to try. A police van pulls up, my heart starts pounding, and I'm scared. The chief gives me a card.

"When you've decided, give me a call."

It's a business card with his address, his email, his phone number, all in blue letters on a sky-blue background.

"Decided what?" I ask.

"I've made myself clear."

And he gets out of my car, he waves to his colleagues. The van inches closer. I don't understand what's happening. The chief peers through the car door.

"Also," he says. "Did you have a nice time yesterday afternoon at the lake?"

"What?"

"Considering how long you were there, you must have had a nice afternoon."

"I'm not going to talk about my personal life with you."

"You didn't see anything special happen?"

And I look at the chief, I know I shouldn't dig myself into a bigger hole, I've learned it in a crime thriller, when you lie, there are seventeen different muscles on your face moving in ways that they don't when you're telling the truth. I think about that moment again, I focus on it, I tell myself that the worst thing would be to try to hide my emotions, I consider that fact, and then I go for it, I shake my head a bit, I still look worried, I act a bit surprised, and I say: "No!" And then I give the chief one last look. He locks eyes with me and then, as he shuts the car door, he says "See you soon." He gets into the van. I keep my eyes on the van as it disappears at the end of the square behind me.

I stay there for a long while without moving. There, in my car, on the square. Unnerved by the chief's words. And even moved by them. What if he was right, what if Grampa genuinely didn't want me, then maybe his words in the garden a few hours earlier, that we shouldn't see each other anymore to reassure everybody around us, had really just been his way of kindly pushing me away . . . We'll let things be for a week, two weeks, a month, we'll focus on other things, and we'll eventually forget each other without realizing it. And actually, since the start of this whole thing, Grampa's been asking questions about the nature of my feelings, he wants to know. I can still see him asking me if I was thinking about him while masturbating into his underwear, asking me if he was the one that made me so hard. And although I keep saying no, there's no echo to my answers . . . Maybe he doesn't believe me. Maybe he just thinks I'd say those things to stay with him and keep getting closer to him. That must have seemed odd to him, this man ready to break all the rules to come sleep in his bed. And Mariette who must be telling him things, piling it on every day. I walk all morning pondering these thoughts. I go get some coffee at Marc's café. There's never that many people in there during the morning, so we can talk a bit. He tells me I don't look well. It's normal, I've been up since four in the morning, I'm walking around groggily, I've been getting hit over the head every day, if not more than once, and this has been the worst. Grampa doesn't want to sleep with me anymore, he didn't even tell me he was missing me. Everything's falling apart. There's a knot in my heart, it's not anxiety, it's grief. I don't want to go back home. Being at home would be worse, but I can't drink coffee at every corner bar. And this morning still isn't over. It isn't even ten o'clock when I decide to go drink some pastis at Brigitte's. I head over to her sports bar in Corignac. Brigitte isn't there, but she'll be back soon, she's just running errands. Her boyfriend, Gérard, who I don't like that much, is the one manning the counter, I look at the time, ten twenty, it's still a bit early for a pastis, I'm going to look like an alcoholic, I don't know what to order instead, something that will perk me up.

"What about a glass of white wine?" Gérard says.

It's not a bad idea, okay, fine. I pick up *L'Équipe*, and I read it from cover to cover, even the golf section, but I don't know what they're talking about at all. With every article, it's the same thing, I start reading it, I see what they're talking about, I'm interested for the first few lines, and then my mind drifts off elsewhere, I see Grampa again all by himself in his bed suscing the whole night, his forehead wrinkled, his sad face, Grampa in the garden in his pajamas, Grampa telling me that we shouldn't see each other . . . A week . . . Or two . . . Maybe a month . . . Maybe never again. Never to see Grampa again. I can't. I feel shitty, humiliated, as if I'd believed in something there was never any reason to believe, a loving idyll without any sex, a desire that would be manifest somewhere other than the ass, that would never be manifest at all, and that would therefore never be extinguished. An eternal desire. But that's probably not possible, that's probably not something to wish for. Maybe desire only occurs when it is accomplished, maybe without being accomplished, desire is merely a futile dream. And with that my special fantasy crumbles to rubble. Maybe I've been lying to myself as a way of staying attached to something that doesn't exist, that will never exist. Once again I focus on Grampa in his bed, caressing him, lying next to him, it's all already starting to feel wrong . . . I bring my mouth to his, I kiss him . . . It doesn't work, I can't do it, that's not what I want with him.

Gérard is busy working, he keeps going between the back room and the bar counter. I'm alone in the café. Eleven o'clock. Brigitte still hasn't come back. I put *L'Équipe* back where I found it. I pick up *La Dépêche*. I read just the headlines, I turn the pages mechanically. I try not to think about anything, just the headlines. I see the chief completely naked, coming out of the lake, as handsome as Poseidon. He didn't see me, he doesn't know that I saw him, he suspects it, I have to keep my mouth shut, but I don't want to forget the poor guy drowned yesterday afternoon . . . What can I do? Go to the nearest police station and tell them what the chief did? I'm sure they'd laugh right in my face, I'm a good Frenchman, I don't think highly of the police, they won't hold their tongue, the chief will be informed right away and that'll be the end of me. Send an anonymous letter? Maybe that's a solution, I don't know if they take those seriously but at least I'll have done something . . . And maybe they'll send a squad to look for the body, if they find a cadaver at the bottom of the lake, they'll take me seriously and then I can guide the investigation without having to reveal my identity. But I don't like that idea. I have to think about this a while longer, I'm afraid of overlooking some detail that might turn this whole investigation against me. I don't have a good impression of the police, but I know they're definitely strong. What if the chief has a watertight alibi? What if nobody can prove anything against him? If the man accused by a poison-pen letter turns out to be innocent, then of course all suspicions would redound upon the letter writer himself. How could I prove that it wasn't me? I turn these questions over and over in my head. In the end, I decide that, even if I stay anonymous, the chief won't have any trouble connecting the dots, he's got his sights on me and he'll know right away that I was the accuser. And, after all, he did see my car. The more I think about it, the less sure I am whether it's the chief who's got me or I who's got him. I still have a week of vacation, the best solution would be go to someplace else. It's noon, Brigitte still hasn't come back from her errands, too bad, well, it doesn't matter, I didn't really want to see her that much. I'm hungry. So I go to have some steak at Jean-Pierre's. And eating it, all by myself on the terrace, it occurs to me to go see my old friend Henri . . . My old friend, I mean . . . More of an old lover, actually, a farmer from Corrèze who's always horny. A very generous lover who never gets tired, rolls around with me all night and then keeps asking for more in the morning. We haven't seen each other in a couple of years, I think it'd put a smile on my face to see him again . . . We'll have a great time together . . . It's been nearly two weeks since I had sex, come to think of it, that's what I want . . . Sure, I could call Paul, but the fact is, today, I want Henri. The nice thing is that he lives a two-hour drive away, I don't want to stay at home. I need to get out a bit. I call him. He picks up, he's happy to hear that I haven't forgotten him.

"So when are you going to come over?" he asks.

I wouldn't have expected anything less from him. I tell him that, as it happens, I've got a few days off and I was thinking about a drive over to his place.

"Come on over," he says. "Jacques isn't here, you can fuck me anywhere you like!"

Jacques is his friend, a guy my age, he's not all that talkative but he's still very nice, and he works in the vineyard with him. They've been living together for at least twenty years but these days they have separate rooms, they don't hook up anymore, but they still call each other "honey" and "sweetie." It's cute when old couples don't get bored of each other.

"You're still topping, right?" he asks. "I'm hoping you haven't turned into a bottom, because that's all there is around here, I haven't been able to find another cute guy with a nice cock to ram it deep in my hole. That's what everybody's doing these days, they all want to get fucked, you can't find a single top anywhere . . . Tell me, you're still a good top, aren't you?"

"Yeah, yeah," I say, not utterly convinced. "If I come over, I'm fucking you."

"Oh, and if you've got any friends, just bring them along, you know me, if I can take two dicks at the same time I'm going to do it . . . So when are you getting here?"

"Well, let me see how this afternoon goes and I'll give you a call, okay?"

"Why don't you come over tonight?"

"I'm not sure, I have to see . . . I'll give you a call."

"Sounds good."

And I hang up. Maybe it's not such a good idea to go see Henri right now. I'm not sure I want to have sex all night. With Henri, if we're not fucking, we're either sleeping, eating, or bored. I'm scared of driving two hours for nothing. I while away the afternoon on my couch with the fan at full speed, the shutters closed, the heatwave is overwhelming, especially in Roquerolle, a nice basin with absolutely no air circulation at all. It's well above a hundred degrees now. And I'm suscing, still suscing. This is how I've always been. I've always liked the idea of leaving . . . For a weekend . . . For vacation . . . For ever . . . But I've never liked actually leaving. I never want to stay at home. I don't know where to go, I don't know who I want to see. I think I don't want to see anybody. When I was younger, I felt like leaving might help me to turn things over in my head, to focus, and even if that didn't help me, at least it would give me the feeling of having saved some time. These days, I know it doesn't help me at all and I don't see any point to saving my time. And, just like that, it's already evening. I don't want to stay at home. And yet I stay. I call Paul. I leave him a muddled voice-mail message that I'm alone, that I'm bored, that he can call me or even come over. When I hang up, I feel like I've told him that he can come over just because I'm bored. He's definitely going to take it that way, I guess. Then I leave him another message to explain that I didn't mean it that way, that he should just call me and we can actually discuss properly. And then I realize he's definitely not going to call me after that. But then he calls half an hour later . . . Just to tell me that he can't tonight. He's really happy that I called, he was waiting to hear from me, he'd gotten nervous that things were over between us. But he didn't dare to call me. It's a shame that I didn't call him earlier about tonight, he could have moved things around, but he can't get out of dinner with his daughter now. But he could make tomorrow work. At the end he asks me again if I'm okay. I tell him yes. And that's the end of it, we tell each other we'll call tomorrow. Then, while I'm still holding the phone, I think about calling Mariette, I want to hear her voice, talk to her, make sure that nothing's changed, that we're not enemies now, that she's on my side, at least a little. But I don't. It's too early, she'll think I want to talk to Grampa, she'll think I'm trying to fool her and that'll just make everything worse. Later, in the apartment's shadows, I watch the sun setting . . . A huge, red sun . . . I drink some Ricard, I think about the British Petroleum oil spill in the Gulf of Mexico, I don't know it it's been stopped or if it's still spreading, I think about a completely black ocean, I think about the end of the world, the end of humanity, actually I'm mostly thinking about my own end. In my mind I can see the nude chief coming out of the lake like a Poseidon at the end of a very long day, I whisper phrases in Occitan to myself, I don't remember anymore how to conjugate the verb that means to follow, *segre*. I pull out my Occitan grammar book and that keeps me busy until it's night and I fall asleep.

I wake up very early, at daybreak. With a massive erection. I had a long dream, one of those dreams I haven't had in a long time: epic, poetic, sensual . . . Many things happened, but only a few powerful images remain. It began on a cliff and, below, standing on another cliff in front of me was the chief watching the ocean. And I stayed there, watching him. I was afraid that he'd turn around and see me but I stayed, it was so beautiful and mesmerizing. Then I came to the Escandolières' house, I was walking, I was delighted by the prospect of seeing them again, I rang their doorbell, no answer, then I saw M. Escandolières's head in the window and then, once he saw me, he immediately pulled back but I had enough time to look at his face carefully, and that just made me want to go in even more . . . I was convinced that he'd seen that I had seen him. I rang again. But still nothing. I stayed in front of the door for a moment, unsure what to do. Nobody came and I became incredibly depressed but shortly after that I was in a square in Montauban that looked awfully like Paris . . . But it was definitely Montauban. Then I spent a good long while at Mariette and Grampa's house. They weren't there anymore. I had the whole house to myself . . . And I treated it like my own apartment, I walked naked through the rooms, I ate the food in the fridge, drank from the bottles in the cupboard. Then I took a shower in a massive bathroom that bore no resemblance to their actual bathroom with a toilet. I was unnerved at the thought that the chief might find me here and I told myself that I was an idiot to take a shower downstairs, that I should have gone upstairs, but by then I was wet, it was too late to switch bathrooms. And I was also fascinated by a basket full of dirty laundry, I was looking at it because I thought I had seen some of M. Escandolières's underwear in it . . . That seemed odd to me and then I really wasn't sure anymore which house I was in . . . And I kept watching this basket because I was sure there was an animal, probably a snake, under the laundry and I was waiting for the basket to move so I could be sure. But it didn't move. Someone knocked at the door, I knew it was Mariette, I didn't answer . . . Specifically so that she would come in and find me naked, I was very proud of my penis, it was as hard as a bull's. She came in and said "Oh, sorry" and went right back out without even glancing at my crotch. I was very disappointed. Just as she was stepping out, I saw her back and saw right then that she was naked as well. But it happened far too quickly, I didn't have time to see anything. After that, I was running down the streets of New York with Cindy, a New York that looked much like Toulouse but was definitely New York. She was very energetic and at home in the city, she pulled me down the streets, amid the skyscrapers . . . I was sad to have spent so much time in Grampa's house without having seen him, I wanted to go back to Trintaud but Cindy wouldn't let go, she said we'd go back there someday and at the end of our trip, I saw that we were in Valparaíso, at the other end of the world, on cliffs that looked just like the ones at the beginning of my dream . . . I was terrified because the chief wasn't there and I couldn't see him anymore. Then I felt like I'd run everywhere and messed up everything and that now I would have to come back from Valparaíso and that the trip would be a very long one.

A horrible anxiety is tying my stomach in knots. I think of the drowned man in the lake, I think of his friends, his family looking for him for two days now, then I think that maybe he doesn't have any friends, any family, or friends and family stuck far away, that they might not necessarily be worrying about him at every moment, or, worse, that they think he's on vacation . . . And if that's true, he might stay there, at the bottom of the lake, for an entire week or even two, and even if someone had noticed his disappearance, he might not have told anyone that he was going to cruise guys at the lake the day before yesterday and if I stay quiet he might decompose in the water. I have to say something. I get up. I write an anonymous letter on my computer.

Monsieur,

I witnessed a crime the day before yesterday, Tuesday July 16th, at Corignac Lake.

I saw the Trintaud chief drowning another man . . .

And then I stop, it just seems stupid, I can't find the right words. And it's pathetic to write an anonymous note that I can't even write, when I reread it, it feels like a letter written by a retard, and there's no point to anonymity because the chief will know it was me. I might as well have the balls to go straight to the police station and tell them what I saw. I even start to hope that nobody else saw the crime, if someone else decides to write an anonymous note, then I'll end up being the patsy here. What if he's been found already? I wonder. Quickly I pull on a tee-shirt and go down to buy *La Dépêche*. Nothing. I go back up to my apartment, disappointed, I really had my hopes up, I would have been so happy for this poor guy not to be decomposing at the bottom of the lake. That he at least had a grave worthy of being called such. And just as I feared, nobody seemed to be nervous about this disappearance, not even two days later. Not even a search notice or something like that. I sit, suscing on my couch. The captain wouldn't hesitate to talk to the chief . . . The chief will suspect that I was the one to send the letter . . . He'd have every reason to, he saw my car . . . And then he'll kill me. Yes, he'll kill me before I talk. I know that's not what he wants, but he won't have the choice. Am I afraid of dying? As I keep thinking about it, I feel like I'm not afraid of dying . . . It's not that simple . . . Let's say that it doesn't scare me any more than never sleeping with anyone again, or never drinking with friends again, or never smoking a cigarette again, or even never seeing anyone again . . . It's the nasty stretch of time right before dying that has me scared shitless. I think about what that has to involve, a knife driving into my flesh or a bullet from a revolver or even dying by strangulation or drowning, and the chief won't kill me in a painless way, I can just see how he'll start off, I'll suffer like a martyr and it will last a long, long time. My stomach hurts. The baton up my ass, the underwear full of shit, Grampa in tears, the chief saying "I know." I shouldn't stay here. I want to go to Henri's. Henri, that'd be too painful . . . Henri's good for when I'm in good shape, not when I'm depressed, he's not the man for that kind of thing. I call Franck, he's on vacation with his family on the Costa Brava. But it's okay because when I called him another idea came to me . . . A much better idea. I call Annie. She's fine with me coming to spend a few days with her but she's back together with Jean-François. I really like Annie, but Jean-François is no go, he's always lecturing and explaining everything. Well, that's too bad, another idea comes up. I call Thierry . . . But he's leaving for Mexico tomorrow. I don't have any other ideas. I pull out my address book, as I look through my friends' names, I think again about going to see Henri, no, that's really not a good idea . . . And then I come upon Serge, an old flame from the Landes, he's gifted with a magnificent cock, but more than anything he's a sweet guy. We could spend hours talking. We fuck and it's wonderful, we talk and it's wonderful, we do nothing at all and that's wonderful too. I have no idea why I don't see him more often. Well, it's as good a time as any, I'll call him. He's happy to hear my voice, his is always irresistible, we catch up a bit. He's getting a bit older but in terms of his cock and his interest, he hasn't changed one bit. And he simply says:

"Why don't you come see me?"

"Hmm, why not?"

"That's right, come on over!"

"Today?"

"Come on, I'll wait for you!"

"All right, all right, I'll come!"

And we both hang up, smiling at the prospect of seeing each other again soon . . . It'll take me a good four or five hours to get to his place. I notice it's already one o'clock. I realize I'm hungry. That's a good sign, I'm alive again. I'm actually happy, I eat everything I can find in the fridge as I pack my bag, I cram it full as if I were leaving for a long trip, and just as I'm about to shut the apartment door, the intercom buzzes.

"The chief!" I say to myself. I don't answer. It buzzes again, I jump. I go sit on the couch. It buzzes one more time. My heart's pounding. I don't move. He's going to have to come looking for me here. Then it stops. I stay put. I hear an intercom ringing in another apartment down below. He's going to get someone else to let him in. I go and shut my door, lock it, and wait. There's some talk downstairs, I can make out M. Gasc's voice on the second floor, his deep voice carries a long way . . . Footsteps on the stairs, I go back to the couch. The footsteps stop on my floor, they're soft, they don't seem like policemen, as I remember it, policemen's footsteps are heavier, but I could be wrong, I'm wary.

There's knocking at my door, gentle at first and then a bit harder. Hearing the knock, I tell myself this isn't the chief, I can't hold still on the couch but I pull myself together quickly, I don't move, there's no way to know that this isn't a trap. And if this isn't the chief, the visitor will have to say who he is at some point, either he'll tell me who he is or he won't, there are three more knocks, and then the fourth one is a bit harder, and then nothing. No more noise, no more movement, no footsteps down the stairs. I stay frozen on my couch, I hold my breath. I think carefully, I don't know who it might be, anyone would have gone back downstairs by now, the chief would have kicked in the door, and, even then, he would have said something first, he would have said, "Police, open up" or something else but he would have said something. My VCR shows that it's already past two. If I stay like this, not doing anything, I might be here the entire afternoon, I think of Serge, I really want to see him, now that we've talked, I can't wait for us to have sex together and then have drinks on his terrace by the water and then have a candlelit dinner . . . And have sex again once night has fallen and then I'll fall asleep in his arms. And Paul . . . Shit, Paul! Suddenly I remember the plans we'd made to spend the night together this evening, I was supposed to call him, and that reminds me, my cell phone is in my bag right by the front door, if it rings I'm fucked. Too bad, I take a chance, I tiptoe over to get my phone, and as I'm standing there, I press my ear to the door. I can tell someone's outside, breathing, a body shifting under its clothes. I can't take this anymore, I have to know who it is, I turn the key without making any noise, it's agonizingly slow, I push the handle, I open the door ready to shut it immediately, and I see Cindy, sitting at the top of the stairs, she turns her head in amazement.

"You've been home?" she says.

I don't answer, I take her hand, pull her inside quickly, close and lock the door.

"Why didn't you open the door?" she asks.

"I didn't know it was you, what are you doing here?"

She takes in my apartment, she walks around the couch, it's dark, just a bit of light comes in through the shuttered windows.

"This is a really great place, can you give me something to drink?"

"What do you want?"

"A bottle of Coke."

"No, I don't have Coke, I have water, Perrier, orange juice . . ."

"Do you have mango nectar?"

"I have mint, peach, passion fruit . . ."

"Peach, then."

While I pull everything I need out of the fridge and the cupboard, she keeps pestering me, asking me questions:

"So, why didn't you open the door?"

"I was scared . . . Not of you, though!"

"What were you scared of?"

"The chief . . . Come on, we're going to sit on the couch . . . How did you get here from Trintaud?"

"Hitchhiked."

I give her a glass and then look at her sitting on the couch, she's wearing her black tee-shirt, the one that's most tight-fitting, but she still went with her ugliest shorts, a white pair that flares at the bottom, clearly she thinks that's the sexiest item she owns. I don't know why she's here, I don't sit down. I say:

"All right, Cindy, drink your glass and then I'll drive you back to Grammy's."

"Oh, don't do that, we've got time, it's not even three o'clock!"

"I have to be in the Landes tonight, I'll be late."

"But I came to see you, not drink some juice and leave."

I sit on the couch, determined to explain things to her as calmly as I can.

"Listen, Cindy, I'm sorry about the other night, but it's impossible, could you imagine if your grandmother caught us?"

"Yes, but that wouldn't happen here!"

"You're too young."

"It's okay, I'm fifteen years old . . . I'm only in eighth grade because I had to repeat fifth grade."

"But I'm forty."

"You're forty years old?" she asks, shocked.

"Yes." I nod. "We're twenty-five years apart."

She leans against me, she grabs my arm.

"But I don't care," she says. "I'm bored when you're not around, I think about you all the time, I can't stop thinking about the other night when we slept together, we were comfy together, weren't we? I didn't want to hurt you, I just wanted to have some fun."

"Some fun?"

"Yeah, I was bored because I couldn't sleep, and I'd never seen such a hard penis."

"Because you've seen so many?"

"Never so hard."

"But you've already seen many of them?"

She doesn't say anything, she doesn't answer, then she looks down at the floor, then she looks at me again and she shakes her head no. She smiles at me.

"I want to make love with you!" Cindy says, painfully serious again and sounding as if this was her desperate hope.

I stand up. Her elbows are on her knees, and I know she's determined, I won't get out of this easily, and I really don't want to hurt her. Very calmly, tenderly even, I keep going.

"Listen, Cindy . . . I am homosexual, you know what that means."

It's not a question, it's an affirmation, because I'm sure she knows what that means, but she seems dumbfounded.

"You have sex with Grampa?"

"Of course not, Cindy, I don't have sex with every man I meet . . . I have lovers, but I also have friends . . . Men I'm happy with but not interested in having sex with. Girls can be friends but I can't sleep with them."

"Why?"

"I don't know . . . There's no explanation . . . Well . . . I've wondered the same thing myself, I've tried to figure it out and the only thing I've decided is that there's no use trying to force things. It's not easy, but it's for the best."

"But if I love you, I have to keep on loving you!"

"That's a different thing. Two people can't love each other if it's not mutual."

Cindy is disappointed, she understands what I'm trying to tell her, I feel like I'm doing a pretty good job. I smile at her and I'm almost ready to get up, thinking that we can end on that note, that this is enough, lesson learned, but no, Cindy grabs my hand.

"Do you want me to hold your penis in my hand now?"

I slump back on the couch, I say:

"You know, Cindy, the problem is that I don't want to kiss you, or hug you . . ."

"Oh, that's okay, I do that with other people."

"You've already had sex?"

She says yes, very proudly. I half believe her. She leans against me again and says:

"Let me!"

I let go of her hand, pull away from her.

"I'll hold it gently, I'll make it get bigger without hurting you . . . Let me, please!"

"You'll see, it won't grow!"

"What about the other time?"

"I was sleeping."

I'm not getting anywhere, I really am not interested in Cindy and yet I don't know what's keeping me from taking her with me, putting her in my Safrane and bringing her back to her grandmother's. I don't want to hurt her, I have to grin and bear it, deep down, I'm excited that I'm going to see Serge again, I don't know what's come over me, I tell myself that so long as we haven't gotten to actual practice, so long as she hasn't understood that this won't be possible, so long as this hasn't happened, we'll stay on this couch, she'll keep on finding some argument, some idea for keeping me with her, she'll say "let me" all afternoon and if I take her by force, I won't be done with her. I take off my tee-shirt, my shorts, and my underwear . . . I sit down on the couch. She looks at me, but she doesn't chicken out, she takes my soft dick in her hands, she has plenty of time. She pulls at it slowly. I stay impassive, cold, and even sneer a bit. After thirty seconds, I say:

"See, it's still the same!"

"Just wait, you're old, you need a little time!"

I'm flabbergasted, I knew young girls were learning about these things at younger and younger ages, but really, fifteen years old. And she's still stroking me, she takes my balls in her other hand, she rubs them, and I stop paying attention and I realize that my dick's slowly growing . . . Cindy's hands feel good and once she's got me hard, she doesn't stop, she looks at me and proudly says:

"Look at you now!"

We smile at each other. I shut my eyes, I let her do it, when she's tired of it, she'll stop on her own but I have a feeling she wants to go all the way. If that's what it takes for her to calm down. I'm still happy and now I want her to go all the way. While my eyes are shut, I feel horny, I think of Grampa sitting next to me holding my hand, then I think of M. Escandolières, he appears in his navy-blue underwear, his cock sticking straight up, I've always imagined M. Escandolières with a huge cock because of his huge nose and his long fingers, I pull it out of his underwear, and then Cindy stops. I open my eyes, she looks at me. She asks:

"Do you like that?"

"Do you think I don't like it?"

"You're not saying anything, so I want to know."

"You know what I would like more?"

She shakes her head, she doesn't know.

"I'd like it if you took it in your mouth," I say.

"Like in porn?"

"Or like in life, people don't only do that in movies."

"But what if you ejaculate?"

"I won't ejaculate!" I say with a smile. "Not in your mouth."

She looks at me for a minute and then she says:

"Okay, good, but you have to close your eyes, all right?"

I nod and shut my eyes.

Cindy shifts on the couch, I feel her hair on my thighs and my chest and then her mouth on my cock. I feel around for her body, I caress her. She sucks me a little with her lips, she doesn't dare to take my whole cock. I slide my hand under her tee-shirt, I rub her breasts, I flick her nipples, and she gets really into it, she gets more and more passionate and goes down deeper, it's nice except for those moments when, in her enthusiasm, I feel her teeth scrape against my head.

"Careful with your teeth," I say.

"What?" she straightens up.

"I can feel your teeth. It doesn't feel good."

"Sorry," she says. "I'll be careful."

And she takes me back in her mouth and I'm daydreaming again, Grampa next to me still holding my hand, no, now he's rubbing my stomach. M. Escandolières showing me his cock at full mast, I suck him and then he gets the idea to fuck Cindy, she's still sucking me on all fours, he does her doggy-style, and when I start coming, I hold back as much as I can, the chief's just popped up in my thoughts, handsome as a Poseidon coming out of the lake. His tanned body, his shaved crotch. Water dripping down his body. I come. Cindy, surprised then disgusted, pulls away, she spits it all out and coughs, and when I open my eyes, I can feel her puke, hot on my belly.

Cindy's sulking. Sitting on the other end of the couch, mouth shut, and when I look at her, she turns her head even farther away in order not to look at me. Of course she'd been yelling at me for coming in her mouth. She'd said that I could have held back or warned her, that I was completely disgusting, that she was only fifteen years old . . . And then she'd gone and rinsed her mouth over and over and we'd wiped the puke off my belly, that was the part that had upset her the most, vomiting. Like a teenager barfing after getting drunk for the first time and suddenly realizing that she isn't all grown up after all. I was still pleased at myself about the trick I'd played on her, of course this wasn't going to put her off blow jobs forever, she liked those too much, but now I was sure we wouldn't have any trouble for a while, possibly forever. I let her wallow in disgust and then, noticing how much time had gone past, I got up and I hadn't even finished telling her that I was taking her to her grandmother's when she said: "Oh come on, not already!" And I said: "Yes, already!" I'd just finished putting on my tee-shirt when she said:

"When are we seeing each other again?"

And then I got really annoyed, I was really sick of her, I grabbed her hand, I told her that this foolishness needed to stop, that I had four hours of driving ahead of me and that she had two choices, either I could take her back to her grandmother's, or she could hitchhike her way back. She said she didn't care, she'd just hitchhike. She refused to get off the couch, I didn't want to be aggressive and push her outside, that wouldn't have been very smart of me, especially since I wasn't sure I'd even get that far. So I tried coaxing her, but it didn't even help when I told her that we'd see each other again . . . That I didn't know when but we'd see each other again, it was a promise, she still didn't budge an inch, instead she burst in tears. I comforted her as much as I could, I hugged her, but that didn't do any good either, she clung to me, she wouldn't let go, and I had to pull her off of me, and she just started crying even harder. My heart was torn, I couldn't bring her back to her grandmother's in this state, I let go of her, I didn't say anything else. She didn't either. Little by little, she calmed down, just a few small sobs, the last ones straight from her heart, and now this is the situation, both of us, each sitting at the opposite end of the couch. I don't dare do anything else. I'm so uncomfortable I even think about calling Mariette, but I immediately change my mind. No, that won't fix things at all. I really do feel real tenderness for Cindy, for her youth, for her passion, for her sadness in love. I don't want to hurt her anymore. At five o'clock, I call Serge, I apologize, he shouldn't wait up for dinner with me, I just tell him that there's a problem keeping me here in Roquerolle, I don't know when I'll be able to leave, definitely not before the evening, or even later. He tells me to come anyway . . . Even if it's late. I tell him I'll call as soon as I leave. I go back to the couch, I try talking to her again.

"Listen, Cindy . . . You can't stay here all day . . . Your grandmother's going to be worried . . ."

"I want a Coke!" she says.

That's better, she's talking again, not angrily, she asks for the Coke in between two sobs, quietly but insistently.

"All right, I'll buy you a Coke downstairs and you can drink it in the car."

"I want to drink it here!"

"And then we're leaving, okay?"

She nods. I smile at her. She finally smiles back.

"Good," I say. "I'm going to get a Coke, I'll be back in five minutes."

She just nods, not particularly happy that I'm going to get her a Coke. I go down to the bakery slowly, it feels nice to get outside, and it's best if Cindy has a few minutes alone to think about all this. At the bakery, they don't have any more Cokes in the fridge or on the counter, every single bottle's been bought already this afternoon, I walk over to the market . . . It's not that far either. Everybody's staying at home with this heatwave, the street's empty, I walk under the plane trees. I hope they do have Coke at the market. And they do. I don't let myself worry, I talk to M. Brunet, the owner's father. A tiny seventy-year-old man who always wears green gardening pants and gray or beige or blue polo shirts. He has hazel eyes, a nice round head, and hairy nostrils. Today, he's not playing pétanque, it's too hot outside, he came to help his son out, in here at least it's a bit cool. He says that this year is worse than usual, it reminds him of the '76 heatwave.

"You wouldn't remember it, you were too little!" he says.

"I do remember it, yes, my parents were farmers, so you can imagine . . . My father even had to dig deeper wells to find water."

M. Brunet is astonished, he says:

"How old were you?"

"I was . . . about ten then."

He calculates in his head, looks at me, he must have thought I was much younger and then, after he's looked me over carefully, he nods as if everything's fine. And we don't have anything else to talk about so I go. There's still nobody out in the streets, all the house and apartment shutters are closed, a few cars go by slowly, I don't know why, then I remember that it's summer, everybody has plenty of time, I realize that it's a good thing I didn't start driving at two o'clock in the afternoon, without air conditioning it would have been sweltering. And that makes me smile. Cindy will drink her Coke calmly, I won't rush her. We'll leave by six, six thirty, that way she won't be late for supper. I'll drop her off at her grandmother's, I won't go in, I'll just drop her off up the street, then I'll start driving, I'll get to Serge's by ten thirty or eleven o'clock, I'll take a shower, we'll have sex, maybe we'll have sex in the shower . . . Yes, this will all work out nicely. So I open the door to my apartment. I walk into the living room with the chilled Coke in my hand, Cindy will be happy. And I see the chief's head, he's sitting at my big white table, next to him Cindy looks disappointed, as if this was her fault. Sitting next to her, the other policeman turns around, it's the young colleague who was the chief's partner the day of Grampa's underwear.

"Are you leaving for vacation?" the chief asks.

At first, I wonder what would make him think that then I immediately remember the bag right next to the front door and then I think: "Why would it be a problem if I left?" I can't imagine why. I say yes. He immediately shakes his head.

"It's not a good time for that."

I lean forward in puzzlement, but not too much, I'm careful not to overdo it.

"We need you while we're investigating the drowning in the lake."

And I understand perfectly. Actually, I don't understand anything but my heart's pounding, I'm mustering all my energy not to let anything show on my face. I stay as I am, seemingly puzzled, I glance at Cindy, she still looks disappointed. I concentrate like crazy, I have to say something, a question, I can't just act puzzled and be quiet this whole time.

"There was a drowning at the lake?"

He nods. He gets up. He taps his partner's shoulder and points at Cindy.

"Take her to her grandmother's, I'll call you when I'm done."

The partner gets up and takes Cindy away. In front of the policemen, she looks at me, I can tell she's wavering at whether to kiss my cheek or something of the sort and then she finally does so, and she follows the partner quietly. She doesn't even say good-bye. The apartment door is barely shut when the chief gestures for me to sit at my table. I look at him in his blue shirt, his head is somehow different again from the one in my memory from our last meeting. This time, I notice that he doesn't really have eyebrows, he doesn't furrow them, they're high above his blue eyes. He doesn't stop staring at me.

"What did you see the other night at the lake?"

Here goes. I hold on.

"Nothing in particular."

"Where exactly were you at the end of the afternoon?"

"On the shore."

"Your Safrane was in the parking lot after nightfall, if you were on the shore, you must have seen something."

"A man came to talk to me at seven o'clock."

"How can you be sure of what time it was?"

"He asked me for the time."

"And you were there the whole time?"

"No, we went into the woods a bit later."

"I was in the woods myself . . . I would have seen you."

I need to act surprised right now, so I do.

"We were deep in the woods, he really didn't want to be seen."

"Which level?"

"Do you know those woods well?" I ask.

"Yes, very well."

He answers with a smile, not sly or mocking . . . Knowing . . . Very knowing, even, we know about each other. He wants to win me over, I have to be careful and act like this is a surprise. I look at him a long while as if I were wondering what to believe.

I reassure myself that I now know the chief didn't see me in person on the lake shore, he only saw my Safrane, he's playing fair and square. I have to not be overconfident, that could be my downfall, I stay cautious.

"Between the little path that goes up on a diagonal toward Martory and the two big twisted chestnut trees."

He nods several times.

"What's his name?"

"Who?"

"The man you were with."

"I don't know."

"You don't even know his first name?"

"No."

He nods again as if he understands. I'm sure there's a trap, I don't know why else he would wait so long before asking another question, there's ten thousand he could be asking. I'm starting to get panicked, I think over what I could say, but just as I figure it out, he asks:

"That doesn't surprise you?"

"Not knowing his name?"

"No, that I'm not surprised that you don't know his name."

"Yes!"

I'm okay again, but I'm still a bit shaky, I set my hands on my knees, they're trembling. I take advantage of that to wipe them on my tee-shirt.

"Well, why?"

"Why I'm surprised?"

"Yes."

"Because normally, when you're playing around with someone, you'd know his name."

"So why don't you know his?"

And I start wondering what the chief is trying to do. I don't let myself waver.

"Because sometimes that's what happens, you're having a good time and you say good-bye without having even asked each other's name . . . Not all the time, but this time it happened . . . And sometimes you feel bad about not even getting the other guy's phone number . . ."

"Did you feel bad about that?"

I look at the chief, I don't answer. I don't really like the way all this is going. "Well?" he asks, as if he's trying to bait me, but I don't bite, I'm proud of myself, I've held my own through this interrogation, I've been able to lie effortlessly, shifting between lies and truths I didn't have to make up, short evenhanded answers with slightly longer, more emotional ones. I really do think the chief believes I haven't seen him. He pulls at his shirt collar a few times to cool himself off. He unbuttons the top button and then another one and then another.

"It's hot in here," he says abruptly.

And he slowly pulls off his blue shirt. He's sending a clear message. I don't know how to act, I have to think for another minute. So I keep my eyes on the top of his bare chest, his neck starting to show his age a bit but he still has beautiful, sculpted pecs and taut nipples. I catch myself, I look back up, I meet his gaze. He knows he's well built, he thinks it's normal for me to look him over so thoroughly.

"Well, that doesn't give you much of an alibi."

I'm thrown off, the bare-chested chief in front of me, this thing about alibis, I don't understand, then I understand perfectly, but I'm afraid of saying something stupid, I ask:

"What's that supposed to mean?"

"We find a body drowned in the lake, the death happened the night before last, between six o'clock and ten o'clock . . . And that same night, I see your car all alone in the middle of the lake parking lot . . . If you don't have a better alibi, then I'm not interrogating you as a witness so much as a suspect."

"A suspect? But how am I a suspect? Why would I have drowned anyone?"

I'm upset, I stand up, he also stands up, he walks toward me, he sets his hands on my shoulders, he says:

"Calm down . . . Right now, I haven't talked about this with anyone else."

I look at his hands on my shoulders. I'm still not sure of anything but I'm getting turned on, I'm getting hard in my shorts. Maybe it's a trap. I shouldn't let myself get distracted, I have to stay focused all the way through.

"What about your partner, the one who was just here?" I ask.

"Don't worry about him, I'll take care of him."

And I feel his hand sliding down my shoulder, then I feel his hand on my bare forearm . . . My gaze is locked on his, I think I should have understood this from the start, his hand on my hip, the chief's beauty is overwhelming me. I want him, I gingerly set a hand on his waist, I'm surprised by how soft his skin feels, I feel bold, I rub it firmly. And I feel all his desire in the blue of his eyes. He's just waiting for me. So I let go, I shut my eyes, and I lean in. Immediately, I'm astonished by the gentleness of his kiss, I'd gone at it more fervently, I relax, I go along with him, I'm gentler in kissing back. And we're comfortable together. We'll draw this out. I've never seen a man kiss so well. It's an early promise of a great love. Under my tee-shirt, his hand is stroking my back and sliding down to my cheeks. I like his skin, I pull him closer to me so I can feel his chest against mine, he pulls down my shorts and, since it's slightly short, he pulls away from me, stops kissing, he pulls my shorts down lower, kisses his way down my chest until he gets to my cock, licks it all the way to its tip before swallowing it and sucking it very gently at first and then, once I'm nice and hard, like he's dying of hunger, like he just wants me to come as hard as I can right there and then . . . The intercom buzzes. At first, I just think I'll let it buzz and then

I remember. "Shit, Paul!" I say. The chief doesn't stop. I pull my cock out of his mouth, I touch his cheek.

The intercom buzzes again.

"Don't answer," he says.

"I have someone coming over."

The chief tries to put my dick in his mouth again, but I pull away gently.

"Wait," I tell him. "I have to deal with this."

The chief gets up, he kisses me.

"I'll deal with that and I'm yours!"

My phone, I run to get my phone from the bag by the front door. I turn it on. There's a message already. It's Paul asking what the hell is going on. I call him back straightaway.

"Where are you?" he asks.

"Listen, I'm not at home, we can't meet up now."

"What about later?"

"No, I can't do later . . . We can't get together tonight."

"What happened?"

"I'll tell you . . . Look, I'll call you tomorrow."

"Why didn't you call me earlier?"

"I couldn't!"

Then I think twice, I realize that's nonsense, I say:

"All right, yes, I could have, but I'd completely forgotten."

That just makes things worse. I can feel that Paul's shattered. At the other end of the hallway, the chief fills the doorway, stark naked. He's even more handsome in the apartment's darkness. I keep talking.

"I don't think I want to see you anymore . . . I've met someone. But I'll call you tomorrow, okay?"

Paul doesn't reply. That was probably a harsh way to put it but it's for the best, I'd only have dug myself in deeper, leaving him with hundreds of questions. This way, at least, it's clear.

"Okay?" I ask Paul.

"Fine!" he says. He's crushed.

I can't be the one to hang up first, I can't end on that note, but he doesn't keep me waiting for long, to my surprise, he doesn't say anything else, he hangs up. I stand there with my phone in my hand. I've known Paul for some ten years, I've canceled on him plenty of times . . . But never like this. The chief doesn't let me stew, standing in front of me, he tells me to come, my eyes slide up his muscular, tan legs and between his thighs, I discover his beautiful cock standing at full mast and his nice, round balls, the gentle light slanting through the shutters etches a sublime torso, it softens his stern face, it's the face of the man I've always dreamed of, I get down on my knees, the head of his cock so close to my lips, I'm this close to swallowing it when he puts his hands on my head, he comes down and starts kissing me tenderly. I've never met a man who kissed so well. I forget Paul, I forget everything, everything from the very start, we caress each other, we rub each other's muscles, we touch each other's balls, we stroke our dicks, I finally suck on his, a wet finger up his ass, and when I feel him quiver on his legs, I bury him deep down my throat but he pulls back out, he hasn't had enough yet, he pulls me up by the shoulders, I flick his nipples with my tongue on my way up, he kisses me again and makes his way back down to my cock, and when my arms and legs start quivering, when I tell him I'm about to come, he goes down on me with even more enthusiasm, pressing his lips around my head, he drinks it all up slowly, then he stays like that, licking his tongue around my head. He goes slowly, but I'm oversensitive after having come and the pleasure quickly turns into pain. I push his head away. I try to do it gently, tenderly, even lovingly. With his hands on my ass, he's not letting me pull away. And it's starting to really hurt. I'm getting freaked out. The baton up my ass. The underwear over my head. I feel like he might bite off my dick with his teeth. I yell in pain and push him away as hard as I can. Then he's sitting against the wall, near the front door, looking at me uncomprehendingly. I can't believe he still looks so handsome.

"What's wrong?" he says.

"Fuck, that hurts."

"I just wanted to keep you in my mouth."

"But it really, really hurts."

"You're really sensitive!"

He says that with a smile. He hadn't wanted to hurt me. I reach out to help him stand up again. And as I touch his body again, I fall in love with him again, once he's on his feet we look at each other, I'm even more aware of his beauty, I can't get enough of his face, his body, I would never get bored of them. His mouth hovers close, I kiss it. A long kiss that lasts and lasts. Then we break apart, we go to the couch, we drink some pastis, we caress each other, I tell him once again that he's an incredible kisser . . . He tells me that it's because I'm an incredible kisser that he's being such an incredible kisser . . . "It takes two to tango," he adds, and then we kiss, another long kiss, and when we feel like we've come to the end of our kiss, one of us always wants to start another one, an even more passionate one. We're huddled close, I'm rubbing his chest, his ass, I take his cock in my mouth and then I feel his tongue in between my cheeks, pressing into my ass. But he feels like he's about to come, he wants me to stop sucking him, so I move my head, stick it between his thighs, and as I spread apart his cheeks, I open up his ass with my tongue. He wants me to fuck him. I penetrate him slowly, I push my cock gently into his hole, he's lying on his back, his legs are on my shoulders, he welcomes me as he stretches his neck, he's sighing in pleasure, I piston in and out of his ass, I pull out my cock, push it back in again. I drive it in as deep as I can, and his moans of pleasure keep me going . . . "You're so good at this, honey," he says breathlessly. I like that he's calling me "honey," I slowly push my dick into his ass as I watch his face in ecstasy. He smiles at me. We're together. I want him to fuck me, too, I pull out, I suck his cock all the way, sliding my tongue up and down his blue vein, and when he's good and hard, I offer up my ass. He enters very slowly, with barely perceptible thrusts of his hips, he fills me up easily and when he's all the way in, he pulls out slowly and then goes back in, he takes me the way I took him, my feet propped on his shoulders, I see him undulating above me, I rub his pecs, he kneads my love handles, and he strokes my cock. I say: "My love, you fuck like a god too." He doesn't reply, he spreads my cheeks with his hands, so he can push in deeper, and when I feel him tensing up, I touch his face, I want to feel him come in my ass. He twists his head, kisses my hands, I place my index finger on his lips, he takes it into his mouth, sucks it gently, he buries his cock to the root, it tenses up, our moans of pleasure mingle, and I love his stern face as he's coming inside me. He relaxes, regains his breath, smiles at me, and then, I don't know why, dark thoughts arise in my mind. When he leans over me, when he places a gentle kiss on my lips, I wonder what will happen now that we've made love. He lies down next to me, his head on my shoulder, his hand on my crotch, and then I think of the man drowned in the lake, I see the two of them again, walking into the dark water, kissing each other quickly like two lovers headed for a swim after making love. What can the chief be thinking about now that he's gotten what he wanted? As I ponder that, I keep him next to me, his eyes shut, his stern face exuding calm and peacefulness. I feel his breath on my shoulder. His skin against mine. I do think that I love him. Even if I might die. Then I shut my eyes as well.

At ten o'clock at night, we both come out of our amorous half-slumber. We're still entwined in each other's arms. The chief kisses me, just a small peck on the lips, he looks at me seriously, he looks outside.

"Is it night already?" He's amazed.

He shifts on the couch, propped up on his elbow, pensive, playing with my hard cock, he gently strokes its sensitive tip, and then he taps my chest lightly, he gets up.

"All right, I have to go. Can you drive me to Trintaud?"

I'm feeling lazy and I don't want to get up, and I really don't want him to go, even though I was sure from the start that he wouldn't stay the night, I don't want to get used to this idea. I caress him, I kiss his chest, I tell him that he should stay. He says he can't. He gets dressed. I watch him. He finally smiles at me. I'm worried that he doesn't love me as much as I love him. With all the pastis we'd drunk, I don't feel like I'm in good shape to drive him and come back, I ask him why he can't call his partner who'd been here earlier.

"Wait, after how we've made love to each other? We're so good together and you'd just have me leave with anybody?"

"He's not just anybody!" I say with a smile. "And honestly, what if your colleagues made me take a breathanalyzer?"

"Come on . . . The checkpoints don't ever start before the cafés close . . . We'll go for a romantic little drive, we'll stay together for a little longer, we won't just say good-bye to each other like that, okay?"

The chief fondles me, our lips come together in a long delicious kiss. It's like we've known each other for ages. Now I'm properly awake, I know I'm not going to fall back asleep. I want to go. And a romantic drive seems enticing. I get up, I put on my shorts and tank top, he's already gotten into his uniform. And we're in the car. At every traffic light, at every stop sign, as soon as we come to a stop, we kiss, sometimes briefly, sometimes for a long while. And then I press on the gas again, impatient for the next stop. At the entrance to Trintaud, I take the little road through Bridou Park, nobody's ahead of us, nobody's behind us, I park the car and we share another long kiss, I've never loved kissing a man so much . . . we don't pull apart. He strokes my cock through my shorts, I slip my hand through his fly. I could stay like that, his cock in my hand, for the whole night. But the chief pulls away abruptly, with no explanation, he says we have to go. But when we get to the police station, not even five minutes later, once again, he puts his arm around my neck, leans in toward me, and says:

"Kiss me!"

I hesitate, I look around, I tell myself that it's risky here. He pulls me into him and kisses me softly, he doesn't care about the cars going by on the road, or even the people talking on a bench further off. I can't keep from worrying that maybe even his wife, his children, or his colleagues might see us. Especially his wife. I keep thinking about his wife. He can probably tell I'm nervous, he finally breaks off the kiss, he looks at me, puts his hand on my thigh. He also seems nervous. I can tell he doesn't want to go.

"See you tomorrow?" he asks.

I'm caught off-guard by the question, I didn't think we'd see each other again so soon. And the thought makes me very happy . . . More than happy, even . . . Euphoric . . . But I can't let my face show it, the chief looks at me anxiously.

"Do you not want to?"

Of course I want to, and I let him see my enthusiasm, I give him my phone number and I tell him to leave a message if I don't pick up and that I can't wait to see him again. I get the impression that he likes me as much as I like him, and that reassures me.

We kiss again, and then he gets out of my car, I don't rush to leave, I watch him going off into the distance. Before going into the police station, he turns around, blows me one last kiss with his hand. I think to myself that he's feeling bold, anyone could see him, and once he's inside I feel relieved . . . Relieved that he's in the police station, relieved that I'm no longer with him, and I can't tell if I want it to be tomorrow already or not.

When I get to Mariette's the bit of wood under the hedge is in place. It makes me think Cindy hasn't left tonight, or that she's already come back. And that's a good thing, she's the one I'm coming to see. The house seems to be asleep, no lights on, the back door is shut but Mariette's left the kitchen window over the sink open for the cat probably. I go in. The sink creaks under my weight. I jump to the floor quickly, I'm barefoot so I land gently. But I don't have time to be proud of myself, I see a ray of light across the hallway. I hesitate about leaving. I don't leave. Not without seeing what's up. I really have to talk to Cindy. I listen. No noise. I go down the hallway as quietly as I can. The bathroom door is ajar, I don't see anybody, maybe they forgot to turn off the light. Then a rustle of clothing. I get a bit closer and see the white buttocks of Grampa, his pants over his thighs, his pajama top hiked up over his cheeks. And I stay there, watching, awestruck by his sweet, pale, smooth ass. A teenager's ass. I'm stupefied as I realize that Grampa has a beautiful ass and I'm mesmerized by this strange vision. From behind, his head lowered, he's moving his arms as if pulling something, I shift my head to see better but even when I have a better angle I can't figure out what Grampa's doing. I think he's doing something with his penis. He might be stroking himself, but his arms aren't moving enough for that . . . Or maybe not the right way . . . And then I tell myself that, after all, he can do whatever he wants, I don't need to know. I don't want to know. I go down the hallway to the steps. The image of Grampa's pale, smooth ass is stuck in my mind. I feel guilty to have seen him, or rather, for having lingered during this time. I shoo away all the ideas popping up around this sight. I go up the stairs. Cindy isn't in her room. But the wood was definitely in place, I don't know why, but I suddenly start suspecting the worst. Without even really knowing what the worst might be. I have to know. I consider waiting for her, but how long would I wait? And even if I do, I have an odd feeling that it won't be any use. I go back downstairs. Grampa isn't in the bathroom anymore. In the cold light of the kitchen, he's sitting at the table, pensive and worried, he's not doing anything, he's suscing. I come in, he looks up. He's surprised to see me.

"Es la pichona que cèrcas?"[26]

I'm taken aback by his question.

"Son paire la venguèt quèrre."[27]

I don't understand, and then I start to see what he's saying.

"Èra pas content. Te cal far atencion que te vòl atrapar!"[28]

"Son paire?"[29]

He nods.

"Aquò's vertat que te siás escampat dins sa boca?"[30]

Grampa asks me that mischievously, smiling, as if it wasn't any problem. I nod, not feeling terribly proud of myself, but Grampa whistles admiringly, he shakes his hand, impish as ever. He thinks I'm bold but he's delighted and then he's immediately serious again.

"M'agradariá que demores per dormir amb ieu, tu pòdes pas saber cossí m'agradariá . . ."[31]

"Lo sabi . . ."[32]

"Non, lo sabes pas."[33]

---

26. Are you looking for the kid?
27. Her father came to get her.
28. He wasn't happy. Be careful, he wants to catch you!
29. Her father?
30. Did you actually come in her mouth?
31. I want you to stay and sleep with me, you don't know how much I want you to . . .
32. I know . . .
33. No, you don't know.

It makes me happy that Grampa's telling me this. I know that I could certainly sleep with him tonight, I'd be surprised if the chief came, but tonight, I'm the one who doesn't want to, I don't know how to tell him that. It's not just that I froze in front of his ass earlier, even though the image still won't go away, it's more that I'm completely in love with the chief now, he's still here in my thoughts and in my heart. He won't leave. Suddenly I remember I have to make sure to call Paul tomorrow. And I have to check in with Serge, too . . . I'd completely forgotten about him. Then I realize that Grampa is my one confidant right now. I really want to tell him about the chief, to tell him the whole story, I'm trying to figure out how I could tell him that and how I could say it in Occitan. It's odd, it's so simple and yet I can't find the words, even in French. I'm afraid that this will ruin something between Grampa and me. Then I realize I'm afraid of clearly indicating to Grampa that I'm gay, for now, we've just enjoyed this vague thing between love and friendship, but I have a suspicion that if I tell him about my feelings for the chief, he'll connect my love for the chief with my love for him, and he'll think that I want him the same way I want the chief . . . And I'll never be able to explain the facts clearly, he'll only ever believe what he wants to and it'll be over between us. Grampa doesn't say anything. I can tell he's worried, I don't know what to say, I feel like this might be the last time we ever see each other, as if tomorrow I would be moving on. Grampa suspects the same thing.

"Es lo darrièr còp que te vesi?"[34] he asks.

The question hurts me. It hurts because I don't want to make Grampa unhappy, and I don't want this to be our last time together any more than he does. I don't know how to answer, and in the silence, we hear Mariette calling from upstairs:

---

34. Is this the last time I'll see you?

"Grampa!"

"Soi aquí!"[35]

"Who are you talking to?"

"Soi dins l'ostal, amb lo Gilles."[36]

I look at Grampa, I don't understand, I want to ask what the hell he's thinking, but he waves at me to wait.

"With Gilles? Have you gone crazy?"

"Si, si, es aquí . . . Lo vòles veire?"[37]

Mariette doesn't come downstairs. Grampa's eyes are welling up, I don't know if it's malice or sadness, probably both, he smiles.

"Te vòli jogar que davalarà pas."[38]

"Me'n vau!"[39]

I get up, I hold my hand out to Grampa, his left hand grips mine, he squeezes it hard with his thick, dry fingers. And that makes me happy, we look at each other for a long while. I think about Mariette, at the top of the stairs, wondering if I really am here . . . More likely she's sure that I'm here, she's just wondering whether or not she'll come downstairs. Grampa's right, she doesn't want to see me, she doesn't know what to say to me, she'd rather that the police handle this. And then I think that it's just too stupid, I don't want things to end like this with her either. If I can't ever come back to this house, at least I'm saying my goodbyes to her. I'm not sure exactly what I need to tell her, and I'm even less sure how to say it, but I have to see her. I step back.

"Li vòli parlar,"[40] I say, and I head up the stairs.

When I get to the top, she's still there, she's stepped back as I make my way up. She's in her nightdress with red and blue

35. I'm here!

36. I'm in the kitchen with Gilles.

37. Yes, yes, he's here . . . Want to see him?

38. Bet you she's not coming down.

39. I'm leaving!

40. I want to talk to her.

polka dots, and astonished that I'd come up to her. She has to think I'm pushing my luck.

"You can't stay here," she says. "The policemen will come, they have a key, I gave them one so they could keep an eye on Grampa."

"And so they could bother him every night?"

"They come over, they don't make any noise, and they leave again . . ."

"And Grampa's sleeping even less."

"Leave him alone. All of this is upsetting him. He's talking in patois again, he doesn't know what he's saying anymore."

"He knows what he's saying."

"Often I don't understand him at all."

"Listen," I say. "I'm not coming over anymore . . . Actually, tonight, I came to see Cindy . . . I didn't want to, I swear to you, I didn't want to . . . I just wanted to bring her here but I couldn't make her budge."

"Oh, if you'd really wanted to, you could have!"

"I couldn't tie her down, could I?"

"I know . . . When she gets an idea in her head, she won't let go, but she's not even fifteen years old yet . . . Did you know that?"

"Yes, I knew . . ."

"So you were forced to ejaculate in her mouth?"

Mariette says that and I'm stunned. I shake my head no, I wasn't forced to, I catch myself.

"But she didn't give me any time . . ."

"Oh, you men! Of course she gave you time! You couldn't have warned her?"

I look down again. Mariette's nothing short of surprising tonight. I try not to look ashamed, I try to stay firm and look her in the eyes.

"And on top of that, you're the one who asked her to use her mouth."

"But if I'd wanted to, I could have just penetrated her."

"You only ever think about your pleasure . . . You're all the same."

"No, I just wanted to be done with her . . . I wanted her to stop liking me and agree to come back here . . . She wanted to have sex so much."

"Why didn't you do it?"

"What?"

"Why didn't you just go and have sex with her? That way she might have learned what that meant."

"Because that wasn't possible."

Mariette looks at me in shock, her eyes go to the ceiling.

"Listen, Mariette, I swear to you, I don't like girls, even young girls, I'm not attracted to them . . . I only like men . . . I'm homosexual."

She's dumbstruck. And I feel weird, it's strange to say that I'm homosexual to Mariette, to say the word to her face. We've never touched on that topic, she only asked me once, early on, if I was married, and when I said no, she said "but you have a girlfriend," as if it was plainly obvious. And when I said that I didn't have a girlfriend either, she acted flabbergasted but she didn't press the question, at the time she didn't make anything of it, at least she seemed not to have done so. But she never broached the topic again. But deep down, I'm sure she knows . . . She suspects it, at least . . . But telling her "I'm homosexual" is as if I had revealed a huge secret that everybody knew . . . More than that . . . It's like I broke a tacit agreement that we would never discuss certain things. I don't know if this agreement worked for me, but I know that since they never asked I never told. But I feel relieved to have told her, like this, in the heat of the moment, and even then I think I've done something terribly wrong.

"Have you told Grampa?" she asks, still looking at me.

"No," I answer immediately.

"You need to tell him."

"But that's not what's happening with Grampa . . . That's just friendship."

"I want him to know."

"Do you really think he doesn't suspect it?"

"I wouldn't be so sure."

Mariette and I are at the top of the stairs, looking at each other, she doesn't seem ready to drop the whole thing, I don't think I've ever seen her so determined. All this has changed her, or revealed who she really is. I'm not ready to drop this either.

"But he'll think . . ."

"He'll think whatever he thinks, but at least he'll know everything."

I shake my head, I still don't agree that Grampa should be told everything. Mariette points toward the steps, she's asking me to go down, I wonder how I'd say "homosexual" in Occitan. And then I stop again:

"But I can't just say to him like that: 'I'm homosexual'!"

Mariette doesn't care, she'll wait the whole night if she has to. I'm feeling desperate, and I go down the stairs, not to go see Grampa, but to leave the house plain and simple, it's too bad, Mariette will just have to deal with this, she can tell him herself if she wants to. But then we hear a door opening. The front door. Footsteps in the hallway. Mariette hushes me, she grabs my hand and pulls me in her room. In the doorway, she says:

"You'll be fine here, don't move. I'll go talk to them."

I don't answer. At first, I'm worried that Mariette will rat me out, I step out of the room to listen to them, I try to figure out how I'd hide. Despite the noise of Mariette's footsteps on the stairs, I can make out a bit of what the chief is saying, he's telling Grampa that it's not good for him to stay up all night, sitting in the kitchen, and then Grampa says:

"L'espèri mas es pas vengut."[41]

"I don't think he'll come again," the chief says.

"If you're so sure, then why did you come?" Mariette asks as she steps into the kitchen.

"We can't be sure of anything in this whole affair."

I wonder why the chief has come to Grampa and Mariette's this evening. I'm actually wondering why he hasn't gone home to sleep, why he's not dreaming about me, why he's not in his bed savoring the memory of those hours we spent together. Why he feels such a need to check in on Grampa when he's sure that I won't come back to see him again. I'm suspicious. As I fell in love with him, I thought I'd come to understand something of the chief, and now it's clear that I don't understand a single thing. I wonder if anyone can really love someone they don't understand at all . . . Or if it's precisely because they want to unravel that enigma that they fall in love with someone. I'm worried. And then I hear Grampa saying:

"Tu lo me daissaràs veire un darrièr còp abans de morir?"[42]

I can't believe he's using *tu* instead of *vos*. Then I wonder whether he's insisting on that *tu* because he wants to make this conversation with the chief an intimate one, or whether he's actually asking Mariette that question. And then I realize what he's asking. And it makes my blood run cold. Grampa's going to die, or at least he knows he's going to die . . . It's hardly big news, but the phrase seems like a revelation, it hits me as misery does the poor world. And then I realize that Grampa's *tu* is meant for me, he knows that I can hear their conversation, if he didn't know it I wouldn't be hearing it, and the meaning's immediately clear, I know I have to be there the day Grampa dies. He's counting on it.

---

41. I'm waiting for him but he hasn't come.

42. Will you let me see him one last time before I die?

I don't hear the answer, but I don't care. I'm lost in my thoughts, only the chief's footsteps in the hallway pull me out of them, the door closes shut, Mariette takes Grampa to his room. Good night. I go back to Mariette's room. I sit on her bed, as if I'd been patiently waiting for her. I'm actually happy to see Mariette's room. The huge oak wardrobe. The white embroidered curtains over the window, a chair that Mariette's set her clothes on, and a photo of her and her ex-husband from their twenties on the nightstand. She wasn't very beautiful either. She looked like Cindy, she's improved with age. When she comes into the room, I don't move. She sits at the other end of the bed, her hands on her knees, she doesn't say anything, she considers her words, and then:

"One last thing before you go. Cindy's father doesn't know the whole story . . . But it would make him upset, and I don't think she'll be able to keep quiet . . . So I'm worried that he's going to do something terrible."

I'm not sure why Mariette wants to scare me. It's not like her.

"I'm not saying this to make you nervous, but so that you'll be careful . . . All right, you should go see Grampa now."

"I'm not telling him."

"I'll be very upset."

"But if I tell him that, he'll think I just want to have sex with him."

"Well, explain all of that to him!"

Mariette won't stop staring at me. I don't say anything back. Then she gets up. I follow her. As we go down the stairs, I pause again, I try to convince myself that I might not ever come back to this house, I think of the chief, I can see Grampa in my mind again, telling the chief: "It's a bit like someone's thinking of me!" Then I see his pale, smooth ass again. I tell myself that even if I don't come back, I should tell him everything now. I know deep down that it won't change anything. It'll just be out in the open.

And it's really better that way. Grampa still hasn't turned off the light, he's not really lying down, his head high up on the pillow, he's waiting. Mariette leaves me in the doorway. I sit on Grampa's bed, right next to him.

"Maurice," I say quietly, "me te cal dire quicòm."[43]

He looks right at me and smiles.

"Diga-me!"[44]

"I'm homosexual."

I say it in a rush and I say it in French because at the very last moment I realize without knowing why that if I say it in Occitan it'll be ridiculous. Grampa doesn't say anything. I look down then back up. He's still looking at me. He doesn't seem devastated by my announcement. He doesn't seem delighted, either. He just nods several times, not so much in approval as to make it clear that something was nagging at him. Finally he asks:

"Perqué me dises aquò ara?"[45]

"Perque lo sàpias."[46]

"Te cresi pas! Alara? perqué me lo dises ara?"[47] He puts the emphasis on *ara*,[48] and when I still haven't replied, he asks:

"Vòles far l'amor amb ieu?"[49]

"No," I say quickly.

"Alara? Perqué?"[50]

I don't know what to say. Mariette is still behind the door, I'm fine with her hearing this, but knowing that she's right there keeps me from talking freely. I consider just stopping there and

43. Maurice, I have to tell you something.
44. Tell me!
45. Why are you telling me now?
46. So that you know.
47. I don't believe that! Well? Why are you telling me now?
48. Now
49. Do you want to have sex with me?
50. Well? Why?

saying good-bye to Grampa, but that's not possible. I can't just leave it at that for the night.

"Marieta voliá que te lo diga."[51]

"De qué se maina ela? Crei que compreni pas res a res?"[52]

Then Grampa figures it out. He tilts his head toward the door briefly. I nod in confirmation. Grampa doesn't want to get mad, he still has to live under the same roof as her for a while, he just raises his eyes toward the sky. Then he gestures for me to get closer, he sets his hand on my shoulder, and whispers into my ear:

"T'aimi ça que la!"[53]

I like that Grampa would tell me that, even if I'm not sure what he means by that. I'm so happy that in a matter of minutes I want to curl up in his arms. But I'm not sure he'd like that. He's still serious, his eyes are welling up, he's holding my hand. No, he doesn't want anything more than that . . . Just my hand . . . Unless Mariette's presence behind the door's also keeping him from expressing his desire. She has to be hearing our whispers and silences, she's waiting, she opens the door, she sees us there, hand in hand. I don't linger, I get up, I wish Grampa a good night. He doesn't let go. I like feeling my hand in his. I'm almost getting hard. And then I remember that I'll see the chief again tomorrow, that makes me happy and makes me worried. I'm even more worried to leave Grampa all alone but I gently let go of his hand, give him one last long look, and leave his room. In the hallway, I'm ashamed to have abandoned Grampa so quickly, I'm most ashamed not to have told him that I love him back. I'm so close to turning around and heading back to his room and then I consider how it would look if I returned just to tell him that, after all this time . . . Back then was when I should have told

---

51. Mariette wanted me to tell you.
52. Why is she interfering? Does she think I don't understand anything at all?
53. I love you all the same!

him. And right now Mariette's taking me to the front door. But then she changes her mind, she decides it's better that I go out through the garden . . . "Through Cindy's entrance," she says. I'd thought from the start that it was odd she hadn't asked me how I'd gotten in.

As I walk down the road, my head's a mess. I feel guilty that I made this decision I'm having so much trouble sticking to, namely, not going back to Grampa's house. I don't know what drove me to decide that, and I don't know if I should actually stick to this decision, and I don't even understand why I felt a need or urge that night to decide this at all. What was forcing me to do it? Why didn't I just let things play out instead of trying to control them there and then with bizarre and painful decisions? In fact, I don't know anymore whether I decided that or whether that decision was imposed upon me. As if it wasn't possible to love the chief and also sleep with Grampa every so often. Where did I get that idea? I feel guilty. I feel like I'm following the established order. It's like a terrible thought eating away at my mind . . . I'd thought it would be better to physically love a well-built chief than to nourish a chaste passion for an old man with a wrinkled body. Then I start thinking about the chief, I tell myself I'm getting into an impossible situation again, a half-assed affair where we'll see each other here and there, when he'll have the time or feel the urge, even though in my heart I can't deny the prospect of a great love. Then I wonder if I love the chief because I actually love him or if it's just because I know it's better for my safety that I love him, I'm starting to doubt my feelings. I know my desires can be determined and driven by things that have nothing to do with the person I love. I know that I can love someone simply because it's necessary in the moment . . . I know that I can love someone as a matter of survival. What then? I don't see what the problem is anymore. Tomorrow, I'll see the chief again, I know I'll love him even more deeply. That this affair might not last long. And that saddens me. And I cry. I make myself cry. I go as far into unhappiness as I possibly can, I wallow in that unhappiness. I'm keenly aware of my loneliness, I dwell in despair, I watch myself crying, pure and simple, my eyes focused on the road stretching out ahead of me. And then I see a light in the night, a streetlight swaying slightly and, behind the streetlight, a policeman . . . No, it's not a policeman . . . It's a cop from the national force . . . The place is full of officers . . . It's a roadside checkpoint for drunk drivers. I pull over. The pastis have made their way into my bloodstream, but they haven't been metabolized yet. .08 grams. I'm screwed. The car's stopped. The kind officers don't want to bother me, they're talking in soothing tones, I have a feeling they can tell I was crying just before the stop. I keep my head down. They say it's not much, I'm not driving too fast or doing anything wrong, that it shouldn't be a big deal . . . Two or three months at most. They pause . . . Drunk tank or not? And then their chief says no, I'm not that drunk, he'll just find me a driver who can take me back to town. Which turns out to be two young guys in a white Golf. I thank them for driving me, they talk a lot, I can't even hear the music on the radio. They say that, with .08 grams, it's a tough one. They're nice, they try to get my spirits back up, ask me if I need my car to work. And then I realize it'll be a pain in the ass to get to work every morning this winter, I'll have to get a scooter. They have a friend who's really good at finding stuff for cheap. I decide that I'll do everything by bike at first, that'll be good for me, and one of the two guys brightens up and says that on the other hand I'll save a lot because cars these days end up being so expensive! What with insurance and gas and maintenance . . . And just like that, we're at my place. The driver lights a Marlboro, he offers me one, as

I take it I think of Cindy's father, who I don't know and who might be waiting for me so he can punch me in the face. I ask them if they'd mind waiting until I'm in the house before leaving. They say no but they're watching me, they can definitely tell from the tone of my voice that I'm nervous, they look around, they start wishing they hadn't said that no, they wouldn't mind, they tell me they don't want to get into any kind of mix-up. So I hurry up, I get out of the car, I say good-bye, I thank them again, it's nice to meet young kids like them. I look around carefully, I take three steps, wave them good-bye, I go into the building. I shut the door. Phew, nothing happened to me. But at the top of the building stairwell, the chief is waiting for me, right in front of my apartment. Still stern.

"What the hell were you doing at Grampa's?" he immediately asks.

In shock, I stammer:

"Where did you get that idea?"

"It's my job to know everything."

I look at him. His eyes are gleaming. I can't tell if he's jerking me around or if he's serious. But it's not worth it to lie.

"I wanted to see Cindy."

"She went back to her parents'."

"I know."

"What the hell were you doing down there all that time, then?"

"I was talking to Mariette and I told Grampa that I'm homosexual."

"Ah!" said the chief, as if thinking that it was just about time . . . As if that solved the problem once and for all. I don't understand why the chief would think, as Mariette clearly did, that my telling Grampa I'm gay would put an end to our friendship. We looked at each other a long while, the chief didn't say anything further, in his eyes the case was closed. I put the key in the lock and I say:

"I got caught at one of the checkpoints."

"Serves you right, if you'd come right back home that wouldn't have happened."

I don't answer, I shrug in acknowledgment, but once we're in the apartment, all I want to do is pull the chief into my arms and hug him as hard as I can. We kiss. We kiss a long while, his kisses are still so delicious. I could never get tired of them. He's the one to pull away.

"Why did you go to see Cindy at night?"

"I wanted to see her about what happened this afternoon."

"Why didn't you wait until tomorrow?"

"I wanted to see her straightaway."

He looks at me. I can't figure out if he believes me or not. And it's clear that he doesn't know if he should believe me, either. But he acts as if he does:

"Did the two of you have sex?"

And I start wondering what Cindy told the police. Even though the fact that he's asking the question implies that she must not have said much. I thought that she would have only talked about the blow job with Mariette and Grampa . . . Or rather, I'd think she talked to Mariette about it, who would then have repeated it to Grampa to belittle me in front of him. But there's still something niggling at me . . . It seems odd that Cindy would have mentioned it to Mariette. It's not the sort of thing you tell your grandmother, after all. So maybe she talked about it to the chief's partner, who would have kept prodding her until she'd told him everything. My head is still a mess. I pull away from the chief.

"What did she say?"

"You don't need to know what she said to answer the question."

"No, we didn't have sex."

I say that while looking for something to drink, and while I've got a bottle of whiskey in my hand, since I feel like whiskey tonight, I offer the chief some, he nods yes, he'd like a glass. He sits down on the couch. And I ask again, I want to know what Cindy was telling them, I settle down on the couch by him, he puts his hand on my thigh. He's taking his time, as if he was looking for an answer, but I think he's actually trying to keep me hanging. Finally he says:

"She wanted to see you to have sex with you . . . But you didn't want to, because you're gay."

The chief stops there.

"Is that everything she said?"

He nods, he looks at me with satisfaction, he smiles and sips. I don't know what to say, I like that, I can see Cindy sticking to a short version with the police. A part of me is proud of her. And then the chief sits up, his hand still on my thigh, he's rubbing it, kneading it, and as he does so he says:

"But if you'd had sex, I'm sure she would have said the same thing."

He looks at me self-assuredly, as if to say: "Don't act like I'm an idiot." He finishes his glass. We're sitting next to each other on the couch. I'm torn between sliding my hand under his shirt or talking. But there's something I want to figure out, so I decide to talk.

"What makes you think we had sex?"

"Nothing," he says.

He turns toward me, he looks at me, still stern, and then I can't figure out why we're spending so much time on Cindy. I tell myself the chief is just a clever trickster, I don't want to keep talking about this, I want him. I pull off his shirt, and just seeing his chest heightens my desire, I kiss him on the neck. He caresses me, we kiss again, and I take him to the bedroom. We spend the night fucking. Sometimes, nestled in the chief's arms, I fall into a half-sleep. In a half-dream, I feel like there's a third person in the bed, who I somehow can't identify . . . Like a ghost who likes being with us . . . But this third man, for it's a man, that much I can say for sure . . . This third man doesn't trouble me any more than that, I get used to his presence . . . But still I wonder if he isn't here to help the chief make me suffer. Because I know that the chief's going to want to hurt me, I don't know when it'll happen but I know it'll happen. And then my desire for the chief wakes me up properly, he wakes up as well, and we kiss again, long intense kisses that we desperately want to make last and that we dive plunge into hungrily . . . And we have sex again until we come . . . And then I slip into a half-sleep again, still bound up in this half-dream . . . And we wake up, in the soft light of my room, I'm astonished by how I rediscover him every time, his face even more beautiful every time . . . I don't think I'll ever extinguish the desire that I feel for him, and we kiss again . . . And so on until we fall asleep for good in the early morning.

And not much later, it seems, the summer heat wakes me up. The chief's fingertips are stroking my hard cock. I take his in my hand, I stroke it mechanically but I can't shake the morning blues. All the memories of our night of passion jostle in my thoughts. I'm worried this won't last, the chief will have to leave to go back to his family, go off to work, and I'd rather that we stay together for the entire day and then the entire night . . . In short, that we stay together all the time. And then I remember I have to go get my car. The chief probably notices that his caresses aren't exciting me so much, he gets up, he says he's hungry, that he's going to pick up a few things, I gaze at him while he's getting dressed, the blues are diminishing gradually, I think that even if the chief leaves today, we'll see each other again very soon. Maybe I'm just fantasizing . . . I tell myself it's crazy how stern he looks even getting dressed in the morning. I wonder why it took me so long to realize that the chief was handsome.

And it's odd that I keep thinking of him as "the chief" after the night we spent together, I really should ask him his name but it'd be weird to ask him here and now. I'll ask him later. He smiles at me and then goes through the door. Then I remember I need to call Paul, I don't know what day it is, I'm not sure if it's Sunday. And it's not great to call on a Sunday morning. But it's important, so I'll call him anyway. I try to figure out how I'll explain all of this to him. I can't tell him it's over between us, I can't imagine not seeing Paul ever again. And I can't tell him it's just a fling, either, that he and I can just hook up again in just a few days. After a few minutes my thoughts sort themselves out, I'll just tell him the truth, I've met someone, it's still very early, but I'm in love with him and I have to see how things go. I've gotten that far when the chief comes back in with the groceries and we pull each other close, we can't stop loving each other, we go to pick up my car, the day goes by, and by nighttime, I still haven't called Paul . . . I tell myself I'll do it once the chief's left. But when we're cuddling on the couch, the chief suddenly says:

"Well, maybe we should decide what we're eating tonight."

The question catches me by surprise. I say:

"You're staying to eat?"

He looks at me oddly.

"Do you not want me to?"

"No, no, I want you to."

And I'm delighted that the chief is staying for dinner here tonight. We have drinks, the chief doesn't talk too much about himself, he doesn't like that, I still don't know exactly how old he is, after seeing him hard as a rock all day, I'd have put him in his fifties, but that can't be right, because he's got gray hair and a gray mustache, crow's-feet around his eyes . . . And because of his name, which I finally learned is Louis. That upset me a lot. First of all, I don't think it's a name that suits him at all, and it's definitely not a name from his generation . . . If he's called Louis, he'd have to be either very old or very young, a kid actually, since obsolete names are only just coming back into vogue. So maybe I assume he's much older even in spite of his perfect body. He doesn't try to get me to talk about myself, he doesn't ask questions. He says we're good together, that he's never had such good sex with anyone and that's all he wants. And we like each other so much that the drinks stretch out, we have dinner at something like one in the morning. After eating, I remember that I still haven't called Paul. And the chief keeps trying to make me come. He strokes my cock, he sucks it, he wants me to fuck him, and I'm drained, I want a breather. And I'm surprised most of all that he's spending so much time with me.

"Is it okay that you haven't gone back home?"

He looks at me oddly for a minute. He doesn't seem to understand.

"Why do you ask?"

"Can you spend that much time away?"

"Why wouldn't I be able to?"

"Maybe somebody's expecting you!"

"Who?"

And as I see the chief clearly failing to understand what I mean, I realize the mistake I made. I don't dare say anything else even as he watches me and waits for an explanation . . . I won't get out of this by being quiet and waiting for the topic to change, so I have to keep going.

"Are you not married?"

"Why would you think I was married?"

I don't know why, I just had the idea in my head . . . That was the impression he gave, he didn't look like a bachelor, he seemed more like a good dad . . . And, of course, I didn't see how anybody could have a career in the police force without being married.

"You don't have to tell people you like men," he says, "but I don't see how being single would be a problem . . . Why is it, then?"

I don't know. I don't know why I got that in my head. I think of the dream I had shortly after the first time we met, I mean after the affair with Grampa's underwear, the dream where we were practically living together, and he wasn't married, and his colleagues even knew about his being gay.

"Why are you so worried about that now?" he asks with a smile.

I don't understand what he's asking, I just shrug my shoulders.

"We spent last night together, and the one before that, and all of today . . . If I was married, do you think I'd have stayed here for so long?"

He's right. I don't have any idea anymore how I managed to think up until now that he was married. I've got my head in the clouds. I feel stupid. I'd like to drop the whole thing but I don't know how to get myself out. Especially because the chief isn't taking this lightly. He knows I didn't just ask this question absentmindedly.

"Are you upset that I'm staying here?" he asks.

"No, no, not at all . . . On the contrary . . . I was just imagining . . ."

I let my words trail off because I didn't know how to finish them and I didn't even know if it was worth finishing. He didn't wait.

"You shouldn't imagine things like that."

"But you didn't say anything either . . . It's inevitable that I'll imagine things."

"All you have to do is ask."

"But when I ask, you don't answer."

"Oh, what didn't I answer?"

"Off the top of my head, I can't remember . . . Your age, that's one, you didn't ever tell me that."

"You never asked."

"I did."

"Then you should have asked again."

"Just now, when I told you how old I was, you could have told me."

"Well, I'm sorry, that wasn't a question . . . Why didn't you just ask me directly?"

"I thought you didn't want to talk about it."

"Because I might think I'm too old?"

"I don't know."

"So how old do you think I am?"

"Oh no . . . That's a dangerous question, I'm not answering that."

"Go on, take a guess!"

He's smiling at last. Things are better now. He puts on a playful face. So do I.

"You promise not to get upset?"

"Why would I get upset? I'm too old for that."

"Fifty-five?"

"Not bad, I'm fifty-two . . . Anything else you want to know?"

I'm not sure I believe him. I think he's fifty-five, fifty-six, but I can't think of any reason he'd lie to me. There are plenty of other things I'd like to know, but that'd get us off track, my desire for him comes back in a huge rush, I'm happy that he's staying with me, I'm happy that he's free, I slide my hands around his balls, he's hard again. I am, too. We fuck all night, between two long kisses, two licks, the chief tells me over and over again that he's never been so happy in any man's arms, that I'm the best lover he's ever met. Only one thing still bothers him, though, he feels like I'm still afraid of him . . . I need to not be afraid . . . Yes, he was violent . . . He knows that, he's sorry, it was before he fell in love with me, he wouldn't do anything like that now . . .

All he wants now is for me to be happy, because my happiness is his. And later, after we've enjoyed a long and tender and gentle kiss, I look in his eyes, and I say: "I love you." He pulls me in tight, then, as my cheek's pressed against his chest, I wonder if I can love someone who's always there, next to me, indefinitely, then I fall asleep terrified at the thought that the chief might never leave.

This morning, the chief got up early, at six thirty, he told me that he had to go back to work, that I shouldn't wait for him at lunchtime, but that he'd be back in the evening, around seven or eight o'clock, and that he'd take care of the shopping for dinner tonight. I was happy to be alone, and I fell back asleep listening to France Info . . . Although calling it "listening" might be a bit much . . . The black flood in the Gulf of Mexico, I didn't know they'd·been able to stop it, and apparently the leak's just broken open again. I remember something that a tycoon like Warren Buffett or someone like that had said: "Everything's going well for the rich people in this country, we've never been so prosperous. There's class warfare, all right, but it's my class, the rich class, that's making war, and we're winning." And then I remember something else that I read somewhere, something that the head of a large company, maybe France Télécom, but I can't remember, had said about his own employees: "They're going to understand that we're at war, and as in any war, there will be casualties." And that reminds me of something I'd heard an Interpol commissioner saying on this same radio show, that we should expect towns in Europe to have the same level of violence as South American towns. All this gets me down in the dumps, I'm thinking about the end of the world again, at least an end of the world that I dreamed up not so long ago. The one where the oligarchy openly jerks us around, they just kill us en masse until they're the only ones left on their desert islands. I don't know what the hell I'm thinking, jerking off in Grampa's underwear or fucking a the chief of a police squad like crazy, I should be working to reverse the way things are going, to find a political alternative. But I just keep feeling powerless in light of how much work there is to be done, I know there's no way I can ever live up to current events . . . And I'll never be able to live up to History. A light breeze whistles through the apartment, bringing in morning's freshness, I curl up in the sheets, I'm so small, I'm terrified. I fall back asleep slowly, not feeling particularly proud of myself, and then when I see that it's nine o'clock, I get up immediately, determined to keep my chin up and do as much as I can before noon.

First, I call Paul on his cell phone, I still don't know what to tell him, I decide that I'll improvise, I'll explain the truth, that's all, without getting too much into the details. But it goes to the answering machine. With a sad, disappointed tone, I apologize for not having called earlier but he can call me back whenever he wants. Then I go down to the cellar to find the bike I bought two years earlier for getting around town and maybe even out a bit, for exercise and for fun. But mainly I'd bought it just to spend some money and because I liked the idea of having a bike . . . I had ridden it around town a few times, even made a few trips further out, and then when winter came I stopped using it and put it in the cellar because it took up too much space in the garage, and it stayed there. But now I'm happy I had that idea two years ago to buy a bike. While I'm inflating the tires, I wonder what I can do with my car. Should I sell it right away or wait for the verdict? Because if it's just a matter of three months, like the police officer was telling me the other night, then I'd just keep it. So I'll wait, and I go ride my bike around Roquerolle in the meantime. At first I'm amazed by how fast I feel like I'm getting around, but I don't enjoy it for too long, I'm still thinking about Paul, it's odd that he's taking so long to call me back. By noon, he still hasn't shown any sign of life. I leave another message telling him that I hope he's all right and that I'd really like to talk to him. After my siesta, I feel nervous and debate about calling him on his land line, but I really don't want to catch his wife. I don't know her. What would I tell her? I'll wait a bit longer. I go down to buy *La Dépêche*, they're talking about the man who drowned at Corignac Lake with a photo of him and his family, his head in a circle, his name is Thibault Lombard, a good-looking twenty-nine-year-old man, a young French teacher appointed to a position near Paris, he'd come back home to spend two weeks of summer vacation with his family, but I shuddered when I read that he was gay and that this part of Corignac Lake was well known for being a gay cruising spot and that the Central Directorate of the Judicial Police (since the Toulouse-area CDJP force was handling the case) suspected that it was either a financially motivated assassination during a casual encounter or even a crime of passion. I'm thinking about the chief. For a moment I'm scared for him, scared that they'll find him. And they'll send him to prison and I'll never see him again. But I force myself to think straight: I reiterate to myself that normally I should report him, there's still time to do so, I could say that I was afraid, that I also wasn't sure of what I'd seen, that I was far away, that it was the *La Dépêche* article that made me react, but then I feel relieved that this isn't possible, they won't believe me, they'll believe that I wanted to settle a score with a chief because they revoked my driver's license, they'll find out that he was my lover for these two days . . . And worse yet, they might dig up the story about the baton up my ass . . . Grampa's underwear . . . And none of that will bring poor Thibault Lombard back to life . . . And I start thinking again about my desire for the chief. I was happy this morning when he left but I'll be even happier to see him again tonight. The question I keep coming back to is whether I like him because I actually like him (as in, would I like him even if . . .) or if I only like him because it's in my best interest. As usual, I still can't decide . . . It must be a bit of both . . . But if I can't bring myself to send him to jail, it has to be because I really do love him. And Paul still hasn't called back. I really am this close to calling him when it occurs to me to see Cindy again, the poor girl must be moping around at her parents', and actually, now that I think about it, I'm surprised that neither her father nor her mother nor the two of them have come to find me yet, even just to see my face. It's perfectly easy to find their address and once I'm back on my bike I head off that way. It's at the other end of town in a newly built housing development I don't know at all. On the way there, I keep repeating to myself how I'll introduce myself, I'm just coming to ask after Cindy, in my head it all comes out right, it seems perfectly logical to come see if she's not too shocked, given that the other night, it was the police who brought her back . . . It seems logical, I'm even offering them some measure of honesty, but as I get closer I start wondering how her parents will take this, is there a risk I'll come across as trying too hard to seem honest, actually? My certainty withers away, I start wavering, I tell myself that it's best if I call first. I bike past the pink and yellow houses in the housing development, and as I pass the fir hedges around her parents' mauve house, I nonchalantly peek as if I were a disinterested passerby. The shutters are half closed and I don't see anybody. I make my way back home. But I don't call, I wait for the chief to come back. I go back to reading Enric Mouly's *E la barta floriguèt*, which I think has to be the greatest Occitan novel of all time, but I'm not really reading it, I'm mostly thinking of Grampa. I see him again in his bed without his hat, suscing, then the image of his pale smooth ass in the bathroom comes to mind . . . An image I push away immediately . . . And I wonder why I'm thinking of Grampa when I'm in love with the chief. Maybe it's tied to the fact that I'm reading Occitan . . . But mostly, I tell myself I must not be that in love with the chief . . . When I'm in love with a man . . . really in love, I mean . . . I can only think about him. I forget all the others. Suddenly, the intercom buzzes. I jump in surprise, I hope it's Paul. No, Paul would have called first. I rush over anyway. An officer from the CDJP, whose name I don't really understand, introduces himself, he wants to talk to me. I buzz him in. There are two of them, actually. The one who spoke is a man my age or maybe a bit younger with an affable face. He's wearing a red short-sleeve shirt and faded jeans . . . And the other is a young woman in a blue dress, a very beautiful dress and an especially beautiful woman, in fact. They come in, I ask if they want anything to drink. They're fine, they don't want anything, and we get to the discussion. They're here about the investigation into the guy who drowned at Corignac Lake. They've been told that I was there the day of the drowning. I'm surprised, aside from the chief, I have no idea who could have told them that and I wonder why the chief would have told them. I stay calm. I tell them the same version of the story I gave the chief. And then I'm afraid of the chief coming while they're still here, I hope he'll think to call ahead.

"And the two of you stayed there, like that, until nighttime?"

"Yes."

"In the woods?"

"Yes . . . We were having a good time together . . ."

"And you don't even know his name!"

"No."

"You didn't even exchange phone numbers to see each other again?"

"I wanted to, but he didn't."

"But he still stayed with you until night fell."

"Yep."

Something's still bugging me. I want to know what makes them so sure it was murder, but I can't just ask that, I'm afraid they'll see that as proof of my guilt. I feel as if I'm putting myself in a sticky situation, I'm positive that at some point I'm going to trip up, make a mistake in my false version of the story. I don't know why I'm lying anymore, well yes, I'm protecting the chief and I'm not sure anymore whether that's a good or a bad thing, I need some time to myself to decide. I miss him already, I can't wait to see him again.

"So you said good-bye to him and went back to your car in the parking lot?"

"Yes."

"What about his car?"

I hadn't considered that but I'm surprised by how quick I am to answer, almost too quick:

"Well, we went down to the path, and then he told me his car was at the other end, on the little road that goes down to the water . . . Sometimes people park there . . . I do, sometimes, it's a bit more discreet and it's a nice drive . . . But it takes a bit longer."

The two inspectors look at each other and then stare at me. She finally asks:

"And you didn't notice anything? No other car?"

I shake my head. I'm still thinking.

"Or even in the afternoon, a man acting strange . . . Nobody suggested going into the water?" she asks.

I'm surprised by the question, I don't know what she's really trying to figure out, it's such a weird question. So I let myself go.

"Hmm, nobody really suggests something like that . . . Not to a stranger, anyway."

"Why not?" the other inspector asks, intrigued.

I wonder where the trap is.

"Well, it's ridiculous."

They're both transfixed and I'm pretty happy with myself. The inspector looks at his colleague. He shrugs. I think they're in agreement with me. And I conclude that the question wasn't a trap. The vibe is really relaxed between us. My phone rings. I hope it's Paul. It's the chief. He tells me he's on his way, he just wants to know if he should pick up some bread.

"Yes, I don't have any more . . . But take your time, I've got company!"

"Who?"

"Two police officers, I'll call you when I'm done."

The two officers wave at me that I shouldn't worry about them, as if they're nearly done. At the other end of the line, the chief hasn't replied. I hang up.

"We won't be much longer," the inspector says immediately. "Right now, you're the only gay man who's actually talked to us, the others are all acting as if they were there by chance . . . We want to know how it works."

"How what works?"

"Cruising in those places," he says.

"Oh, it's just like with straight people except it happens a lot more quickly."

"But you don't all necessarily know each other?"

"You know, I tell myself that every time, I feel like I've seen them all, but I'm always surprised to see new faces."

"What about Thibault Lombard, had you really never seen him?"

"Never."

"But he came here every summer."

"Maybe he didn't spend every afternoon at the lake."

"Well, of course not."

"And I don't spend every waking minute cruising either."

They both smile at me as if it was evident, they almost feel bad for having thought that, and then the inspector pushes back his chair.

"But even if you didn't know him, I'd have guessed that in such a small world like yours you'd all stick together a bit . . . From the outside, we tend to assume there's some solidarity, some fraternity between you guys . . . So I guess I'm must say we're a bit surprised."

He looks at his colleague, she nods, then she looks at me. He goes on:

"We feel like this whole drowning doesn't really seem to have affected you."

The inspector's hit home. I feel shitty but I have to say something.

"It's hard to be upset about the death of a total stranger!"

"But he was like you, he was gay . . . In the prime of his life, athletic, a good swimmer, that has to make you a bit nervous."

I look at them sadly. I don't know what to say. Well, yes . . . I'd like to ask why that should make me nervous or make all us gay men in this area nervous, but I'm afraid that this will get the interrogation going again, and, even just thinking about it for two seconds, I know why it ought to make me nervous, and besides, I tell myself the inspector will tell me more without my having to ask. But he ends the conversation there, he gets up, his hand in his pocket.

"All right, we'll stop there . . . If you think of anything else, a face, a detail, here's my card, just call me."

And he pulls out his business card. I'm astonished it was over so quickly, I was almost feeling good with them. But we've run out of things to say. His partner gets up as well, she looks at the Enric Mouly book I'm reading.

"Can you read Occitan?" she asks.

I wonder where the trap is again.

"Yes, why?"

"No reason, that's nice."

They smile and head toward the door, shake my hand, and she says:

"Adissiatz!"[54]

"Adissiatz," I say back.

After I shut the door, I realize I need to make sure I don't lose the inspector's card for any reason . . . In case things go wrong with the chief, I think I might be able to confide in the two of them . . . I actually think it's the two of them that I'd like to tell everything. But then I immediately feel bad having thought that. Why would things go wrong with the chief? And indeed, if I'm worried things might go wrong, why wouldn't I report him directly? I call him to tell him that we're good, I've wrapped things up with the police. And I put the Enric Mouly book away, I get the feeling he wouldn't like seeing that on the table.

At first, things are strained with the chief. For one thing, he was upset that I might have suspected he was the one to send the inspectors over. He'd never say that he went cruising by the lake, because on top of revealing that he was gay, it would raise suspicions that despite being a policeman he might be a suspect. So he wasn't very happy but he didn't really get upset at me personally, and after we talked and he reflected for a bit longer, he understood how I could have thought that. But I could tell he was still, deep down, a bit irritated, that meant there was an unexpected witness who could have seen him hanging around the lake until late. And then he told me that maybe it was the guy I'd hooked up with. But I reminded him that we didn't even tell each other our names. The chief told me that the guy might know me without me knowing him, and as I still didn't understand he added that I was well known in the tiny gay community here. That caught me off guard. I'd never have thought that, but he was right, it was possible, and I finally said that it probably wasn't serious, given that I wasn't the one to drown this poor Thibault

54. Good-bye!

Lombard. And since this still bothered me and I couldn't talk to anyone other than him, I asked the chief what could have made them think that it was a murder. He was a very good swimmer, they hadn't found any indication of a heart attack, and his friends all insisted that he would never have gone out swimming to the middle of an empty lake by himself. He was afraid of the deeps . . . The fear that arose when you realized just how much water was below you. I had no idea that kind of fear existed and I still think it's odd that someone could be a good swimmer and still have that kind of fear. All the same, there were enough things to make them suspicious. And as the chief didn't say anything further and I really wanted him, I kissed him. He really wanted me, too, we had sex and it was even better than the night before, this day apart had done us both good. And now we're drinking some red wine. I'm watching him prepare dinner. Every so often, I help with something, but not much, I give him a plate or a fork or a cooking utensil. He still doesn't know his way around my place, he doesn't know where to find everything. We don't talk. Sometimes we kiss each other quickly or I press my chest against his back while he's peeling garlic or, between two tasks, he's the one who comes over and has a sip of wine and when he's finished, he puts his hand down my shorts. We kiss again and then he goes to flip the sliced potatoes in the pan. When he cooks, I'm surprised by how much younger he suddenly seems. He also seems younger at the table. I wonder if it's because of the smiles we've been trading or if it's because he's in his element, it's something he enjoys doing and he's just having a great time. I can't figure out whether the chief's still young or if he's already old. But as someone I can't remember said with absolute clarity (and I love this quote): "The problem with getting older is that you still feel young." But with the chief . . . Or Louis (I should remember to call him by his name but it so doesn't fit him that I can't get used to it) . . . So with him, it's like he's another man in the kitchen or in bed or in the car or in the police station. I think a lot about that. And then I realize that this isn't terribly new, every time I fall in love with a man, I see him with a new intensity, I'm always surprised to see him from new angles, with new faces, attitudes, ways of being different, and I'm always astonished at how easily I get lost in the other man's complexity and subtlety. And I think I actually like that. I like that but I can't stop thinking about Paul. Two days have gone by, which makes me really nervous. I want him to call even though it would be a problem if he called now, while I'm with the chief. But I don't know why I'm thinking that because part of me knows that Paul won't call again. That would be just like him, he could just disappear, think that something like this was bound to happen one day or another and just bite the bullet so as not to upset me . . . And vanish without a trace. Except that I've left three or four messages at this point, asking him to call me back. It occurs to me that he might be dead. I shudder.

"What are you thinking about?" the chief asks, a wooden spoon in his hand.

I come out of my torpor, my eyes land on his belly button, and sweep up his torso, his neck, and then his own eyes. I still want his body . . . I'll never get enough of it.

"About you," I say.

He smiles and I smile back and he comes to place a kiss on my lips. My smile fades away as I start wondering if Paul really is still alive. Why am I getting this premonition here and now, as I'm watching the chief cooking? He notices that I'm still worried, his smile fades away too.

"Is thinking about me making you so worried?"

I shake my head no, but I don't think he believes me. He keeps watching me for a minute, pours himself another glass of wine, and another for me as well, we clink glasses, we kiss. And then dinner is finally ready and we sit down at the table. Then we have sex again and I fall asleep in the chief's arms, but before I fall asleep I wonder why he killed Thibault Lombard.

It's my last Sunday of vacation. Tomorrow I go back to work, which is depressing to think about. It's not the work in and of itself that bothers me, but knowing that I'll have to leave my sales job for manufacturing work. "It's the crisis," my boss had told me, but the crisis really is just a convenient excuse, I don't know why they'd need more people in production than in sales. It's logical, if there are fewer orders then there has to be less production. I don't understand why this decision was made, nobody wanted to tell me anything and it's upsetting. On top of that, I'm losing forty percent of my salary. I don't understand why the most painful work is the worst-paid. It's not new, I've never really understood, but in the past I just bore it, I told myself that I should have worked harder when I was in school, I also told myself that managerial positions were much more stressful and that the salary was supposed to compensate for the stress. Now, the injustice of this basic rule of our world just feels even more wrong to me. And I wonder how I'm going to manage. My apartment costs seven hundred euros a month, which will leave me just five hundred euros for food, water, electricity, not to mention books and DVDs . . . I'll never make it, I'll have to sell my apartment and I'm not even sure I'll be able to sell it and even if I do, I don't know where I'll live instead. With just twelve hundred euros a month, I can't stay anywhere that's more than four hundred euros, is there even anything available for four hundred euros a month . . . I'll have to move into a studio apartment and it's upsetting to think that I'll have to go live someplace so much smaller than here. And then I realize that I can sell my car now that they've taken away my driver's license, it's been revoked for a full year. I should be able to get a good four thousand euros for it, that'll help me for the time being. I go for a walk in the countryside, I try to take advantage of this last day of vacation. But the sun's setting, there isn't much time before night comes and then it'll all be over. I think I've missed "Stade 2," the sports show on TV that always marks the end of the weekend for me. When I was younger, I tried to make the weekend stretch as far as I could, staying in cafés and drinking pastis with my friends until way too late at night, sometimes until the café closed and I went to sleep completely wasted, and that way there was less of a transition between the weekend and the working week. And then I had fewer and fewer friends to see for Sunday-evening drinks, or simply drinks at all. They got married, they had children. The kids always needed to be bathed and fed early so they could go to sleep before it was late. So I started watching "Stade 2" and sitting at home alone to wait for the weekend to end. I'd get anxious while watching "Cinéma de Minuit," I kept putting off my bedtime so I could have just a little more weekend. But then with age, I'd gotten used to it and I wasn't even so upset at the thought of having to go back to work the next day . . . Well, the truth is I did keep feeling anxious, but I'd just remind myself that in five days a new weekend would come along and then a new week of work and then another weekend and so on forever. Yes, we get used to everything . . . And I've gotten used to this. Until now. I'm alone and I don't want to see anyone. I don't go back home until it's evening, I'm walking along the banks of the Alzou, there's some wind in the trees, the setting sun turns everything yellowish, it'll be fall soon. In the distance, I see a man sitting by the water. At first, he reminds me of Georges, a man I met by the lake shore, a man I talked to for a long while over several encounters and two full summers and ended up not hooking up with because he wasn't gay, but it was fine, it was actually nice. And the closer I get, the more the man reminds me of Paul. I know he can hear me coming, we're alone on the banks, but he doesn't look up, he's still suscing, he's staring absentmindedly into the water. I walk a bit further and now he reminds me of Louis (I've finally decided to stop calling him "the chief"). I sidle right up next to him without knowing whether it's Louis or Paul. I stare at him but he still hasn't turned toward me, I can only see his silhouette and I can't get a clear view of him. Why won't he look at me? I don't dare to call out, I don't know what I would call him, and I'm afraid of getting it all wrong, I crouch down next to him, I wrap my hand around his shoulder, and he finally looks at me and right there and then I see that it's Paul, and I'm stunned by how much Paul looks like Louis. And then he says very sharply, even harshly:

"Qué fas aquí?"[55]

"Me passegi."[56]

"Ont as metut ton òme?"[57]

He's talking in impeccable Occitan and I feel like we can finally get along again. I answer:

"Tu siás mon òme."[58]

He shrugs. And then he goes back to staring at the Alzou's black waters. The sky, too, has darkened.

"Lo foguèri pas jamai!"[59] He tells me this without looking at me.

And even though I want to tell him no, that's not true, he continues:

"Ieu auriái volgut t'aimar fins a la mòrt!"[60]

"Es pas acabat."[61]

"Aimas tròp d'òmes a l'encòp, cossí poiriái trapar mon sèti dins ton còr?"[62]

"Pr'aquò l'aviás trobat!"[63]

---

55. What are you doing here?
56. I'm walking.
57. Where did your man go?
58. You're my man.
59. I never was!
60. I wanted to love you until I died!
61. It's not over.
62. You like too many men at the same time, how could I have a place in your heart?
63. But you do have one!

"Non, jamai . . . Tu vòles viure amb de trèvas, ieu vòli viure amb d'òmes de carn et d'òsses."[64]

"What the fuck is this?" I think to myself as I listen to him. He really has some nerve saying things like that, but I force myself to keep my mouth shut, I know that if I say anything Paul will dig his heels in and the conversation's just going to get even more difficult. I use a really gentle tone, as gentle as I possibly can right now, and I don't know where this comes from but I say:

"Mas las trèvas pòdon venir de carn et d'òsses."[65]

"Pas cap d'òme poirà èstre lo que sómies, ni mai ieu."[66]

"Ni mai tu?"[67]

As I tell him this I try to touch him but I can't, I'm scared that might make him leave and I want him to stay near me, I'm desperate for that but immediately after I'm in a room caressing Grampa's penis, a little hairless pink penis and he ejaculates shit that flows over his balls and I have to wash it but I don't know what to use.

I'm woken up by Louis moving around, he pulls away from me, sits at the end of the bed, then he gets up and leaves the room. I watch his muscular back and sublime ass walking away as I wonder how long this will last. I don't want to go back to the horrible dream I had, I keep my eyes open, I see the sun breaking through the shutters, it illuminates circles on the bedroom wall and I think it looks beautiful. But I can't stop thinking about Paul. I miss him. So I get up, I sit down by Louis buttering some bread, I rub his back, his shoulders. We kiss. And again I'm astonished by how soft his kisses are. But I remember that when he leaves, I'll have to call Paul, and I'm nervous even as I'm leaning into Louis's warm

---

64. No, I never will . . . You want to live with ghosts, I want to live with flesh-and-bone men.

65. But even ghosts can become flesh and bone.

66. Nobody can fulfill your fantasies. Not even me.

67. Not even you?

body, and I think of the shit coming out of Grampa's penis so I pull away from Louis to go check the thermometer on the balcony. It's already seventy degrees out, it's not even seven o'clock yet. I look back at the chief eating his buttered bread, I don't know anymore if this corresponds to the idea I have, or used to have, of happiness, and I still don't know if I really want happiness and I tell myself that this can't possibly last long so I might as well enjoy it. He goes to take a shower and then gets dressed . . . One last kiss and he leaves to go to work. He just tells me that he'll call when he's done. I'm all by myself. I think It's probably too early to call Paul, so I go back to reading the Enric Mouly novel, but I can't stay focused, I keep rereading the same page. I don't understand any of it. I give up, I go back to sleep. I wake up annoyed that it's already ten o'clock, it's hot in my room and I'm pissed that I'm wasting my life like this, I only have a few more days of vacation, and I can't even bring myself to enjoy them. And not a few seconds later, I feel bad to have gotten annoyed about so little, after all, vacations are specifically for not having to get up early in the mornings. In the mail, at last, there's a letter from Paul, I can't say I'm happy but at least there's some news. In tiny handwriting on the back of a beautiful postcard reproduction of Raoul Dufy's *Red Orchestra*, Paul's written that he's very saddened by our separation, that he still loves me and will always love me, and he ends by wishing me years of happiness with my new friend. That word irritates me . . . Only Paul really knows how to push my buttons like that. I don't understand why Paul isn't more aggressive, why he's giving up so quickly when we've known each other for nearly ten years. I'm annoyed enough that I immediately leave a message on his phone, I tell him that his note is just ridiculous, that he knows what I'm like, that after all these years he should have suspected that it wouldn't last, or maybe it would last but that wasn't any reason to just kiss me off with a postcard in the mail, and then I get mixed up because it occurs to me that maybe Paul's had enough of seeing me ditch him for other guys only to come back to him after making him suffer. Last night's dream comes back. And I realize that rather than me leaving Paul, Paul's leaving me with this postcard. I stammer, I get muddled up, I stop myself and tell him that I want us to talk and I hang up. But I'm not proud of the message I can't even remember completely, which had to be incomprehensible, which might even make Paul nervous . . . Too bad, I dial the number for his land line without thinking, and wait. It rings, and then it picks up. It's his wife. I introduce myself, I start telling her that I'm an old colleague of Paul's but she cuts me off.

"I know who you are."

I don't know what to say, she adds:

"He's told me about you!"

"May I talk to him, please?" I ask quickly to avoid the awkwardness.

"I'm sorry," she says, "I wanted to call you, but . . ." There's a long pause. "He's deceased."

"What happened?"

"He hung himself . . . I found him last night as I came back home."

She's close to tears. I can't believe it. I don't know what to say. I try to find the right words to say. I want to hang up without saying anything, I just say:

"Oh no!"

"He didn't leave a note, I didn't see it coming, he really loved you, you know!"

And it hits me even more that I'm on the phone with the wife of the great love of my life and that he committed suicide because I cast him aside like a piece of shit the other night and, on top of that, I can't muster a single phrase of comfort or compassion. She finally says:

"Come see him later this afternoon!"

"Okay, I'll come and see you in the afternoon, good-bye."

"Good-bye."

And I hang up. Immediately after, I realize I'm scared shitless . . . Not just walking into Paul's house with his wife and maybe his son and daughter and friends, but also most of all I'm scared shitless to see him dead. Maybe I shouldn't go. And the thought that he's no longer alive makes me feel so weird. First of all, I don't see exactly what that means, I stay like that for a while, on my couch as I try to imagine it but I can't . . . I see the moments we spent together. With Paul, I had come to only feel a purely physical desire, the time for love had long since gone . . . Of course, he stayed my friend, but friendship is a slippery thing . . . And it's also a weak feeling. And as we got older, people who were strictly friends became less and less interesting to me. I still had a lot of desire for Paul, but for a while now I hadn't really needed him much . . . I just wanted him, and that's why our relationship was better . . . And so relaxed. We could go a month without seeing each other and that was fine, and at the end of that month we'd be together exactly as before. I tell myself it'll take me some time before I really know what it means to me that he's dead. Right now, the only thing that affects me is knowing that he committed suicide because of me. I'd gotten used to telling him everything. Anyway, I couldn't keep it a secret that I loved another man and telling him was the only solution. I'd also gotten used to his falling by the wayside, his unobtrusiveness, his silent suffering in his own little corner, since he couldn't possibly live with me all the time, he thought it was normal that I went cruising elsewhere, even though that meant he might lose me forever. And we both lived with that. We'd talked about it plenty of times, we stopped talking about it, and life went on. And then I think about his wife again, telling me: "He really loved you, you know!" I couldn't believe it, that he'd ever talked to her about me, and if he told her these sorts of things, then she must have thought it odd that she never saw me at her house. It's becoming increasingly clear that Paul must have really loved me completely . . . Loved me, pure and simple . . . So it looks like Paul still loved me with all his heart. Being so patient with me, going along with me, was the only way he had of keeping me and I'm reminded of my dream from last night and the note I got this morning . . . And I'm reminded of the memories I had been reliving when I left my last message on his answering machine. The prospect of life without me had been unbearable for him. But I can't shake the feeling that I'm giving myself too much credit if I think he put an end to his life solely because of me. And I spend the day mulling over that thought, so that late in the afternoon I decide to go see his dead body after all. I don't know, I feel like that might help me and I also want to meet his wife, his children, his family. The truth is that I've already seen his house, I've been there when his wife was gone, but that was a long time ago. The house makes me think of the beginning of our relationship, when we saw each other every day and we couldn't bear to be apart from each other. But I don't think of those times as happy years so much as painful years, a relationship doomed from the start, and I tell myself that now I'm really lucky to have found a man who's available. Maybe Paul's death isn't such a bad thing for me, it's cleared the slate so I can love Louis but it freaks me out and I'm immediately ashamed to think such a thought. When Paul's wife sees me, at first I can't stop thinking about how beautiful she is, I'm speechless in front of her exhausted and worn face, and it's not only worn down by these last few hours, you can feel that this didn't happen overnight and that she hasn't always been a happy woman. She's staring at me in a particular way, and I understand that she knows what I meant to Paul and that she's known it for ages. I feel an outpouring of compassion for her, for her loneliness as a wife recently widowed and also as a wife long since abandoned by her husband keen to find elsewhere what she'd never been able to give him anyway. And now that I've seen Paul's wife, I want to leave again, but she takes me to the room his coffin is in. As we make our way, she introduces me to their son and their daughter. They seem surprised to see a friend of their father's they haven't met already, as if he couldn't have had a life outside his family. "What if they also knew what I represented for their father?" I suddenly think. They're younger than me, thirty, thirty-two years old . . . But they seem pretty savvy. I'm afraid of their questions but they're polite enough not to ask anything. And I've ended up in front of the coffin with Paul inside wearing a black suit with a tie. I've never seen him dressed up like that. At first I'm caught off guard by the shape of his face, but even more so by his soft, peaceful expression, as if it wasn't really him but a statue of him. And then I remember that's how the dead always are. I always feel like they're not in their bodies anymore. I don't want to stay. I stay there, looking at him, because it wouldn't look good to leave after just a few seconds. Now I know why I was so reluctant to see Paul dead. I'm coming to understand that this doesn't change anything for me. So long as I haven't really experienced his loss, I won't know what it meant to have lost him . . And now all I have is this embarrassment at being in this house amid a family I don't know at all. I realize it doesn't necessarily bring people together to have loved the same person. What was I thinking? I don't want to be here anymore, I step back, I start making my way to the front door, I don't care if I haven't stayed for long enough.

"Had you not seen him for a long time?" his wife asks.

I look at her, wondering why she would ask me that, I turn around and look one last time at the coffin. But I'm too far away, I can't see Paul at all.

"A week, a week and a half . . . I would never have thought that he'd do that."

"Me either . . . He hadn't been doing well for the last few days, but for him to do that, I just don't understand."

I wonder why she's saying that to me, now. She has to suspect something.

"Yes," she says. "He came home Friday night even though he'd been planning to spend the night in Bordeaux with his brother, he was upset and he seemed worried all weekend . . . He wouldn't answer his cell phone when it rang . . . But he didn't say anything, he just said it was a passing bout of depression, which happened to him every so often. And Sunday night, he seemed to be doing great . . . We went to eat with our friends, he was laughing and talking, and Monday morning he got up in a good mood, he ate properly, he went for a bike ride and he came back in good spirits . . . Like everything was going well. As if it was all over."

Paul's wife looks at me. She wants me to say something, but I don't know what to tell her. That seems so much like Paul, this way of just being, taking all the responsibility, waiting for things to settle down, and always making sure that things do settle down. But mostly I start being suspicious. I'm no longer so sure that Paul's wife knows what was going on, for a second I consider trying to find out but immediately realize just how ridiculous that would be.

"I don't understand," she says at last.

And I just want to not be here anymore, but I try my best not to look like I'm trying to rush off. I ask her when the funeral will happen. There won't be a funeral. He'll be cremated tomorrow at three o'clock at the Roquerolle crematorium. A vision comes to me of Paul burning in a massive oven and the image pains me because it feels like an entire part of my life going up in smoke. I don't know what's come over me, in a burst of tenderness I take his wife's hand in mine, I hold it firmly, then I see their son and daughter at the end of the hallway walking toward me, I shake each of their hands. We look at each other oddly, I probably look embarrassed. And they're still wondering who I am and I'm sure they're waiting for me to leave so they can ask their mother. I go.

On my bike, I think about Grampa, alone in his bed, I speed up so I can get home and call him sooner, but once I'm in front of the apartment building I decide there's no use, I can't think of anything to talk about with him, there's not much to say beyond a quick catch-up, I know what he'll tell me and it'll only be two minutes before the conversation's over, and then I'll have to wait a few more days to call him because there's no point calling every five minutes. For half a minute, I debate about biking over to Trintaud, but night is still a while off and I don't want to be all alone at my place. I'm crying too much these days. Things really aren't okay. I go around town a few times. I try to stay under the plane trees or in the shady streets near the center of town. I try not to think about anything but it's hard, I have to focus on the road, the houses, the cars, the strangers I go past . . . And also the people I know because I want to steer clear of them, I don't want to talk to them, not even to say hello. So I head away from the center so I can relax a bit, I end up going by the pink and yellow houses in Cindy's housing development. As I bike past her front door, I look and I see her, and she sees me as well. Her hands are on the rail and she's kicking her legs in boredom. She quickly makes her way down the steps, I go around again and just as I come to the end of the hedge of fir trees her voice comes from behind them, saying:

"Stop there, my mother's upstairs, we can't let her see you . . . Why don't you act like you're fixing a flat tire."

I'm always amazed by how alert Cindy is, I pretend to check my bike's tire. And I hear her mother:

"Cindy!"

"What's wrong?"

"Where are you?"

"I'm here."

"What are you doing?"

"Looking at the trees."

Then she asks me, quietly:

"Can you come see me tonight around midnight?"

"No, I can't."

"But I want to see you."

"Listen, Cindy, we can't do this, the two of us, it's not possible . . ."

And Cindy's mother upstairs cuts me off.

"Why are you looking at the trees?"

"I'm looking for a maybug!"

And then she whispers to me:

"She's coming!"

I put away my bike pump, I get on my bike, and I head off. I hear her mother saying:

"Since when did you get interested in bugs?"

And Cindy answering:

"Well, I'm really bored."

I shouldn't have biked past Cindy's, it's just made me even more depressed. And really, I shouldn't have even let her jerk me off, let alone ask to suck me off. Actually I shouldn't have ever done plenty of things. I stop by Gaston's café to have a beer, and as I sip it I wonder if I'm going to just spend the rest of my life doing stupid things. With my second glass, I decide that if I'm doing these stupid things maybe it's because I can't not do them. And with the third one, I don't know why I'm asking myself so many questions, after all, it felt really nice to come in Cindy's mouth, it's been nice to have sex with Paul all these years, and it was fantastic to jerk off in Grampa's underwear. And since nothing interesting ever happens at Gaston's café and even if something interesting did happen I wouldn't actually be very interested, since I'm not in the habit of having a few drinks in a row anymore, I go back home and just wait for Louis. He called me half an hour ago to tell me he was coming. As usual, he'll take care of dinner, he just asked if I had cumin because he was planning to make something with cumin. I don't read, I don't watch TV, I don't listen to music, I watch through the window, I'm anxious the way somebody would be upon seeing a man they're completely in love with for the second time . . . Except I've already seen him four or five times now. I don't know if I should tell him about Paul's suicide or not. I tell myself it's not normal to be hesitant about this. It ought to happen naturally, normally when we receive such a hard blow we should talk about it with whoever we love. And then I start questioning my love for Louis. I love him when he's here, and when he isn't here I hold onto the idea that it will be good to see him again but I don't live in that expectation. I feel like we went too fast, as if after just three days we were already living like an old couple . . . And I'm already scared that our desire will die out. I don't remember if love needs something more than desire. I don't think so. For a long time, I thought that for there to be love, things had to go well in bed and we had to share things like political ideas or sports or drinking together, or maybe we didn't have to agree on everything but we had to be able to talk enough not to get bored in between bouts of sex. I had something like that with Paul, but that's not what it took for things to last for the two of us . . . It was because we didn't spend all our time together. Our passion never got dampened. But love, yes . . . At least for me . . . The love I felt turned into a kind of friendship with very good bouts of sex. The love was at the beginning, when I couldn't do without him, physically . . . When there still was a need. But does desire only arise from the physical? Does it arise from an alchemy that blends the physical and that person's way of being? And worse yet, if someone has a physique we love, can't we invent a way of being for them that would correspond to our desire? And even worse, couldn't we let ourselves be won over by someone else's body because at that moment we needed love? Or not even love, just human warmth . . . But at another moment, at a moment when the need wasn't so pressing, that same body would have left us indifferent. I consider the question for a long while. Without the baton up my ass, without Grampa's underwear, without my thwarted desire for Grampa, without Grampa, without Mariette, without Cindy . . .

Would I still love Louis? In fact, I really do feel scared that my desire for him might be extinguished . . . I'm scared because I don't know how I'll be able to keep that desire intact forever.

I'm at that point in my thinking when Louis buzzes the intercom. He comes in, I leave him enough time to drop off the groceries, then I kiss him and pull him close, I could stay like this for a long while since I feel so good. But he pulls away.

"I'm thirsty," he says.

So we open some beers and drink. I caress him, he notices, he caresses me back, I can tell he wants to tell me something and then he says:

"You don't seem happy."

"It's been a hard day."

I still don't know if I should tell him about Paul's suicide. I don't dare to. I don't know what's holding me back, also, I don't know how long I'll be able to keep this to myself, and I tell myself that it'll seem even more ridiculous to tell him this in two hours. But I don't say anything. He sees that I don't want to talk, he shoves his hand down my shorts, he gets me hard and when I'm completely hard he puts me in his mouth, and he sucks me as masterfully as ever but I go soft. He keeps trying but nothing works. He looks at me, worried. I shrug. I'm trying to think of something intelligent to say but I'm not coming up with anything, so Louis goes into the kitchen, he pours himself a glass of red wine and starts cooking dinner. We don't talk for a minute, I come and hug him from behind, I kiss his neck, and then he asks:

"Are you still in love with Paul?"

I don't understand why he's asking me that right now. My heart swells, I loosen my hold on him, and then I realize something.

"How do you know about Paul?"

"I don't know him," he says immediately. "You were talking in your sleep last night."

I get even more flustered.

"What did I say?"

"You said 'Paul' several times and then some words I didn't understand, they were in a foreign language."

"What made you think I was in love with him?"

"The other night, the first night I came here, he called you, you told him you were seeing someone else . . . I knew what that meant."

I drink some red wine, he does as well, he comes over to me.

"Are you still thinking about him?" he asks.

He's not really asking me, it's more like an affirmation but he says that in a very understanding tone. I nod. I take a deep breath, and then I spit it out:

"He committed suicide!"

Louis puts down the spatula, he turns around, and takes me in his arms. At first I'm surprised that he's reacting this way even though I can't say why, I chalk it up to awkwardness, I don't know how I myself would act if my new lover told me that his ex had just committed suicide, he holds me tight.

"Why didn't you tell me earlier?" he asks gently.

Why would he ask me that when he knows that the question will embarrass me? But maybe he doesn't know what to say even though he has to say something.

"I didn't know how to tell you . . . I didn't dare to, I don't know you very well yet."

"You can say anything when you're in love."

I prefer not to say anything else. Louis doesn't, either, he doesn't say anything else, he holds me tight, his hand stays on the nape of my neck. I feel an infinite tenderness for this man. I could stand here like this forever. Except that we hear the noise of dinner boiling over. Louis gently steps away and picks up the spatula. After that, I tell him a lot about Paul, how we met, in a rest area on the roadside . . . How we met up again and fell in love and how I came to live here so I could be near him if he didn't want to leave his wife . . . how I broke up with him repeatedly only to return every time with even more desire for him . . . And then how things finally calmed down for the two of us and we only saw each other every so often to spend an afternoon or night or weekend together like we were an old couple that had never actually lived together. Louis listens. And as I tell him about the trajectory of my relationship with Paul, it hits me that I'll never see him ever again . . . Yes, that's when I finally truly understand it and I tell myself it's a good thing. I hesitate to tell Louis that. I think of Thibault Lombard and in the end I hold my tongue. Over dinner, the anxiety fades away, I get rock hard again, and then, in bed, I've never been so good in my life, pulling at every part of Louis in wistful urgency and in a sensual freedom that hints at the promise of infinite happiness. He finally comes deep up my ass while muttering loving words that terrified me in my ecstasy. Now I'm lying in bed, Louis kneeling over me as he keeps on stroking me, he really wants me to come. I hold back, I'm afraid that if I come now, the urge will take too long to come back . . . In fact, I'm even a bit scared it'll never come back. I want to keep my desire for Louis intact. But he's nervous, he asks me if I'm okay, if this is good, if he's doing a good job of stroking me . . . And then he wonders if I still want him . . . If I don't come, it must be because I don't want him anymore. So I understand that I have to come, I shut my eyes, I think of Grampa. A younger Grampa with smooth skin, soft lips. I dream that it's his mouth sucking me off while M. Escandolières licks my balls. And when he feels that I'm coming, Louis places his mouth just at the edge of my piss slit and I feel my sperm shooting past his lips, along his tongue and down his throat. Then he keeps me in his mouth for a long time, without moving. Now he knows how to stroke my cock after coming without hurting me and he does exactly that until my cock's completely soft. And as all this has been happening, I've been unable to understand how a man who could make me come so hard could also have drowned Thibault Lombard. And then I'm drowsing and dreaming that there are three of us in this bed, although I don't know who the third one is . . . At moments I think it's Paul, at moments Grampa, and that makes me happy but I'm nervous that Louis might realize that Grampa is with us, until I think I've figured out that it's Thibault Lombard. I really don't want him in my bed but I tell myself to accept his presence because that way I can finally learn why Louis killed him.

In the crematorium, the room is full but as I look around I can't tell how many people are here, at first glance I'd have thought that Paul had more family members, more friends, more neighbors. I start counting heads, but I quickly stop because I'm thinking about my own circle of acquaintances. I try to figure out how many people would come to my funeral . . . And after a quick mental rundown, I decide that a good hundred people or so would be present now, but in twenty or thirty or forty years I'm not so sure. Still, I hadn't really thought about it before now, and now that the ceremony's actually happening here in the crematorium, I think I'd much rather have a burial, and maybe even a funeral ceremony at a church, even if I'm not a believer. At the church, the ritual would actually seem significant, it would go on, there would be songs, litanies, prayers, all that amid paintings, old stones, altar candles, and priestly garments. I've been feeling bad for not being Christian for a while since I like being in churches so much, at the same time, since I've received all the sacraments aside from marriage and ordination, I know I could get back on the bandwagon without any trouble and become a proper Catholic again, even if it didn't happen until extreme unction. I still feel like the older I get, the closer I get to death, the more likely it is I'll become a mystic again . . . I say "again" because I was certainly very mystical when I was young. I'll never feel like a stranger in a church. But I can't bear this crematorium. I feel all alone amid so many people who must all know each other and who must be wondering who I am, I don't dare to turn around because I'm terrified of people looking at me oddly. The only person I could feel even remotely close to is Paul's wife, but she's too busy, she simply nodded at me coldly. As if I was nobody. So I feel even worse. I don't know what I'm supposed to do at this sort of ceremony, I just have to wait for it to end. And not much is happening. I look at the white coffin on the white stage in front of a white wall, cut in half by a black curtain. Being incinerated might feel reassuring to yourself when you're still alive, but it's not reassuring at all to those who are still here. Paul is dead. I'm still trying to think of everything that means. I remember the shape of his peaceful face in the coffin, his body dressed in a black suit. I don't even know why I loved him so much, so I don't know why I'll miss him. I tell myself it's better this way. It's been ages since I fell out of love with Paul. And my desire for him has long since ceased to be desire, it had become physical habit, the reassuring routine of lifelong companionship. Now I'm free. The coffin moves slowly and disappears behind the black curtain then the man in charge, who hasn't said much until now, tells everyone who wants to gather with the family to go into the next room. Then people leave the crematorium. So I understand it's over, and I don't have to stay. I leave. In the last row, I recognize the two investigators from the CDJP. I wonder what they're doing here. I gesture to them with my hand. They catch up with me. Outside the inspector asks me if I have a few minutes. I say yes. And we decide to get some drinks at the Café des Platanes, not a long walk away.

I relax almost right away. I'm actually happy to be talking to these two. They're tactful enough not to talk about Thibault Lombard and the lake affair immediately, they take their time talking to me about Paul, the inspector asks if we were close, I tell him he was a friend. And then she asks me if we'd known each other for a long time.

"Almost ten years."

"And you'd never met his wife?" it's a surprised question.

I don't really understand the question, or rather, I understand it but I don't see why it's being asked here. I smile with evident embarrassment, I shrug my shoulders and hope that'll be enough, but she asks again.

"Really, it's odd that a wife wouldn't have met a friend that her husband had known for ten years."

My heart starts pounding. But I nod. She's right, it's odd.

"Were you lovers?" she asks.

"Did his wife tell you that?"

"I'm asking you."

My heart pounds even harder. I say yes, but I still want to know.

"So did his wife know?"

"We don't know," the inspector replies. "We try not to ask too many questions right after a death."

Suddenly it's clear that the police officers are actually here about Paul and not the lake affair. I'm surprised it took me so long to figure this out, like something I was scared of but didn't dare to admit. I ask:

"What's happening?"

"Do you know of any reasons that he might have been compelled to take his own life?" the female inspector asks.

I look down, then at them, I don't want to lie to them, I just want to know and I'm in a rush.

"I had told him that it was over between us."

"When?"

"Friday night."

The inspector and his partner look at each other, they're surprised but stay calm, he looks back at me, calmly, gently, he asks me how it happened. I don't see why I would answer a question like that, it's really their turn to answer some questions now.

"But what's happening?"

"We have some doubts about the suicide."

"And you think I could have killed him?"

"Wait," the inspector says, still very gently. "We're not saying that just yet, we're just trying to understand."

"His friends were very surprised by his suicide. What do you think about it?" his partner says.

I quickly realize I really don't know how to answer this question. I don't know if I'm surprised. I try to remember the feelings I had the day I found out. I think for a long while, I flood my brain with images, I see all of it in a jumble, I think back to the dream I had last night where Paul was telling me that I wanted to live with ghosts while he wanted to live with flesh-and-bone men, there was a deep sadness in his face and then the image of Paul hanged in his garage crosses my thoughts for the first time, I can even see Louis pulling the rope around his neck. For half a second, I panic inside. My gaze crosses the inspector's. He seems to have noticed my distress. I catch hold of myself, in any case, I don't see how Louis could have known Paul, at best he had a first name to go on and that's not a lot to find anyone. I pull myself together, the police officers are watching me, they're trying to perceive my distress again, I can tell, they're not staring at me but they're still waiting for my answer. And I think of the resigned note that Paul sent me, where he told me that he wished me years of happiness with my new friend.

"To be honest," I say, "it's not his suicide that surprises me . . . It's that he did it because things were over between us, we weren't seeing each other much anymore but I know that he wasn't very sure about where he was in his life but I'm shocked that he hanged himself."

"Why?"

But as the inspector asks me that, I realize that I don't know and then I think that I'm not so surprised after all by his hanging himself. And then the vague idea comes to me that I decide to tell the police officers but I put it together as I'm talking.

"I feel like hanging himself was a way of upsetting his wife . . . She would have to be the one to find him and she would be the one to deal with that image of him hanged in the garage for years . . ."

Why have I gone off on this tangent? It seems far-fetched, and they seem to be thinking that as well, but since I can't just stop there and they don't seem to really understand what I mean, I wrap up with:

". . . while she has nothing to do with it."

The female inspector doesn't wait a second, she hurries to help me, and goes:

"Maybe he wanted not to hurt you in particular!"

First of all, it's not clear why she's saying that, but then I think I understand she's validating the suicide hypothesis. That seems really strange. I'm not interested in shifting the investigation toward the possibility of murder, but something self-evident comes to mind, the other inspector is about to say something, but I cut him off:

"And I'd already done this to him before, told him that it was over and I was leaving him, either because it just wasn't going to work anymore or because I'd met another man . . . It was almost a given between us, he knew it could happen at any moment. It's true that this time I was particularly harsh about it, but I'd tried to call him several times starting the next day . . . I left more messages than I could count on his cell phone . . . It's odd that he didn't call me back."

"As it happens, we haven't been able to find his cell phone." the inspector says.

The way he says it, this seems really serious.

"Would that explain why he didn't call me back?"

The inspector shakes his head.

"His wife is positive that he had it with him the whole time . . . Even the morning of his death . . . She was just puzzled that he never took any of the calls."

"Yes, she mentioned that . . . Do you think he got rid of it?"

"Why would he get rid of it but keep all his emails, even the most personal ones?"

And that sticks in my mind. I think back to our emails, the love letters we'd sent early on and even the nude photos Paul relished taking of me and my erect cock. I think to myself that I too will have to remember to clean up everything before I die. It could happen at any moment, and I'd rather that my mother not find particular things. But the point is that it's one of the first things I'd do if I was contemplating suicide. I wonder why the police officers beat around the bush for so long before telling me that. I think back over the entire interrogation (at least I try to), to figure out where the trap was. But I can't see it anywhere and then my phone's ringtone makes me jump. I hold it in my hand, waiting for the police to give me the go-ahead.

"It's fine," the inspector says, "you can answer it."

It's Louis. He's just left the Intermarché store, it's cool, he got everything for dinner, he even picked up some more pastis because we were out, he asks me if I'm at home. I tell him I'll be there in half an hour, looking over at the inspector for confirmation. He nods.

"I'll wait for you downstairs if you're not there," Louis says. I hear him smooch.

I kiss back and hang up, wondering just when he could have met Paul or found his address. I don't see how it could have happened. But that doesn't keep me from seeing that image again of Louis coming out of the lake, water dripping from his tan and muscular body. Distress overwhelms my thoughts again, and to keep a poker face, I tell the inspector:

"You should have started with that."

"With what?"

"That you'd found photos and letters . . . That's how you knew about Paul and me, I'm guessing."

The inspector nods.

"But we had a feeling when his wife said that she'd never seen you," he clarifies right away.

"That changes a lot of things."

The two officers look at me, they're waiting for me to say more.

"Paul wouldn't have committed suicide and just left all that there . . . He'd never have wanted people to find out!"

"Or he specifically wanted people to find out."

It was the male inspector who'd said that, and his partner nods in agreement. I don't have any idea where they both want to go with this train of thought. But I act like I understand, I'm sure that if I ask them about it then this will go on for a good while and I'm a little sick of this, and really, the more I think about it, the more I feel like I know what they're getting at . . . I have a sneaking suspicion that I'll understand everything once I'm alone and certainly soon enough.

The inspector gets up, and his partner follows, they say good-bye, I'm surprised that we're ending on this note, and once I'm on my bike, I go through all the questions in my head. Paul had lied for a good part of his life, so would he have actually wanted this truth to be found out after his death? I almost want to say that does seem like him even if it ends up being very violent for his wife. But actually, I tell myself that it would actually be most like him to not have thought about it at all . . . Or maybe to have convinced himself that it was better not to think about it. In any case, I think it's a really good thing that Paul's dead, I'd never have been able to let go of him otherwise . . Now a new life is holding its arms out to me. I'm just worried by the investigators' attitude. I'm not sure if it's a technique the CDJP developed, cutting their interrogations off before the end as a way of confusing the people they're talking to right before saying good-bye. I still don't know if

I'm actually a suspect, but it's clear that they'll come back to ask more questions, maybe they're following me to my place. I check behind me. Nobody. But to make sure, I turn off onto one of the small side streets in the center of town, they still know where I live but at least I can give them a bit of a runaround, and if Louis is waiting in front of the apartment building, I can get him upstairs before they see him. And when I get there, Louis is right in front of the building door with the grocery bags on the floor, he's tapping out a number on his phone. Just as I get close, my phone rings and he's startled by my being there.

"That was me calling you," he says with a smile.

"Have you been waiting a long while?"

As I usher him inside with an eye on the street, he says no, he's just arrived.

"It'd be nice if you gave me a copy of your keys," he says.

As I put away my bike, the suggestion echoes violently in my thoughts. My heart's pounding, I'm trembling again, I should be confident enough to tell Louis it's a bit soon for that, that my place is my place and his place is his . . . But I just smile, I mumble sure evasively. He asks me why I'm so tense. I calm down. I tell him that I'm not tense, that I'm just impatient to be alone with him, and I pull him into the stairs. We kiss on each landing, and as we enjoy a long kiss on the last one, I hear some footsteps coming down, and I've just pulled away when I see Cindy, a few steps above us, leaning on the wall. She's watching us.

My first thought is to hope that she didn't see Louis or that she at least didn't recognize him, but those hopes are quickly dashed, I see him go up past me and I don't understand why he's not staying behind me. Cindy steps back. Louis stops, he doesn't say anything, I don't understand what's going on. Cindy stays in place, stupefied . . . She looks at me furtively but immediately turns back to Louis, as if she didn't dare to let him out of her sight. Then Louis turns toward me, as if he's waiting to see how I'll handle the situation. I walk up to Cindy, I want to put myself between her and him.

"Cindy, you can't stay here . . ."

"Yes, I'll take you back home," Louis says as he sets down the groceries.

And Cindy shakes her head no, she looks at me, she doesn't want to see him, she steps down, she clings to me so she can hide from him.

"Are you scared of me driving you home?" he asks flatly, as if he didn't understand. And I'm amazed that he doesn't understand.

"Did you come on your bike?" I ask.

She nods but I know she's lying. She's standing awkwardly, her eyes are darting everywhere, and I don't see how she could have gotten out of her parents' house with a bike. But Louis comes down the steps.

"Come on, I'll drive her back. If anyone finds her here, you'll just get in even more trouble."

I don't know why Louis put it that way . . . He's not being very subtle. I wave at him, as discreetly as I can, in exasperation, and when I turn back to Cindy, I realize she's kept watching me the whole time. And there's terror in Cindy's eyes. At first I wonder if she figured everything out after Louis's last words . . . I want to reassure her, tell her that the chief is cool now, that things are good, everything that happened at Mariette and Grampa's is in the past, that everything's better now and he can't possibly hurt her, but I don't really believe that . . . And then the idea occurs to me that her terror is stemming from something else, an encounter the two of them had that I know nothing about . . . And maybe she's trying to get me alone so she can tell me about this.

"All right, let's go!" Louis says.

And as he says that, he starts going down the stairs. I'm worried that Cindy's going to start screaming. I'm worried that our neighbors will open their doors and see us like that on the steps . . . Two older gay men with a terrified teenager. I step in front of her, I tell Louis:

"It's fine, we don't have to do this . . . I'll call her parents."

I look at Cindy to see if that's okay with her. As she thinks, Louis seems surprised, but all he can do is nod. And Cindy starts to relax, I tell her to come inside. She walks up the stairs.

"Why won't you drive me home?" she suddenly asks.

"My license was revoked . . . Listen, Cindy, it's better this way, I'd rather your parents come here, at least they'll know I'm being honest."

"But I'm going to be in trouble."

"You'll be in trouble either way."

"She's right," Louis says. "We might as well save everyone the hassle."

And as I turn away from Louis, I glare as angrily as I can at Cindy, she looks down. I really can't let her leave by herself. I have to find a minute alone with her, without Louis. I don't know how to make that happen. As no answer comes to mind, I settle on my original idea, and I pull out my phone.

"Okay, what's your parents' number?" I ask Cindy.

She doesn't answer. I ask again. Still nothing. She's really pissing me off.

"Do you want the chief to drive you back?"

I let that slip, I realize. I'm sure Louis wouldn't be glad I'd suggested it, but I don't look at him. Cindy shifts on her chair, she looks at the ground, finally she spits out her parents' number. I dial it.

"Do you have any idea what's going to happen to me?"

"All you had to do was stay home," I say, and then Cindy's father answers.

"Hello, are you Cindy's father?"

"I am."

"I'm Gilles Heurtebise, Cindy's here. Can you come pick her up, please?"

"What's she doing with you?"

"You can ask her."

"All right, I'm coming, where's your place?"

I'm amazed that he doesn't know my address. I tell him, and then I hang up.

As I go down the stairs, I feel a sense of satisfaction. This idea to call her father has gotten me a few minutes to talk one-on-one with Cindy, and I don't know why, but I really needed it, I would have been sad to let her leave without having gotten to talk to her alone. If she has something to tell me (I'm still stuck on that event I might have missed), she can tell me without any worries. Louis just watches us go down the first steps. He hadn't insisted on coming down with us, that would have been odd.

"Have you been with the chief for a long time?"

I'm taken aback by the question, even though I'd been expecting it. I give a straightforward answer.

"No, four or five days . . . A week . . . I'm not really sure."

"Why didn't you tell me yesterday?"

"Why would I have told you?"

"So that I wouldn't come see you anymore."

"But I couldn't tell you . . . Don't you see why?"

And she doesn't see why. She doesn't get why I didn't tell her, she doesn't get why I'm with the chief, she doesn't get anything, she just looks at me with her eyes screwed up and her lips trembling and then she bursts into tears. She collapses into my arms, her head against my chest, she's sobbing, and when she's all cried out, she takes a long deep breath.

"Grampa wants to see you," she says quietly.

Outside, we hear a horn honking. Cindy jumps. That's her father already.

"He told me over the phone this morning."

"You came here just to tell me that?" I ask as I hug her.

"I wanted to see you, too!" She cries harder.

Outside, the horn honks again. This time, I'm the one who jumps. I'm ashamed of how I've acted toward Cindy, I could have thought of something besides calling her father, in any case, I really should have been more considerate.

"You're not afraid of the chief anymore?" she asks abruptly.

Again I'm hardly surprised by that question. I'm more surprised that she waited so long to ask me. I keep hugging her, but I pull back slightly to look her in the eyes.

"Yes, I'm afraid."

And I let go of her. She really doesn't understand anything anymore, she doesn't even seem to know what she's doing here, she wipes away her tears, sniffles a bit, she tries to distance herself from all this, as if it wasn't worth getting so upset over it. I feel like I shouldn't have said that . . . This poor kid who's probably blowing all romantic entanglements out of proportion. But I nod again so that she knows I'm not bullshitting her. Cindy is my only confidante right now. I had to talk to someone about this . . . And you never know, maybe she'll be able to bring herself to talk about this, if I'm ever killed. I drag her away, I open the door. And I see a man stamping his feet in front of his blue car, he hasn't turned off the ignition and he looks deathly serious. It's clear right away that's Cindy's father. I say hello to him. He doesn't care. He doesn't even answer. He's staring at me, like he wants to memorize my face, he's trying to figure out what could be so special about me that his daughter would run away without saying anything. I'd have thought he would be younger, he's a good fifty years old, and then I realize that has to be right, Mariette's a good seventy years old, she can't have a son in the bloom of youth. When he gets in the car, I smile at Cindy one last time, but she's not in the mood, she looks down at her feet, I see her shoulders shaking, apparently she's crying again. Her father hits the gas right away, he makes a tight U-turn right onto the main road. As he passes he gives me a dirty look as if he's trying to make an impression on me. It doesn't work. I was expecting far worse. The sun turns the rear windshield into a huge square reflection and I can't see anyone inside the car anymore and then it disappears around the bend in the road. In my head, I see us again, Cindy and me in the stairwell, hugging each other, me saying "Yes, I'm afraid," her not understanding a thing. It reminds me of last night, when Louis asked me if I still liked Paul. I don't remember the exact situation where he was asking me this but I do remember that I thought it was odd. I go through our conversation again, I try to figure out where we started. That was where it started. That exact question. And I still don't understand how he knew Paul's name. I go through the last conversation I had with Paul on the phone, the day Cindy gave me a blow job, the night I had sex with Louis for the first time. The scene's too distant now but I know we didn't say much and I know that I never said Paul's name at any point. I know that some sort of decency had kept me from saying it in front of Louis . . . And even in front of any other lover, I probably still wouldn't have said it . . . Not at that moment. My mind goes back to Paul's cell phone. What if Louis had it? And listened to the messages I'd left for him the other night? What if he heard my last message, where I was telling Paul that the relationship I had with a new guy likely wouldn't last long? I'm stuck on this thought for a few minutes . . . Standing terrified in front of the door to my building. It's still very hot, the light isn't the same but I'm reminded of those autumn Sunday afternoons when I was a teenager and I had to go back to school the next morning. I feel my desire for Louis fading away . . . A desire that left just two seconds ago. I don't love him anymore. I don't think I ever loved him. Well, no, I did love him for real. I'm afraid. I decide to go back up to my apartment. Maybe it's not completely gone yet

. . . It might still come back . . . Maybe I don't want it to be over. But when I walk into my apartment and I see Louis sitting in front of the Enric Mouly novel that I'd left on the table, next to my dictionary and my Occitan grammar book, it's clear to me that I'll never be able to spend the night with him.

"Brushing up on your Occitan?" he asks with a smile that feels like a sneer.

"Yes . . . Why?"

"Did you hear it's a dead language?"

"Oh, there's plenty of people who still speak it."

"Grampa?"

"Grampa and a few younger ones."

"But you can't talk in that patois every day, or anywhere."

"So?"

"What's the point of studying a language nobody speaks anymore?"

"It was my parents' mother tongue . . . I don't feel like giving it up."

"And you think that a few of you are going to get it going again?"

"I don't know . . . I don't think so . . . It's just that I like this language and I want to practice it."

"But you're not practicing it . . . Nobody speaks it."

"People have written in it, and I like reading them."

"Is this some kind of nostalgia?"

"There's probably some of that. It takes me back to the countryside life I gave up. It's part of my culture. It's a way of life, and I don't intend to forget it."

"Why did it die out?"

"Because it was battered to death."

"You sure about that?"

"Yes."

"You sure it's not because it was supposed to die out?"

"Nothing's meant to die out."

"If the Occitans wanted to keep their way of life and their culture so much, like you're saying, they'd have fought for it."

"They did fight."

"Not enough."

"Maybe . . . But I want it to survive."

"For a language to exist, you need a people, do you think there's an Occitan people?"

"There used to be one, in any case."

"And you think that every people will survive . . . Do you think they all want to survive?"

"I don't know . . . But the one thing I'm sure of is that they don't lose their language because they decide to . . . They are always forced to."

"All right, but once the language's gone, is that really a problem?"

I don't know, I shrug, maybe he's right, I have to think about that. But right now I'm too upset, I can't think, I've never seen Louis talk this much while we're alone together, I don't see where he's going with this. He doesn't let me take a breath, he keeps going.

"The important thing is that people keep on talking . . . That as many people can understand each other as possible, right?"

"Right!"

"So what's the point of studying dead languages?"

"I don't talk in Occitan when I'm in a store or negotiating with a client."

"Of course not, nobody would work with you."

"When I read an author in Occitan, like Mouly, I feel like I'm sharing an experience with him, and with many other readers, and forever."

"Because he's talking about your countryside, but if he'd written in French, that would be the same."

"No."

"Of course it would be the same."

"No. We share something more, it's part of his style . . . That's what moves me the most about his novels."

"What about Grampa, is that what moves you most about him?"

It's odd, he doesn't say that to be provocative, he says that in all seriousness, he's not mocking me, or being ironic, much less cynical, he just wants to know if Occitan plays a part in my feelings for Grampa. And he's waiting for an answer. And I say yes, I think so.

"You think so or you're sure?"

"Yes, Grampa moves me more when he talks in Occitan."

And I don't know why, but it's clear he doesn't like that at all, he's annoyed, he pours himself some whiskey.

"Do you plan on growing up at some point?"

"I don't have any say in the matter, I'm already grown up."

"But are you going to spend your whole life chasing after fantasies?"

"What else would I chase after?"

"You might chase after things that are actually possible."

"And how would anyone know what's possible and what isn't?"

"It's not that hard to figure out."

"But how?"

"Grampa, that's not possible!"

Louis is pissing me off, and I shout at him.

"What about loving a guy after you shoved some underwear full of shit up his ass with your police baton, is that possible?"

Louis is frozen for a minute . . . Completely frozen. Then he frowns at me, intensely and for a long while. I'm not intimidated, I meet his eyes . . . The ball's in his court now, and he buys himself some time with a pitiful:

"Don't you bring that back up!"

My whole body's shaking but I'm not giving up.

"You should be happy, come to think of it, that I'm chasing after fantasies . . . Otherwise, you wouldn't get to sleep in my bed every night."

"Listen, Gilles, that doesn't have anything to do with this, I already told you I was sorry about that . . . And the fact is that's not why we're in love with each other."

"That's how we met."

"Stop being so difficult."

"But it is! That's how it all started."

"No, I was only interested in you much later . . . I had to see you one or two more times."

"And here I thought you were interested in me from the beginning."

"No, are you crazy? You think I'd want to hurt someone I'm interested in?"

"You wouldn't be the first one."

"You really think that?"

"Oh, yes!"

"Does that mean you think I could still hurt you?"

"Yes, that much I'm sure of."

"And torture you?"

Louis looks at me sadly and incredulously. He's genuinely saddened by what I've been telling him. And I'm starting to think that I might have gone too far and I might be making what I had suspected a reality. But I also get the feeling that if I backtrack right now, I won't see the end of it, he'd have the upper hand again and I'd never wiggle out of it. I have to go all the way. He asks again.

"Do you really think I could torture you?"

The question's become harrowing. I know I'm hurting him a lot. I keep thinking, I can't let myself waver, I have to be subtle, my hands keep shaking, I put them on my thighs and I very calmly say:

"Yes."

"Physically?"

I can't answer again, I just nod. He understands, he gets up, he walks around the room.

"You already did!" I say.

"But that was because I thought you were one of those little fags pissing off old people with their creepy obsessions."

"So?"

"What?"

"I did piss off old people with my creepy obsessions . . . But you shouldn't have handled it the way you did."

Louis stares at me in shock. He looks up at the ceiling, wipes his forehead, as if I was being a hypocrite and there was no talking to me. It doesn't matter, I keep going.

"You also tortured Grampa!"

"Don't be silly, I didn't torture him."

"You forced him to shit in his underwear . . ."

"Torture is worse than that."

"And now you bother him every night to see what he's doing . . . And if you bothered him like that from the start, it's because you had an inkling of his feelings for me."

Louis is looking at me now like I'm a total stranger. It's really freaking me out but I can't stop now.

"Are you the one who hanged Paul?"

He looks at me, stunned.

"Are you crazy? No . . . He committed suicide."

"We have doubts."

"Who has doubts?"

"Me . . . the police."

"Do they suspect me?"

"I don't know."

"Do they know we're together?"

I nod. It's a lie but at the same time it occurs to me that the investigators probably do know already, that they likely already suspect Louis and that's why they're so interested in me. My thoughts are a mess. I can't stay where I am, I'm confused. I'm scared he'll notice, I go to find something to drink.

"Did you tell them?"

"No . . . You're not terribly discreet when you come here . . . I'm sure the neighbors think we're living together."

"And why would I have killed Paul?"

"Out of jealousy."

"But you broke up with him in front of me, the other night, on the phone . . . Why would I be jealous of a man you don't love anymore?"

I've gone too far. Louis looks at me incredulously and yet not that incredulously. He seems genuinely upset by this conversation, and disappointed that I could think these thoughts. He knows it's the end of our relationship, I can see it in his eyes. Except he doesn't want it to be over. He's sure of that.

"Why?" he insists.

And I don't know what to tell him. I'm stuck in this mess I made myself and I know I'll just get myself in deeper. I start to think that Louis might not have killed Paul. Maybe I said his name on the phone the other night, but even if I said it, it still wouldn't have been enough to go on, how could the chief have found him? I'm just making things worse for myself.

"You might have thought I still liked him."

"Oh, are you able to love two men at the same time?"

I shake my head no.

"So?"

"Hmm?"

"So why would you think something like that?"

And I still don't have an answer. But mostly I'm full of doubt. I've gone too far and there's no way I can fix this now. Louis holds my gaze, he's waiting for me to say something. I stutter something.

"All right, fine, I'm just talking nonsense . . ."

"You? Talking nonsense? You heard everything you accused me of just now. That didn't just come out of nowhere."

"I'm not in a good place right now . . . And you just attacked me about knowing Occitan and then about Grampa . . ."

"And you're suggesting that I'm guilty of torture and murder! What's wrong with you? I don't understand."

I don't understand, either. I know I was right earlier, but I can't put my finger on why. At one point, I think that the only way to get out of this would be to go all the way to Thibault Lombard's murder, to tell him that I know, and then he'd have understood. I'm painfully close to telling him but after a long minute, just as I get ready to speak, he gets up, puts both his hands on the chair, and says:

"All right, I think it's best if I go sleep at my place tonight."

And I'm amazed it's over this quickly, he adds:

"You need to get some sleep . . . I do, too!"

He puts his hand on his face like he's trying to get a grip on reality but as he walks out, he still looks haggard and lost. As for me, I must not look much better, I really think it's best for us to stop here and each of us to sleep at our own place. I nod and I try not to show my relief . . . But I don't have too much trouble hiding it because deep down I'm not relieved at all. First of all, I suspect it's not going to stop there, even after he left with just one last glance back, I expect he'll come right back any minute now. And I'm also scared that I'll miss him.

On my balcony, I watch night fall. I make sure not to drink too much so my thoughts are clear. And so that I don't drink, I smoke cigarettes while looking at Roquerolle's roofs, the church, the Foch high school, the old shuttered factory. I look at it all as if this was the last time . . . I tell myself to think about this as if it were the last time. I want to die but I'm unable to kill myself so I tell myself that I must not actually want to all that much. I'm waiting for the dark of night, I'm waiting until it's time to go see Grampa. One thing is for sure, I can't die without seeing him again. Now, after the chief's gone . . . Long after, once I was sure that he'd gone for good, I found myself even more anxious than if he'd stayed. I thought this wasn't good, I should have kept him here, even if just to keep an eye on him. I began to feel freaked out, I called Mariette, I was hoping to find some reassurance in her voice but what could she have said? She was simply surprised to hear me, as if she thought our friendship was firmly over, and she wouldn't see me again anytime soon. And I didn't know where to start. I didn't even know what exactly I wanted to tell her. It would have been nice if, by the workings of the Holy Ghost or something else entirely, she'd somehow known everything there was to know, and with some gentle words she would offer me her friendship again, or even a bit of her affection. But no, she wasn't ready at all. After that long silence, she asked me what I wanted. Not aggressively, but not tenderly either, just in a neutral tone. I almost said at first that I didn't want to be by myself and I wanted to come sleep at her house, but I wasn't sure whether to simply express my hopes and say "I'd like to sleep at your house," or if it was better to directly ask: "Can I come sleep at your house?" And then I realized that I'd just look even more stupid . . . And make things even more uncomfortable. If I wanted any chance of sleeping with Grampa tonight, I needed to not act like that. So I told Mariette to please take good care of Grampa, to keep people from coming into the house . . And since she didn't understand what I meant, I added:

"Make sure the chief doesn't come into the house."

"Oh, that. There's no danger."

"Yes, there's danger," I said. "Especially tonight."

"He doesn't have the keys anymore if that's what you're worried about," she said.

"How does he not have the keys?"

"He gave them back to me."

That wasn't reassuring at all. On the contrary, it made me even more nervous.

"When? And why would he have given them back to you?"

"Why are you asking me this?"

"I'm scared for Grampa."

"But why would you be scared?"

"I just have a feeling, I don't know why, there's no way I could explain it."

"Okay, listen, Grampa is doing just fine, if that's all you have to tell me, then there's really no point . . ."

"Can I talk to him?"

"Did something happen?"

It took me a long while to answer, I kept wondering how I should put this . . . How could I tell her about the entire affair as briefly as possible? And even if I didn't summarize it, I still didn't have an answer. All I could bring myself to say was:

"I have to talk to Grampa."

But as I said that I knew she wouldn't put him on the phone. I was ready to keep trying, to tell her that it was a matter of life or death and that if she wasn't willing to put him on the line, I'd go to her place right away, but just as I was about to say so, she surprised me.

"Fine, I'll put him on."

"Thank you . . . And shut all the doors and windows in the house."

And Mariette went to give the phone to Grampa, and when Grampa started talking to me, when he said "Cossí vas?"[68] and I replied "E tu?"[69] and he said "Languissi!"[70] in such a weak voice that I only understood because I knew what his answer would be,

68. How are you?

69. And you?

70. Languishing!

and when there was nothing else to say, when we were silent again on both ends of the line, then I realized that the phone was good for small talk, catching up on local gossip, or making plans to meet, but for real love the phone was no good. And as I didn't think I had much time, since Mariette could come get the phone at any minute, I just told Grampa:

"Te vau venir veire dins doas o tres oras, espèri la nuèch negra, te picarai tres còps als contravents."[71]

"Òc ben, a tot ara!"[72] Grampa whispered as I wondered if I'd said it right in Occitan.

And Mariette picked up the phone to tell me:

"Listen, as long as you stay far away from the house, Grampa has nothing to fear."

I was surprised by the way she talked to me . . . This harshness. I wasn't used to that from Mariette. More than it surprised me, it hurt me, and I didn't even have the time to react before she hung up without saying good-bye. Any other day, I would have called her right back, I wouldn't have accepted that from Mariette. Or anyone else. But right now, it seemed like Mariette had become distant and unimportant to me . . . After having meant so much . . . And I don't think she's ever had any idea. It's a shame for her. It was over, and I didn't really give a fuck, in fact. I'd realized that Grampa wouldn't live for much longer. I was afraid of not seeing him again. Not even one last time.

And then I thought about calling the investigators of the CDJP to tell them the whole story. As if that might somehow stop everything, including Grampa's impending death. I'm looking for a confidant, a confessor, a savior. I feel like I could somehow justify all my states of mind, all my thoughts, my calculations, my

---

71. I'm coming to see you in two or three hours, I'm waiting until the dark of night, I'll knock on your window three times.

72. Okay, see you soon!

fears from the very beginning. And I'm sure they'll understand the difficulty imposed by my desires, the fact that my love for the chief had kept me from revealing the answers all along. But my perennial laziness hasn't disappeared, for starters I tell myself the police probably won't easily accept the denunciation of the squad chief of the police force, I know it'll be complicated, that they'll make me stay for a long while, interrogate me for days on end until, even with my watertight report (but are the facts actually watertight?) I'll end up being accused of Thibault Lombard's murder, since at that moment I wasn't even having sex with a stranger in the woods. And in the meantime Grampa will have died either at the chief's hand or of natural causes, and I won't have even gotten to see him one last time. And I'm not all that sure anymore that the chief intends to kill Grampa tonight, no more sure than I am that he hung Paul . . . But if he has to kill him, then I should be there to prevent him from doing it . . . But what would I be preventing? I don't even know what I believe and don't believe anymore, all I know is what I want . . . I'm waiting until it's time to go see Grampa, I'm waiting for the deep night. Far off, over the roofs of Roquerolle, lights pierce the shadows, I can barely make out the divide between sky and earth and when I can't make it out at all anymore, I think to myself how I've never seen a night darker than this. I rush out. As I start my car, I wonder if I'm being stupid, with the luck I've had lately I'll end up at a police checkpoint and all my hopes of seeing Grampa tonight will be dashed. I even think about walking the whole way but ten miles on foot in the night . . . I'd rather take the risk of driving. I maneuver out of my spot, the steering isn't working well, I have a really hard time turning the wheel. I get out. The four wheels of my car have gone flat, the valves have been cut open. It's a signature. I look around, I wonder if he's still in the area, spying on me. I pull out my phone and call him, in the nighttime darkness I might have a chance of hearing his phone running. It rings and as I wait I suddenly remember that

I shouldn't talk to him about the flat tires, otherwise he'll think that I'm taking the car and he'll figure out where I'm going. I shouldn't talk to him about anything, I'm worried that he'll pick up, I want to hang up but I know that if I hang up now, with his brand-new cell phone, he'll immediately know I was the one calling. He'll call me back and I won't be able to get out of explaining. So I let it ring. I listen to the street noise. Nothing. No muffled ringing. Then even though my phone's far from my ear, I hear him saying:

"What do you want?"

A thousand thoughts run through my mind, every one of them equally stupid, saying that I meant to call someone else and I made a mistake, or asking him where he is and what he's doing. And since I can't bear to hear him, even with his distant voice, I put the phone in my shorts pocket without hanging up . . . That way I can say the phone dialed him by accident, it'll annoy him but, given where I am, that's the best course of action. The good news is that he's not killing Grampa as we speak . . . And he isn't in the area spying on me either. And that gives me the resolve I need to keep going. I use heavy black tape to hold a pocket flashlight on my bike's handlebars and I head toward Trintaud. While I'm in the village, everything's fine, the night is warm, I can see everything easily, but when I get into the real shadows, on the road that follows the Alzou, the cool breeze keeps me alert. I'm surprised to be in good shape, I'm pedaling effortlessly, it feels like I'm actually going at a proper speed, but then I realize it's only because of the pocket flashlight that doesn't shine very far into the darkness. And on this little road, there aren't any markings on the ground to help me in the darkness. And every time I hear a car engine in the distance, ahead of me or behind me, I turn off the light and hide in the ditch. I don't know, I'm sure the chief isn't going anywhere tonight, he's convinced himself that with my four flat tires I'm stuck in Roquerolle . . . Although I know that he won't come after me, after everything I told him tonight, when I reminded him that the inspectors probably knew we were together

. . . I tell myself this, but I can't stop thinking that I should expect anything and everything from him. As I'm in the ditch with my bike beside me and I'm huddled in the dry grass with noisy engines and blinding headlights passing right over my head, I remind myself that this is ridiculous, that if the chief was looking for me, he wouldn't have any trouble finding me. And then when the car's far off in the distance, I'm happy to be here, I'm actually proud of myself, and I get back on my bike, pedaling as hard as I can, happy at the thought of seeing Grampa again soon. But it's still odd that the chief hasn't called me in the meantime. I mean, at moments it seems odd, at other moments it seems perfectly normal. Once I get to Trintaud, I leave my bike behind a dumpster for recycling glass, in a dark corner. And I keep going on foot, making my way under the plane trees. I got off the road just in time, I see a police van slowing down at the other end of the square. It's easy for me to get to the small road behind Grampa's, but once I get there, it's a nasty surprise to find Cindy's entrance filled in with all sorts of trash, there's no way I can get through. With the pocket flashlight, I check the entire hedge, but there are no gaps. Finally, I get in through the neighbors' backyard, and I finally end up in Grampa's garden. I knock three times on the shutters. Very gently at first but I don't hear anything inside, I don't dare to knock harder, and then I hear Grampa talking, I don't understand what he's saying, his voice is too weak. I press my ear to the shutters, and I hear something like:

"Gilles . . . Oh . . . Pòdi pas . . . Mon paure, pòdi pas venir."[73]

I don't understand why he can't, maybe he gave up and decided to follow Mariette's directions not to let me into his room anymore, I try to push the shutters open, I check to make sure that the door's locked properly. Unfortunately, it is, and as I'm standing there a light turns on upstairs. I look up. Mariette's looking at me from her bedroom window.

---

73. Gilles . . . Oh . . . I can't . . . Poor thing, I can't come.

"What are you doing here?"

"I came to see Grampa."

"What did I tell you earlier?"

"That doesn't make a difference, I want to see him . . . I have to see him, and he wants to see me, too!"

But I'm not so sure about that last assertion, and then I hear Grampa yelling weakly:

"Marieta . . . Daissa-lo dintrar!"[74]

Grampa's voice cuts to my core and I realize that Grampa didn't come to let me in because he's unable to . . . Physically.

"Please!" I say to Mariette.

And Grampa yells again:

"Marieta!"

And then he adds something else but I can't understand his quavering voice, as if he were pronouncing his last words . . . And I'm so upset by Grampa's weakness that I look down. I look at the shuttered windows. I tell myself he's right there, just a few feet away . . . And I know he's thinking the same thing. I'm scared of failing when I'm so close. I'm not going to give up here and now. When I look back up at Mariette, she isn't at her window anymore. I call out her name once, twice. She doesn't answer. Another minute goes by, her window is still open, the light's turned on, I wonder if she's had a heart attack, a stroke, something like that. I scan for a way to get up to her room. Grampa's yelling "Marieta . . . Gilles," he's surprised that he can't hear us anymore, he's panicking. And just as I go to answer him through the shutters, I hear a door opening . . . the door to the garden. And then I see Mariette's silhouette in the doorway. I walk toward her, she watches me, I look at her imploringly. Grampa's still yelling my name, and then hers. He's wearing himself out. She steps back to let me in.

"Come in."

---

74. Mariette . . Let him in!

"Thank you."

"But don't stay all night, okay?"

"Can we talk to Grampa about that?"

I try to meet her gaze, but she looks away.

"Yeah sure! He doesn't know what he's saying."

"But I have to keep an eye on him . . . Can't leave him alone . . . Did you lock every door properly?"

She nods, I go to check the front door anyway, and the windows facing the road. She follows me.

"What's wrong?" she asks.

"I don't know . . . I don't want Grampa to die."

"And how long do you intend to keep him alive?"

"However much he wants."

And then we hear Grampa yelling weakly:

"Gilles, siás aquí?"[75]

"Veni,"[76] I say quickly as I glance at Mariette.

"Fine, go on . . ." she says. "Take care of him . . . And once you've seen him moaning and suffering all night, you can tell me if you still want to see him live for as long as he wants."

"All right," I say. "Go to sleep, I'll take care of everything."

Mariette doesn't seem pleased. I can't tell if she's conceding to me or if she just wants to go back to bed. She shakes her head, she doesn't answer, she opens the door to Grampa's room, she says:

"L'as aquí! Bona nuèch!"[77]

And she goes, she walks up the stairs.

When I see Grampa in his bed, I'm dumbfounded. He's not the Grampa I remember at all, I try to figure out how long it's been since I saw him last, it's only been a few days, but just how many? Something's changed in his face, I can't put a finger on it,

---

75. Gilles, are you there?

76. I'm coming.

77. He's here! Good night.

he doesn't really look sick, I think he's just tired, very tired, as I could tell from his voice . . . Actually I think he's at the end of his rope. He's gotten much older and much younger at the same time, his face is smoother but his thin, purple lips have hardened and although the crow's feet around his eyes have deepened, his small eyes aren't really gleaming anymore in their sockets. Grampa's shoulders and head are propped up on his pillow like an invalid receiving a visitor. As he smiles, his tongue darts between the few teeth left. His tongue moves frenetically. He has trouble breathing, when I lie down next to him, I hear his breath rattling in his throat. It's sounds like the small sound of a breath that can't make its way out easily. He takes my hand.

"Alara?"[78] I say.

"M'as mancat, sabes?"[79]

"Tu tanben, mas soi aquí, ara."[80]

"Demoraràs tota la nuèch?"[81]

I nod.

"Dormiràs amb ieu?"[82]

"Òc ben!"[83]

I stroke his hand.

"Te vòli pas quitar."[84]

"Te quitarai pas! Te prometi."[85]

Grampa smiles, he lets go of my hand, he tries to shift himself on the pillow, or to make some kind of superhuman effort to turn over, I don't really understand what he's doing.

---

78. Well?
79. I missed you, you know.
80. And you as well but I'm here now.
81. Are you staying the night?
82. Will you sleep here with me?
83. Of course!
84. I don't want you to leave.
85. I won't leave you! I promise.

"Cossí te vòles metre?"[86] I ask.

He touches my hand and points to a spot right above his head, as if he wanted to explain what he's trying to do but the words won't come and he drops his hand and makes a "tsss" sound with his tongue between his teeth in exhaustion. He's fed up.

"Me pòdi pas mòure!"[87]

And then he tries again, using his elbows to try to move himself on the bed, he slides toward the bottom of the pillow this time. He closes his lips tight, I can tell that something's bothering him or maybe he's in pain.

"Quicòm te dòl?"[88]

He slowly shakes his head as if to say no or, as far as I can tell, no more than usual, his mouth contorts into a grimace and a groan comes from deep in his throat, and then I see him start to relax and go slack and I hear some noise from his stomach and guts, then the smell of shit enters my nostrils as Grampa looks at me in embarrassment.

"Me pòdi pas netejar tot sol," he finally says sadly. "Te cal sonar Marieta."[89]

And I don't see myself waking up Mariette to ask her to clean up Grampa's shit, I have a feeling that's partly what she meant when she was talking about caring for old people, that I would know by the morning if I actually liked it. And besides, I'd promised that I would take care of everything.

"Lo vau far!"[90]

"Tu?"[91] He's shocked.

---

86. How do you want to lie down?
87. I can't move anymore!
88. Does something hurt?
89. I can't wash myself on my own. You have to call Mariette.
90. I'll do it!
91. You?

"Vòles pas?"[92]

Grampa is still shocked but he's thinking. He doesn't know whether he wants me to or not.

"Perqué lo fariás, tu?"[93]

"Per qué soi aquí . . . E pensi que Marieta dormís ara."[94]

Grampa is still thinking.

"As paur que veja ton cuol?"[95]

I smile as I ask him that, and he finally relaxes, he smiles in turn, he shakes his head no, that's not what bothers him.

"Alara? Ont es lo problèma?"[96]

Grampa doesn't answer, he's still looking at me with his round, moist, deep-set eyes, I have a feeling that somewhere in his head he's thinking what I'm thinking, he must be thinking back to the underwear full of shit over my head. But it's starting to really stink in his room and I have to do it at one point or another. So I get up, I pull back the sheets covering him, I gently pull off his pajama bottoms, I see his thin, white legs streaked with purple veins. Then I laboriously slide a towel under his butt and then I pull off the diaper and I don't even retch when I see Grampa's yellow shit, I'm focused on my job, I'm not thinking about anything else, I go to find a washcloth in the bathroom. It's the first time I've gone in since the baton up my ass, but it's fine, I go quickly, and in any case, the place doesn't have a bad feeling, it's just a typical bathroom with toilets. And then I clean Grampa's ass and when I'm done with his ass, I use the washcloth to wipe his balls and his small penis, which is tiny and very brown . . . Like his balls. He lets me do it without making a sound, at first he's staring at the ceiling but when I say "Siás tot propret,

92. Do you not want me to?
93. Why would you do it?
94. Because I'm here . . . And I think Mariette's asleep right now.
95. Are you afraid I'll see your ass?
96. So? What's the problem?

ara!"[97] he smiles as if to thank me. And I can't keep myself from stroking his penis with my hand. His face gets serious but he doesn't stop looking at me. His head falls back against the wall, his eyes lost in the distance, I can't tell whether he's getting some pleasure out of this or just waiting for it to be over. I slide a finger between his cheeks. Gently. I'm worried that Grampa will slip through my hands, I'm scared that he'll get scared and ask me to leave his room. I find his asshole, Grampa lets me do it, his eyes are still lost somewhere in a corner of the room. I want him to turn toward me, to look at me, I want to see his loving gaze, his desire, I want to see the little gleam that was in his eyes the night that he asked me "Soi ieu que te fau quilhar coma aquò?"[98] And when I push the tip of my finger into his ass, I hear him groan and he turns his head toward me. And he finally smiles. My eyes meet his, I keep stroking his penis, I pull back the foreskin to see his head, which is even darker than all the rest, I push my finger in deeper but he shakes his ass. His smile gets stuck.

"Me vòles fotre?"[99] he asks me, quietly, gently.

"T'agradariá?"[100]

He's serious again, worried even, maybe sorry, then he shakes his head. And then, even more quietly, he says:

"Cresi pas!"[101]

So I pull out my finger, I let go of his penis. I went too far and I'm not proud of myself. I'm still not sure what came over me. I was carried away by an odd urge that I don't even completely understand, I have to set things right, it would be horrible if Grampa kicked me out for a finger up his ass. I lie down next to him, propped up on an elbow, I rub his body gently.

---

97. You're all clean now!
98. Am I the one making you hard like that?
99. Do you want to fuck me?
100. Do you want to?
101. I don't think so!

"Perdon, Maurice, te vòli pas fotre . . . mas coma sentissiaì qu'aquò t'agradava, te voliái donar de plaser."[102]

"M'agradava!"[103]

Grampa says that with absolute seriousness. And I wonder why he's saying that when he doesn't want me to fuck him. I look at him in puzzlement, I want to know more, but Grampa doesn't say anything further, he just keeps looking serious and dreamy, his eyes lost in the ceiling. Come to think of it, I don't see what's so surprising . . . Stroking him makes him happy, but he doesn't want to be fucked. Nothing could be more normal than that. I slide myself closer to him.

"Sabes çò que m'agradariá?"[104] I whisper as our eyes meet.

He looks me over, he doesn't know, he's waiting for me to tell him.

"Voldriái dormir tot nus al prèp de tu."[105]

Grampa doesn't think twice, he nods, he whispers "Òc ben."[106] I hurriedly take off my shorts and my tee-shirt, he looks at me from head to toe, he says:

"Tu m'agradas, sabes aquò!"[107]

And just as I lie down next to him, he says:

"Despolha me, ieu tanben."[108]

At first I'm surprised by Grampa's idea but it doesn't take me long to pull off his pajama top and then we get under the covers, my head against his chest, I stroke his withered body, he sets his hand on my cheek, I stroke his stomach, and I hear a moan in

---

102. I'm sorry, Maurice, I don't want to fuck you . . . But I felt you liked it, and I wanted to make you happy.
103. I liked it!
104. You know what I would like?
105. I want to sleep completely naked right next to you.
106. Of course.
107. I like you, you know!
108. Take off my clothes, too.

his throat, his lips pressed shut, a slow groan with a short breath. Then other groans from the bottom of his heart . . . I don't know if it's just now or if it's always this way, but it seems like I can detect intense pleasure. And I stay there, getting hard against Grampa's ass, I let myself slowly sink into a half-sleep. It's a soothing half-dream where the two of us are all alone in a huge bed . . . Nobody around, either upstairs or downstairs, even Mariette's left the house. Nobody can do anything to us anymore, we'll stay like this for a long, long while. Outside it's night but we can see everything like it's daytime and it's not scary at all, Paul isn't dead, nor is Thibault Lombard, and even if they're dead (because I'm not completely convinced that they're alive), none of that matters anymore. After a while, I can't hear Grampa's moans anymore, then I don't hear his breath anymore, then I don't even feel his stomach moving anymore, not the least tremor. It's over, I think to myself, he's sleeping. My heart trembles. I wanted Grampa to wait until daylight to sleep. It would have given us more time to really be together. But I feel more alive than I ever did, and ready to wait for him to wake up, with my hard dick against his skin. That's when a man joins us in the bed, like a ghost surrounding me with his naked body. At first I don't want to believe it, but then his hands, his skin, his breath, his warmth all convince me that he's there and I should accept his presence . . . Especially since I knew he would come . . . And I think that it's always the same, I can't sleep in the arms of just one man, I always need a third and I wonder when it will all end, when I will finally be able to sleep calmly. I accept his presence in the bed, yes, but I can't kiss him, I'd feel like I was betraying Grampa even though Grampa and I never will never kiss. And this is my greatest regret . . . Maybe Grampa will be the greatest love I've ever had in my life, and I will never get to live that love. The thought stuns me in its incontrovertibility . . . Grampa and I were made for each other. And what did it come to? Not much at all. What kept us from it? Nothing . . . Trifles. And this enormous truth settles in me as I feel the chief's cock trying to push into me, but I clench my ass and nestle closer to Grampa, I hug him tight, I know that I have to extricate myself from the chief's hold, I'll have to fight, but I don't feel capable of it. I know that if I fight, I'll lose, and I also know that if I don't free myself now, then it'll be too late, but I'm so happy in this great laziness that's come over me . . . All I want is not to let go of Grampa. And the chief doesn't try again, he's already gotten what he wanted, he doesn't care about fucking me but just when I feel like I'll finally be at peace with Grampa, I feel something cold on my penis and then it burns and it really hurts and the pain becomes unbearable, I can't pretend anymore, I have to wake up because I really hope this will go away upon waking. But nothing's gone away. My blood's pouring out of my cock in huge spurts and when I try to stop it with my hands, I just feel my cock cut in half, it's only held together by a bit of skin, I try to hold it in place but with the blood pouring, I understand quickly it's a lost cause. I'll never be able to put it back together. My body empties out and then beyond the feeling of my blood flowing out, I smell the odor of shit, an odor I've never smelled before, and when I realize that Grampa's body is completely cold, I know it's a smell of death. It occurs to me to yell and I yell hard, I push out all the air I can from my lungs, but it's like I'm screaming inside myself and anyway the chief holds his hand over my mouth and my nostrils and pulls me in close, he whispers words into my ear. I can only make out that he's talking about Thibault Lombard and Paul, he's also talking about love. But they're just words that disappear in my head. I can't really figure out what he's telling me . . . And I'd like to but I'm too focused on trying to keep breathing, everything's buzzing in my head. I'd like to know why I'm dying before I can't think anymore, it feels like it's important to know the last secrets, the last mysteries before dying, but being that it's too late, I stop struggling, I stop crying, and then I feel the blood flowing more slowly out of my cock, I don't hear the chief talking anymore, I just hear his breath in my ear, a soft breath then in the silence, when I'm focused wholly on his breath, I notice his naked body twitching against mine. Gently, very gently, and his breath catches again, I know he's crying. And that he won't talk to me ever again. And I won't have been able to get to the heart of his mystery . . . Or rather, that's exactly what I'm doing. Deep down, I've always known that one day someone would come and he would hurt me horribly. And from the start, I've known that the chief would end up killing me, I couldn't love him forever. I've never really been afraid of death or only when I was very young when I thought that it must be horrible to no longer exist at all, and as I got older I calmed down about that . . . I was afraid of my demise, the exact moment when I would cross from life to death, I was afraid of suffering, pain, my death throes, but no longer really afraid of regretting life, the people I loved most, the earth and everything I could still have done. I don't have anything else to do. And I wonder whether dying without regret means that I've done everything I meant to do or whether it's more that I haven't had such a great life. And then I wonder if it's really so important to die at the end of a full life, if it's so important to die happy. I don't know if I'm dying a happy or an unhappy man, I don't hurt anymore, I don't know when I stopped hurting, I can't even feel the blood draining away anymore . . . While I still have the strength, I slowly put my hand on Grampa's stomach, the chief lets go and frees me at last. I let my head fall against Grampa's chest. I still want him . . . I want to stay with him forever . . . That's it, I've gotten my eternal desire. And I don't know for sure if this is happiness, but I do think that tonight, I'm happy to die beside Grampa.

UNDIES ARIA

Bruce Hainley: Considering Alain Guiraudie's *Now the Night Begins*—thriller meets philosophical essay on desire's flow—it appalls me that many have found something "wrong" about the novel and its subjects. I want to force-feed it, graham crackers, to those with too delicate stomachs, symptom of our (American, gay, and gay-American) cultural pusillanimity. Guiraudie questions so many received assumptions: what is a novel? what is the drift of an id across a countryside and all it contains? what is softness, tenderness? how does it connect to "old age"? when does "old age" begin and why is there an assumption that sexuality or desire (too feeble?) ever ends? He's finely attuned to the variegated frequencies and nuances of erotic drive, its wonderful "dumbness" (mute, stupid, transitive, *material*). With his use of Occitan, one of the book's crucial melodies, entailing a discussion about "dead" languages and dialects, Guiraudie champions literature, its wayward allowances and *douceurs*, against Law's edicts, ignorance, finitudes, and markets. In *Now the Night Begins*, no elegy, Guiraudie sounds a nocturnal reveille for language, reading, writing, their bodily consequences. The troubadours would be so alive to his strange taking up of their music and song.

Wayne Koestenbaum: "I touch Grampa's underwear": this outré book is funny and uplifting. A mood elixir. Guiraudie's *récit* lands on the truth, a feat that always repays a sentient reader's investment. I'm continuing to think about those salvific undies—my homeland; Genet's mausoleum; the Everard Baths; the scapegoat; a minor literature.

Gramps deserves to be desired!

The undies represent the possibility of translation and cross-fertilization between generations, between languages (dialect and the dominant tongue). Seriously!

BH: Provençal undies, which Ezra Pound never knew how to put to use.

Tenderness, care, and soft eroticism tucked into the "dead" dialect of Occitan.

Guiraudie "passports" the undies for illicit border-crossings, providing transport between the living and the dead, between bodies usually kept apart, between the social and what remains of the intimate. I want an undies quickie to snap me out of our national miasma.

WK: An "undies quickie" says it all—

Guiraudie's film *Stranger by the Lake* is partly based on this book. No film since *Taxi zum Klo* has so effectively and authentically limned the quotidian, improvisatory, embarrassing nature of cruising. In *Taxi zum Klo*, cruising is twinned with pedagogy; in *Stranger by the Lake*, with crime. In this late stage of civilization's undoing, long after sexual-liberatory promises have been broken and idealisms quashed, please observe that cruising—the love for Gramps's illicit, foreclosed undies—must be coupled with fatality, abuse, dismemberment.

I'll save further thoughts for email, lest I spill my seed in merely spasmodic utterance—though this thread is our test drive—

BH: Is Gramps, like the contemplative, ready-to-chat loner on the rocky shore of the lake, a figure for philosophy, thinking *as a body and its vulnerabilities*? Let's not forget Guiraudie's astounding next film, *Staying Vertical*, with its Gramps-like parallels, its wolves at the door.

WK: (e-mail): If a scholar-revolutionary can't jerk off on Gramps's undies, where is the possibility for learning from history by desiring its seamed shamed stretched-out over-laundered cotton?

I'm passionately siding with the undies—as the subaltern.

BH: My yarn-broker father always warns that because we long ago outsourced the cotton and the underwear industries, all any invading power would have to do is cut off that import supply. Says Dad: "It would get pretty rank very fast and bring us to our knees."

WK: Not that we need to remain on this "serious" frequency! *Now the Night Begins* is important because it issues a call for a literature of the future—a sexually unpoliced future.

Your dad is right about rankness and cotton.

BH: Guiraudie's undies make me flash on Guibert's bunny and lambikins.

WK: A literature of peace!

BH: A literature of suscing! Rare sonics of suscing, score of the future.

WK: Suscing: the sucked fecal stones in *Molloy*.

BH: Fecal testicles. Stones. Balls. Sacs. Sascing. Sucking. Suscing.

WK: Susc out (suss out):

Scat and susc = to be in synch with the unsayable—

BH: Put the unsayable to lute, hautbois, and electronic drums!

WK: One origin of modernism.

BH: Gramps and Gilles in bed suscing: a lost Toulouse-Lautrec.

WK: As Ezra put it—

"And then went down to the ship / To susc"—

BH: Tiresias, a Gramps figure, watching from the piers, flaunting his dugs.

WK: Tiresias is totally Gramps. Born suscing in a trunk.

I Could Go On Suscing.

A Suscer Is Born.

A Suscer is Waiting.

Ziegfeld Suscer.

BH: *BUtterfield Suscer.*

WK: *BUtterfield Suscer* is the best: "I was the biggest suscer of all times! And I loved it!"

BH: Suscer writes on the mirror with the product of his suscing: NO SALE!

The anticapitalist roots of suscing.

WK: Also: cow-rumination (Stein and the sucked syllable)—

The fecal immersion of Gilles (the rape) is a demonic (Black Mass) inversion of *Tender Buttons.*

BH: Missing button: plum brandy: salvific drink of relaxation, after-dinner calm; apotropaic, antiseptic—*it smarts*! —balm to the anal degradation and punitive brutalization by Law.

What shall we do with Law—local police chief, "bi" hunk, and vicious menace?

WK: It would be fun to remain forever in the land of the paradisiacal undies, but we must indeed face the chief's obscenity, and his dramaturgical (eschatological?) necessity. Not that desire *requires* a force to shut it down. But Guiraudie has the political wisdom (and unsentimentality) to note that "we" desire the Law even if the Law destroys us. Guiraudie rewrites Genet's *Funeral Rites*: the obscenity of the chief, as the yearned-for fascistic monster, pumps the narrator's desire-machine. Are we programmed to desire the monster? No. Though Sylvia Plath thought so.... John Waters, Dennis Cooper, Samuel R. Delany, Jean Genet, Rainer Werner Fassbinder, Pierre Guyotat, Gary Fisher, Hervé Guibert, and few hundred others, couldn't help but think of filth and "gayness" in one breath... The end of *Fox and His Friends*: *auteur* gay-bashed on the Metro floor.

BH: Elfriede Jelinek provides a feminist optic on such subjugations, crushes. With Gramps, Guiraudie inverts Tony Duvert, sourcing, *suscing* old age as an "innocence" calling out for its diary.

WK: Literature at its best can never be separate from the besmirched, ritually borrowed undies—lending library of the Provençal clothesline—Bibliothèque Nationale, finally deterritorialized.

BH: Guiraudie is airing dirty linens. About class, love, family. What does it mean to make an example of one who airs his dirty linens in public (the act which begins Gilles's "problems"). To err one's dirty linens in public…

Guiraudie thoughts, courtesy of Joe Brainard:

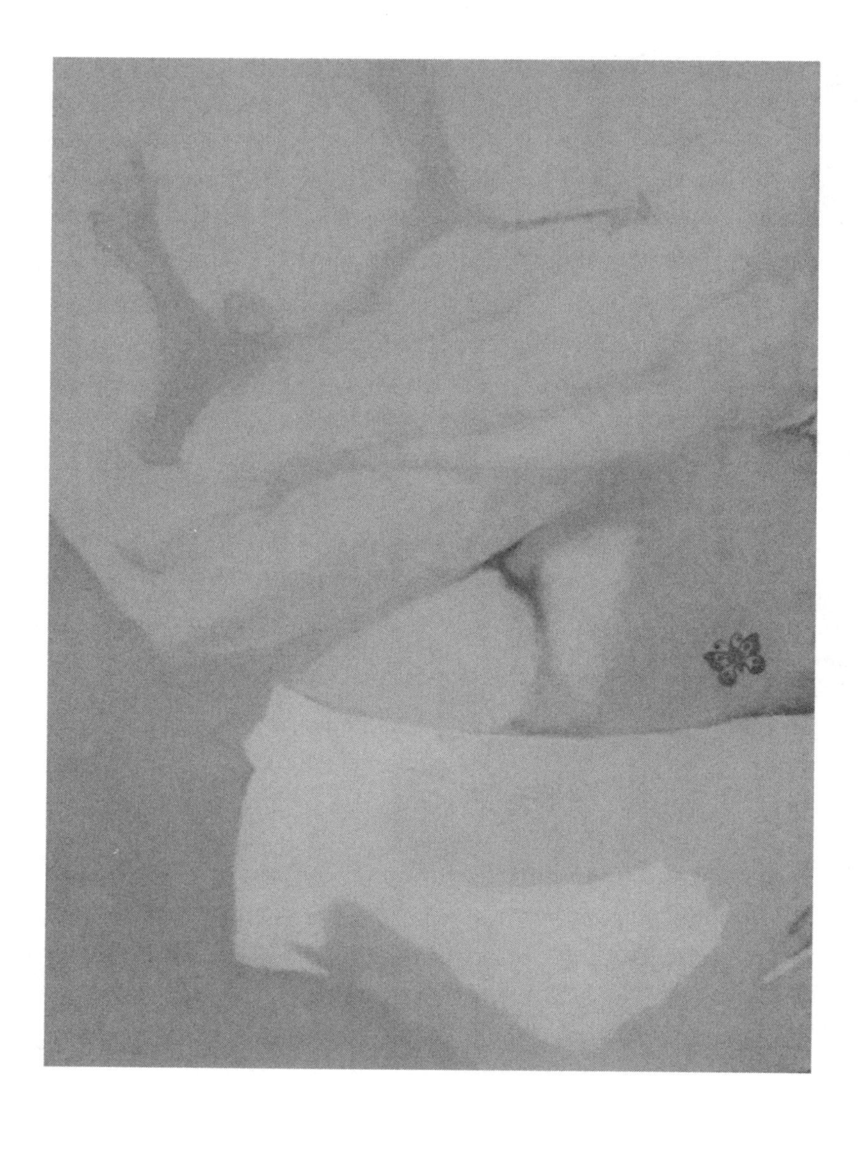

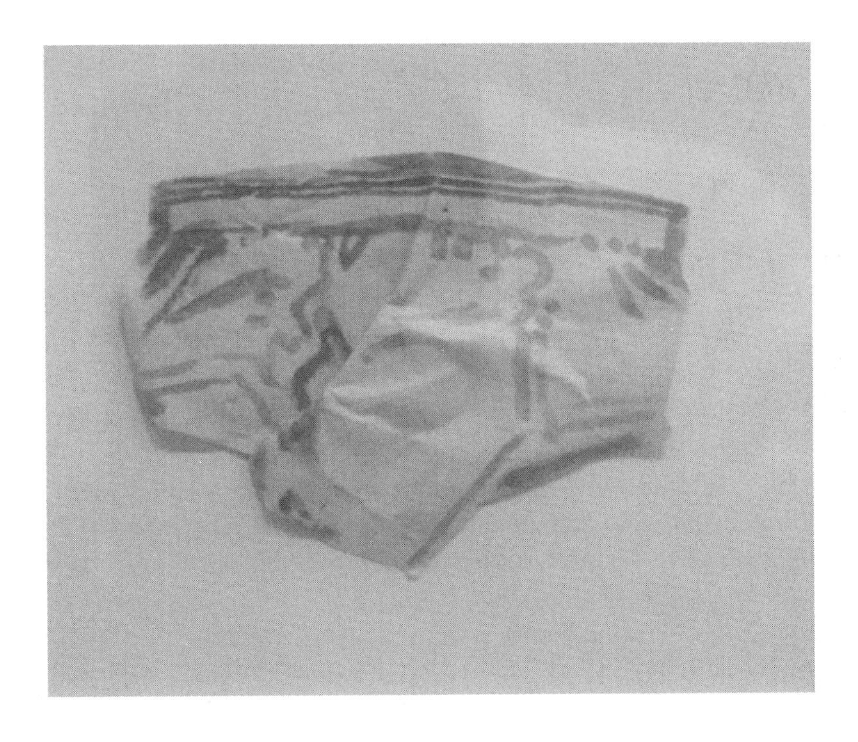

WK: *Undie art*, a phrase to fondle to death:

Undo the (oft-claimed) "death" of art.

Untie art (via undies) from its prematurely imposed death-shackles.

Via Undie—a small street in Udine, Italia...

BH: It leads to a clothesline in rural France, a sentence hanging in midair.

WK: Guiraudie's Gramps-undies lead us back to Guyotat's "beat-sheet," *In the Deep*—where the text's raw page is also the cum rag.

Cum sonnet; cum epic; cum elegy; cum sestina; cum pantoum; cum ode; cum hexameter; cum iamb; cum alexandrine.

ABOUT THE AUTHOR

Alain Guiraudie is a French film director, screenwriter, and novelist. His films include *Staying Vertical* (2016), *Stranger by the Lake* (2013), and *The King of Escape* (2009).